Praise for *Goc*

"*Good Girl* lures you in with its excellent sex scenes, but it seals the deal with its authentic portrait of what it feels like to be a young woman in the world. Sex, friendship, family, work—who knows what to make of any of it? Anna Fitzpatrick's debut is both funny and titillating, and, like so few early sexual encounters, totally satisfying."

—Emma Straub, author of *This Time Tomorrow*

"On feminism, loneliness, and the question of kink, Anna Fitzpatrick bluntly probes the contradictions of sex-positive culture, baring the many ways that shame feeds arousal. *Good Girl* is a sensitive girl's hardcore."

—Tamara Faith Berger, author of *Queen Solomon*

"*Good Girl* is an intense ride, with more twists and turns than a pile of rope at the end of an orgy. Plan to be unable to put it down."

—Stoya, performer and author, *Philosophy, Pussycats, and Porn*

"*Good Girl* is a brilliant debut—sharp, funny, sexy, and unnerving in the best way. Unsentimental but achingly real. Fitzpatrick is a daring new writer to watch."

—Zoe Whittall, author of *The Spectacular* and
The Best Kind of People

"I'm calling it, Anna Fitzpatrick's novel *Good Girl* is going to be a cult-favorite if not on many people's must-read lists. . . . Fitzpatrick takes romance tropes and flips them on their head — then slaps them."

—BuzzFeed

"*Good Girl* is very funny, original and fully absorbing. A brilliant and surprising debut novel that is smart, unaffected and full of the joys and uncertainties of being human."

—Iain Reid, author of *I'm Thinking of Ending Things, Foe,* and *We Spread*

"Yes, *Good Girl* is a book about sex . . . But it's also, more broadly, about the difficult work of self-validation, and about a young woman teaching herself how to be, rather than waiting to be told what to do. . . . And for all its razor-sharp edges, *Good Girl* is also a uniquely gentle portrait of a complex, complicated young woman just trying to get things right. Plus, it's incredibly, intensely, laugh-out-loud funny."

—Rebecca Tucker, *The Globe and Mail*

"Funny until it hurts, *Good Girl* brilliantly captures the vivid details and fuzzy feelings happening in the mind of a person on the verge of becoming herself."

—Haley Mlotek

"Anna Fitzpatrick has accomplished an incredible balancing act. *Good Girl* manages to depict sex and sexuality that is both painful in the way Lucy wants it to be and painful in the awkward and hilarious reality of what it means to navigate relationships and life. Buy this book (unless you are Anna's parents, and then, maybe skip it)."

—David Iserson, screenwriter, *The Spy Who Dumped Me*

"*Good Girl* pokes fun at the contradictions of life as a contemporary twenty-something, only to sincerely engage with the timeless questions that come with growing up: What do I want? Are they the right things? And what if the right things aren't enough? This is a clever and truly funny exploration of desire, shame, power and becoming. The sex scenes are good, too, which never hurts."

—Madi Haslam, *Maisonneuve*

Good Girl

Anna Fitzpatrick

Flying Books

First edition published in 2022 by Flying Books Inc.
www.flyingbooks.ca

This U.S. edition published by ECW Press Ltd.
www.ecwpress.com

28 27 26 25 24 23 22   1 2 3 4 5 6 7 8

Library and Archives Canada
Cataloguing in Publication

Title: Good Girl : a novel / Anna Fitzpatrick.
Names: Fitzpatrick, Anna, author.
Identifiers: Canadiana (print) 20210351500 |
Canadiana (ebook) 20210351543 | ISBN
9781989919033 (softcover) | ISBN
9781989919040 (PDF) | ISBN 9781989919057
(Kindle) | ISBN 9781770417533 (U.S.)
Classification: LCC PS8611.I89195 G66 2022 |
DDC C813/.6—dc23

Also available in electronic format

Series design: Lisa Naftolin and Leanne Shapton
Author photograph: Arden Wray
Typesetting: Mark Byk

Printed and bound in Canada

This book is funded in part by the Government of Canada. *Ce livre est financé en partie par le gouvernement du Canada.* We acknowledge the support of the Canada Council for the Arts. *Nous remercions le Conseil des arts du Canada de son soutien.* We acknowledge the funding support of the Ontario Arts Council (OAC), an agency of the Government of Ontario. We also acknowledge the support of the Government of Ontario through the Ontario Book Publishing Tax Credit, and through Ontario Creates.

For Heart

And because some things cannot be triumphed over unless they are first accepted and endured, because, indeed, some things cannot be triumphed over at all, the "story" must be told again and again in endless pursuit of a happy ending.
—Mary Gaitskill, "Victims and Losers: A Love Story"

I hope life isn't a big joke, because I don't get it.
—Jack Handey

1

Tell me what colour underwear you're wearing.
I look down at the incoming message on my cell, blocking the screen with my hand even though there is nobody around to read over my shoulder. *Blue, Sir,* I reply. I put the phone on lock, slide it into the back pocket of my jeans, and resume reshelving the books in my arms.

"Excuse me, do you work here?" A sixty-something woman approaches me. I have been studiously reorganizing the bookshelf in front of me for the last half hour. I nod and smile politely.

"What can I help you with?"

"I'm trying to find a book. I can't remember the title. It was by a woman author and had a green cover."

My phone buzzes in my pocket.

"Is it a recent release?"

"I think so. It was reviewed in the paper. Or no, the radio. A few months ago? It was something about the transportation industry. I want to get it for my son. He's into that sort of thing."

My phone buzzes again and I squirm.

"Hm." I affix a look of concentration on my face as if her green book were the only thing that mattered. "There have been a number of books by women published in the last couple of months with green covers. A lot of our popular new titles are in the display by the front. Have you looked through those?"

"I suppose I'll try that, but I was hoping you would be able to help me."

She turns and heads to the front display as my phone buzzes a third time. I drop my stack of books on a nearby table and pull it out.

Show me.

That's an order, slut.

Now.

I'm at work, Sir, I text back, and I prepare to put my phone away when another message comes in.

Is that an acceptable excuse, slut?

I look over my shoulder. The store is slow today, but it's not "pull down my pants and take a picture of my panties" slow. Nora is taking her lunch break in the backroom, and the lighting in the bathroom is terrible. I scroll through the photos on my phone, and there are a few good sexy shots, but none featuring blue underwear. Ignoring the order isn't even an option. I head to the magazine stand and grab the latest *Vogue*, flipping through it quickly. There's a shot of Gigi Hadid wearing baby-blue bikini bottoms and a crop top on the beach. Close enough. I pull out my phone and focus the camera on her hip and thigh, hoping the sand in the background isn't obvious. Gigi's ass is considerably smaller than mine. I zoom in until it fills the screen and text the picture to Henry.

Well done, slut. But you took way too long to obey. Be at my place 7 pm sharp, for punishment.

Yes, Sir.

Good. Now get back to work.

My navy panties get wet at the order. I wonder if anyone would notice if I took a quick break to go to the bathroom and rub one out.

2

"I found the book." The older woman is holding up a copy of *The Girl on the Train.*

"Oh, great!" I shove my phone back in my pocket. "Was that everything you were looking for today? Let me cash you out."

I spend the rest of my shift rearranging cookbooks to distract myself from thinking about dick. My annoying colleague Danny has the day off, and so I'm working with Nora today. She's in her early fifties and has been working at Prologues since she was my age, as she frequently points out. I tell her this is only a temporary job until my writing career takes off. She says she said the same thing when she was twenty-five.

A lot of people think Nora owns the store, or is at least my boss in some capacity. Technically I guess she has some kind of seniority, having been here longer, but Nora has no desire to be anything beyond a bookseller. "With great power comes great responsibility," she told me once, "and who needs that?" We do enough work to keep the store running while Marcella, our very rich and very absent boss, is off doing whatever she does, and we spend the rest of the time either reading or complaining about people we hate. Today, for Nora, that's her teenage daughter's current boyfriend.

"I don't give a shit that she's having sex, you know? We had the talk. She's on the pill, and I bought her condoms. Ribbed for her pleasure because, fuck it, girl power, you know?"

"Uh huh," I say, scrolling through Henry's Facebook page on the work computer.

"What I hate is that her boyfriend is such a nerd. And not a cool nerd like you."

"Watch it now."

"He's like a theatre kid, except he doesn't actually do theatre. He just has that vibe where he needs to be the centre of attention. I never know what he's talking about half the time, and when I say as much, he goes, 'Mrs. Goldstein, I was just quoting *Doctor Who.*' He's a . . . Do you youths still say narc?"

"I dunno. I'm not a youths."

"Bullshit, sweet pea. I could get a pretty penny for your skin on the black market."

"Um, ew?" I click through Henry's tagged photos. His profile picture is him at a work function wearing a suit. Henry is older than I am, in his late thirties, and has a real job, a corporate nine-to-five thing. In the next shot he is at a very different party, wearing a top hat, leather vest, and boxers, flanked by two women dressed in what appears to be lingerie designed by Tim Burton. I go to close the tab, but Nora sees it before I get the chance.

"Another narc." She's pointing at Henry's giant corny grin. "Where the hell was this photo taken?"

"I still don't think narc is the right word." I squint at the picture. "And it looks like some kind of dungeon? Is that a flogger in the background?"

"Like a sex club thing?"

"I guess so. I always pictured sex clubs to be classier. Filled with people who look like models wearing masks and stuff."

"You're thinking of *Eyes Wide Shut*," Nora says. "No sex club looks like that in real life, trust me."

"Do they all look like they could have been sponsored by Hot Topic?"

"Only the fun ones. Who was that guy anyway?"

I tell Nora that I met Henry a few weeks ago. At least, we matched on Tinder. We still haven't met in real life; tonight will be our first date. My pulse quickens whenever I remember that, but I try not to reveal to Nora how nervous I am. I would prefer that she think of me as a carefree libertine rather than a narc.

Henry had the word *kinky* in his profile, alongside long irrelevant descriptions about who he was as a person. *Kinky* is one of those words that frequently turns up in my porn searches and something I had never tried pursuing in real life. His pictures were bad; the guy didn't know his angles. But he wasn't unattractive, with olive skin, symmetrical features, a strong nose, and a warmth to his brown eyes, and I was bored by the conversations I was having with other men on the app. *What's the harm in chatting with someone new?* I thought. *Nothing needs to happen.* We matched immediately.

What do you like? I sent him as an opening message.

I like lots of things, he said, followed by lists that made my eyes glaze over about living life to the fullest and learning not to take things too seriously and this one band, have I heard of this one band?

No, I mean, do you like being bossy, or being bossed?

Oh, im very dominant.

Hi Very Dominant, I'm Lucy. Would you like to tell me what to do?

haha i love funny girls. I bet he did. I bet I could be hilarious for him. *I'm going to bed now. more texts and orders to follow soon.*

Yes, I started to type, and then hesitated before adding a *Sir.* I stared at the words on the screen for a second and hit send.

Good girl, he replied, and I exhaled.

We started to sext for real the next night. He was bad at it. He put winky-face emojis in where there didn't need to be winky-face emojis.

im gonna make u choke on my cock ;)

I'm gonna make u scream out in pain and pleasure ;P

I wanted to tell him to cut it out, but I didn't know if that was allowed in our dynamic. A couple mornings later, I tried to switch up the tactic.

I want to make myself cum, but I have to catch up on all this laundry. I've been pretty bad when it comes to finishing my chores.

Do one load of laundry, and then you're allowed to touch yourself.

Yes, Sir

Do you have other things to do this morning?

I replied with a detailed list.

Here's how your morning is going to go. No putting on panties until you finish washing the dishes. Then I want you to do another load of laundry. Text me when you're done all that, and then we'll plan your afternoon.

Yes, Sir.

I had my most productive day in months. I wondered if this was the secret behind the most successful people, the key to being a stand-up member of society: just have a really tall person order you around.

"So let me get this straight," says Nora, when I finish an abridged version of our correspondence. "You've never met this guy in person. You met him online. All you know about him is that he's a sadist. Literally. And you're going over to his house alone tonight?"

"It's not like that," I say, fully aware that it's exactly like that. "Tinder says we have three friends in common, and I never said he was a sadist. I said he was a service top who might potentially have sadist tendencies, which is a huge difference. Read a book." Nora rolls her eyes. "I already told Sasha where I'm going to be tonight." Sasha is my best friend. "We have a rule. If I don't text her by midnight, she sends the cops to his address, which she hopefully won't need to do because obviously we both think cops are terrible."

There is no way to explain to Nora, who is so grown up, so present in who she is as a person, that I've been waiting my whole life for someone like Henry, with his terrible taste in music and his winky-face emojis. Nora lost her virginity at fourteen. Sometimes her boyfriend, Christopher, comes to the store. He is very male and rugged but, like, in an elegant way. Like Wolverine. They have uninhibited, animalistic sex. I know this because she tells me. One morning she came into work, bleary-eyed but excited, and held up her sweater while yanking down the side of her skirt. There, against the translucent skin of her hip, was the soft blue-and-yellow remnant of a bruise. "Isn't that wild?" she asked, while my stomach fluttered, imagining a scenario in which Christopher had hit her, perhaps after tying her up, perhaps after forcing her to submit to him, but in a super-consensual feminist way. Turns out they had just accidentally rolled out of bed during some particularly rambunctious fucking, Nora's delicate hip being the first point of contact with the ground. For Nora, her ideal rough sex looks something like a wrestling match, with both sides fighting for dominance. The rough sex I fantasize about has one other person roughing me up while I just take it.

Nora thinks I lost my virginity at eighteen. This is because I told her I lost my virginity at eighteen. She blinked when I told her this and said, "From the way you talk, I just assumed it was younger." Then she told me I was smart to have waited till I was older so that I could "do things on my own terms," as if I would have any idea what my terms would be at eighteen. She doesn't need to know I lost my virginity at twenty-two. Of the four men I've had sex with, I was able to get one of them, my first boyfriend, to half-heartedly choke me as he came inside me, only to collapse on top of me and sweatily kiss my forehead. He thought I had also finished. This is because I told him I had also finished. It was absolutely nothing like the porn I had watched, where the woman was roughed up into a screaming orgasm. Again, in a consensual feminist way. With Henry I'm playing a role, one with a limited script and minimal character development, but one that gives me room to tell the truth.

"He has a girlfriend," says Nora, snapping me back to reality.

"Excuse me?"

"Your new boy toy." She points to his Facebook page. "It says right there, he's in a relationship."

"I knew that." And it's true, I did. "It was on his Tinder profile. It's called polyamory, Nora, and it's a perfectly valid form of sexual expression."

"Men having lots of sex without their partners is hardly revolutionary."

"The idea is that women can have lots of sex too," I say with a confidence that isn't really earned, imagining myself in the ranks of "women who can and do have lots of sex like it's no big deal," yet another role for me to play. I click over to Henry's girlfriend's profile.

"Violet Nurmi," reads Nora, over my shoulder. "That sounds like the name of a nineteenth-century infection."

"That's not fair. She's not my enemy. I'm the one sexting her boyfriend." Still, my stomach drops when I notice how beautiful she is. Henry has a sweet awkwardness to his look, but Violet is a bombshell. Most of her Facebook posts are public, and I have no trouble lurking her profile. There's a recent picture of her that, according to the caption, was taken at her twenty-third birthday. She's two years younger than I am. Not that I care about stuff like that, obviously. Her eyes are cartoon-character wide, and her boobs are big enough that—no, I'm not doing this.

"She looks like a porn star," says Nora.

"That's not cool."

"No, I'm not trying to insult her. I'm saying, it looks like that's what she does as a profession, for money, which I know you're about to say is empowering if that's her choice." She wrestles the mouse out of my hand and clicks on a photo farther down Violet's profile, enlarging it. Violet is wearing a lot of makeup, pasties, skimpy underwear, stockings, and heels, and is leaning back in a giant martini glass on what looks to be a very important stage in a total showgirl pose like Dita Von Teese.

"She's a burlesque dancer," I say, and a few more clicks through her photos prove I'm right. Violet in a spotlight wearing a skimpy campy costume. Violet in a lyra hoop doing things with her legs I didn't think legs could actually do. Violet looking fun and easy and sexy and free in each of her photos, having the time of her twenty-three-year-old life, her equally hot friends commenting on all her photos with things like "You are cray, girl!" and "Love ya bitch!" and her breasts managing to defy gravity in even the skimpiest of bras that—no, that doesn't matter.

"So her job is being hot," says Nora, once again taking control of the cursor to minimize the window as I slump to the floor behind the counter. Nora always lets me indulge my dramatic side. I think I entertain her, which allows me to believe our relationship is something approaching reciprocal. That and I've always found the floor the most comfortable spot to be. "Your job is being smart. Some men are into that."

"My job is selling books to hot people so they can post them on their Instagram."

"You have substance, sugar. And what does she have? Tits? An incredible pair of tits?"

"That's the patriarchy talking. Trying to pit women against each other and assuming that looks and intelligence exist in an exclusive dichotomy."

"They are truly phenomenal though," Nora muses, and I look up to see she's opened Violet's Facebook page again and is clicking through more of her photos.

"Whose side are you on?" I gently kick her shin.

"I thought you said there were no sides." She kicks me back.

"So I'm a big fucking fraud. It'd be way easier to be a better feminist if my boobs weren't so tiny." I reach up and grab Nora's outstretched hand, and she pulls me back to a standing position.

"You're lying to yourself, sweetheart." She brushes the dust off my shoulder. The bell above the door tinkles as a pair of customers come in. "I've got double Ds, and I'm a real asshole," she whispers to me, before turning to greet them.

2

I'm in Henry's basement apartment. He didn't tell me he lived in a basement. Based on his job, I would have assumed someplace above ground. I ask if he's been living here long, and he says he's only been here since the divorce. He didn't tell me he was divorced either.

He's across from me on the couch while I sit on the significantly lower footstool. I'm there because he told me to be there. I'm not allowed to move without his permission. He's got his hand on my thigh, the spot between stocking and garter belt. My hand is on his. I'm still wearing my dress, but it's hiked up to useless levels right now.

"Before we get started, I need to know your limits and safe words."

"Right." Henry has experience with kink, which so far seems to mean he approaches everything in a drawn-out, formal way. This is fine, so far. Rules turn me on. "No drawing blood, no bathroom stuff, no anal, at least not right away." I continue, "And if it gets to be too much, I'll shout, 'Rhubarb!'"

"Rhubarb is good. I personally like to use the red, yellow, green system."

"Sure. We can do that too."

"Green is for when everything is going well," he says. "It's usually not necessary to say, but if I'm doing something you want more of and you don't want to break character, you can just say green."

"Cool. And yellow is for slow down, and red is for stop. Got it. Let's go."

"Don't interrupt me," he says, and I instantly reply, "Yes, Sir," the words reverberating in my cunt.

"Green means good or keep going," he continues. "If you say yellow, that means you need to stop for a minute, and we can check in with each other about how we're doing. Do you understand?"

"Yes, Sir. I'm ready to have sex now."

"Now red," he says, and I try not to roll my eyes in frustration. Listening to him talk is its own exercise in masochism. "Red means you want to stop completely. It doesn't necessarily mean we have to finish for the night, but it does mean you need to break for a while. I don't want you to be afraid to use any of your safe words. I'll never get mad at you for using your yellow or your red or your rhubarb. Okay?"

"Yes, Sir." He makes me repeat it back to him to prove that I understand, and I do. We've been sitting like this, talking, for over an hour. Henry says it's important to get to know each other before we play—he calls it playing because this is a game and nothing more—but all I want is for Henry to stop talking and to grab me. I worry that the more I learn about him, the less I'll be willing to give him control over me. Not because I'd be scared of him. Because of the opposite. I can only commit to a game of make-believe for so long while keeping my clothes on.

"Excellent," he says. "Now, the second system I like to use is a numerical scale to rate personal levels of pain."

We do eventually get to the good stuff. He doesn't even take his clothes off, but he doesn't need to. He ties me up, spanks me, raises my dress, and shoves his fingers into my conspicuously wet vagina while I'm bent over his coffee table. Then he makes me wash and dry his dishes while I'm wearing nothing but panties and stockings. He watches, his arms crossed over his chest, giving no indication if I'm on the right track as I scurry around his kitchen in my underwear trying to figure out where each pot and glass goes. His apartment is like a warped funhouse filled with secret compartments: he takes the top off a footstool at one point to reveal a selection of collars and leashes. A secret drawer slides out from under his bed to show off his collection of paddles. "This one is custom made." He hands me a large, smooth fraternity paddle with a smile. He is trying to keep his dominant voice on but can't help letting some boyish excitement come through. "Pure oak."

"It's . . . nice," I say, unsure exactly how one is supposed to compliment a paddle, wondering if oak is known for its particularly painful qualities. I add quick a "Sir," and he nods, satisfied that I seem impressed with his collection of punishment toys. He ties my wrists behind my back and orders me to kneel by his plug-in fireplace while he goes to the bathroom.

I look around his living room. There's a record player sitting next to a stack of alternative-rock records from the nineties. There is artwork hanging on the wall, a very particular kind of art: Disney princesses in a mall-goth style, their corsets revealing their cartoon cleavage. I try to remember how old Henry is. Thirty-seven or thirty-eight? Thirty-seven, I think. What's the cut-off line for horny Disney fan art? Probably thirty-seven and a half. Does the fireplace even work?

There aren't really windows in a basement apartment, and there's a lot of space between the two exits. I wonder how hard it would be to escape if there were a fire. I wonder how hard it would be to escape if I were tied up.

I start to squirm, my wrists pulling against my restraints, my pussy soaking through the thin layer of fabric between my thighs, and despite being alone in the room a girlish squeal escapes my lips. I'm stunned at myself. I've never made *that* noise before. The collar feels tight on my throat. Maybe that's it. Maybe the collar is cutting off the oxygen to my brain, and it's turning me into a squealer. It's not a bad feeling; it would explain the lightness in my extremities, the contradictory sense of security that comes with being terrified. The Disney princess artwork is even starting to appeal to me.

"Good girrrrrrl," Henry says, his voice almost a purr, as he reenters the room and sees me kneeling where he left me. He crouches down in front of me and starts scratching me behind the ears like I'm a little dog, and I find the whole thing confusingly erotic. "Such a good little girl."

"I was so scared, Sir," I say in a breathy whisper I don't recognize in myself. *What the fuck, Lucy?* But then he pats my head again, and it's so nice and reassuring, and he calls me a good girl again as I nuzzle up against his hand, and it takes me a minute to realize that now I'm the one who is purring.

3

I take orders from Henry nonstop for the next week. We're playing the same game we played before, where he texts me orders, but now it's in hyperdrive. He's the first person I contact when I wake up, giving him a list of everything I have to do, and he responds with a minute-by-minute schedule of how my day is going to go. I'm to update him every time I finish a task or if I'm running behind schedule, and he always responds within minutes. If he's busy with his burlesque-dancing girlfriend, he doesn't show it. When I finish a task on time or ahead of schedule, he replies with a succinct *good girl*. If I stray from what I'm supposed to be doing or forget to tell him something I have to do that day, he lets me know he is very disappointed in me. At the end of the day, he allows me to have certain rewards (usually permission to masturbate to completion) or punishments (sending him nude pictures of myself in compromising positions). Then he'll order me to get to bed. This last part is the most demeaning, being given a bedtime, and so it turns me on the most.

I don't go on any dates or message any other men or even see my friends during this week because Henry hasn't given me permission to do so and I haven't thought to ask. Sasha texts me a few times to hang out, saying she's having weird side effects adjusting to her new birth control and needs someone to rewatch *Buffy the Vampire Slayer* with, but I make up excuses. I don't know how to fit her into this new schedule. She's sex positive enough—she owns like six vibrators and follows Amber Rose on Instagram—but I anticipate a feminist rant on following orders from a man outside the bedroom. It's already almost too much talking to Nora about it.

"Isn't this getting a little excessive?" Nora asks one day at work as I pull out my phone for the thirtieth time that shift to give Henry an update.

"Are you slut-shaming me?" I say, not looking up from my phone. I'm joking in that way where I mean everything I say. "I know your MO, Nora. You should be supporting me having hot sex."

"I want you to have sex!" she practically shouts, causing the lone customer browsing in the science section to look over with raised eyebrows. "I want you to have all the hottest, filthiest, kinkiest sex your young libido desires. But is this even about that? You told me you haven't even sucked this guy's dick yet."

"But the part *around* the sex makes the sex part hotter. That's true for everything. Last week you told me just the sight of Christopher on his motorcycle made you have to throw out your panties, and then *I* said couldn't you just wash the panties, and *you* said I should stop being so obtuse and that you were just making a joke, and then *I* said yeah I was also making a joke and then—"

"Christopher's motorcycle doesn't control all my actions throughout the day."

"But *that's what makes it so hot.* My guy, not yours. No offence."

"Offence definitely taken."

"Look," I say. "Have you ever seen the movie *Secretary*?"

"You're talking about that romantic movie they made based on an incredibly bleak Mary Gaitskill short story? I was your age when that collection came out. You are not in a position to be teaching me about the transgressive literature of my generation."

"Forget the story for a second. The movie is nothing like that. Mary Gaitskill is a talented writer and all, but it's like the two aren't even the same." Actually, "Secretary" is the only piece of Mary Gaitskill's writing I've read, after I watched the movie on TV late one night when I was in high school and became obsessed. I had never watched porn before and was aware of BDSM in its corniest manifestations, like with dungeons and floggers and the stuff of Henry's Facebook pictures, but had never seen it play out on screen the way I did in the movie. I read online that it was based on a story from a collection called *Bad Behavior*, and the next day I found a copy at the public library. I flipped to the story, hoping to read something modern and hot and exciting. I was ready to be seen. Instead I found a depressing short story and only read a few pages before putting it back on the shelf. Then I went home and rewatched the movie.

"So, *Secretary.* Maggie Gyllenhaal plays this woman who just gets out of a mental hospital," I start.

"Oh, that sounds like a perfect movie to model your love life on."

"She gets out of the hospital," I continue. "But she liked it there. She liked the structure and routine and rules and feeling of safety. Anyway, she is living with her parents but gets a job as a secretary for a lawyer played by James Spader. And he's really intense and bossy and starts to control how she dresses and carries herself, but he also takes care of her. And then soon he starts, like, spanking her, and she's totally into it. Oh, she used to cut herself, I forgot to say, but she stops when he starts punishing her. Anyway, in her 'real life' she dates this boring vanilla guy who is nice but just totally wrong for her, and she's supposed to marry him, but she doesn't. She leaves him for James Spader, and they live a full-time dominant-submissive relationship, and she's happy."

"And how sustainable is that?" asks Nora.

"She doesn't get bored of it. They never get sick of role-playing with each other." It's not even role-playing, I think. Not really. It's just her life.

"What happens when she can't get that high feeling from him? What happens when he's not around to keep her stable?"

"Well, I guess there is one part of the movie where he leaves her and she becomes super depressed and starts self-harming again and tries to seek out sex with all these awful dangerous guys who are bad for her." I check my hair in the reflection of my phone screen. I have what is technically my second date with Henry tonight, although with the constant communication it's as if he's always present. The knowledge that I will once again be seeing his physical self—and that said physical self will hope-fully be hitting my physical self with physical objects—is a reminder that, game or not, this is real too. "But then he comes back and everything's fine again."

"Sweetheart, do you not see the problem with this?" Nora says. "Look, have a good time, but you're treating sex the way we used to treat drugs in the eighties, which you'd know if you actually read any of Gaitskill's books. It's fine and fun and no big deal until it becomes an addiction and you can't stand to be stuck with yourself."

"Yeah, I get it, Nora, you're hardcore," I deadpan.

"Listen to me, Lucy," she says, now serious. "This is one of those things I have more experience in than you. You can't base your entire happiness, all your well-being, on whether or not this guy is willing to pay attention to you. When the sex stops being about sex and starts becoming the only thing keeping you stable, then you're in dangerous territory. What happens when Henry isn't around?"

"I don't have to think about that right now. Henry isn't going anywhere."

Henry is going to South America with his girlfriend.

"Didn't I tell you before?" he asks me that night while I'm hog-tied on his kitchen table. "I could have sworn I told you earlier."

"You did not." I struggle against the ropes. "I would have remembered you telling me you were leaving the country for two weeks next Tuesday. And can I also just add: rhubarb."

He unties me, and I start rubbing my arms. He sits down on the couch and motions for me to join him. I curl up next to him and he puts his arm around me.

"It's a big deal for us as a couple." He absentmindedly plays with my nipple. I straighten a little. Did he just refer to us as a couple? I wasn't thinking about us in those terms, but the idea of the stability offered would refute Nora's warning.

"It is?" I ask.

"This trip. It'll be the first one me and Violet are taking together. Which is nuts! I'm head over heels in love with her, like nothing else I've ever felt."

"Oh," I deflate. He doesn't seem to notice.

"I can't wait to go with her. You would love her. Pretty much everyone does." I can't think of anything to say to this, so I say nothing, which he does notice. "You good?"

"Yeah, I'm fine." I shrug his arm off my shoulder. "I'm just . . . I'm gonna miss you, you know? What am I going to do if you're not giving me directions all day?" I give a dry laugh like the whole thing is just some big joke, I'm just so cool and chill and laid back, I could be a burlesque dancer with how hot and cool I am, but I feel like it wouldn't take much for me to cry.

"I will be coming back." He reaches out and squeezes my knee. It's easy for him, a natural gesture, the way he can touch even the non-erogenous parts of my body like they belong to him, another move I'm unsure how to reciprocate.

"It's just a long time to go without getting laid. I mean, I'm totally still dating other people," I lie. "But I'm not doing what we're doing with other people." I massage my wrists, the imprints of the rope still visible, little marks that will fade overnight and disappear by morning, like Henry.

"Well." He deepens his voice, and his grip tightens around my knee so that his fingernails start to bite into my skin. I can feel myself getting wet again. "Maybe a time out from sex is exactly what an insatiable little slut like you needs."

"Yes, Sir." That's it. That's the solution. Gamify my loneliness. Turn it into another kink. "What should I do instead?"

He is silent for a moment as I snuggle back into him, and he holds me, his fingers tickling up and down my spine. "What's something you've always wanted to do?"

"I've actually never been with a woman before, but I'm really curious. I think I would be good at it." Visions of Violet's chest pop into my head.

"No, dummy." He smacks my upper thigh. "No sex, remember? What's something in *life* you've always wanted to do."

"I want to be your good girl," I say, partially because it's how I genuinely feel in the moment but also because I'm not sure what he's getting at. We have never had a full conversation that wasn't about sex.

"You're a writer."

"Who told you that?"

"It was in your Tinder bio. And yet, I know how you've spent every minute of your life for the last couple weeks, and not a second of it was spent writing."

"I have a day job." I did put "writer" in my Tinder bio because it sounded more romantic and elegant than "bookseller," and also because it seemed impressive enough without intimidating the types of men I wanted to spank me. "Writers don't always have to be writing. Writers drink. Writers rant. Writers phone. Writers sleep. It's this whole thing. *Speedboat*. Renata Adler? Sir."

"Writers seem to have time to scrub their whole apartment and masturbate three times a day."

"I was following orders!" My voice rises in pitch. I haven't yet had to explain my choices to him. He was supposed to be my reprieve from that. "I did an internship during my undergrad, and I've freelanced a little since then. I'm no Woodward and Bernstein," and I immediately regret saying this because it makes me think about *Deep Throat*, which makes me think about sex again.

"When was the last time you wrote anything?" I shrug. "I want you to keep a journal." My nose wrinkles. "Let me say that again. I'm ordering you to keep a journal, slut. And I want you to write in it every day that I'm away. They don't have to be long entries, but they have to be honest. One new, honest, intimate thought per day. And when I come back, I'm going to strip you naked, make you stand perfectly still, and have you read the whole journal start to finish without stopping. Then I'm going to fuck you. Hard. Is that clear, slut?"

Exposure is a turn-on I can recognize. "Yes, Sir," I answer.

"Good." He kisses my forehead and sends me off to do his dishes again, and I am happy to have a job that doesn't involve me explaining my choices to anyone.

4

The next morning, I buy a pocket-sized Five Star notebook from the 7-Eleven down the street before Henry has even left for his trip. I start writing as soon as I get home.

Dear Sir,

I'm sitting at my desk, naked except for my stockings. I know you didn't tell me I had to do that, but I thought it would be extra hot. I like feeling controlled and owned by you. I guess that's my honest thought of the day. I want you to consume me, completely and wholly, until I am nothing more than your disposable fuck doll. Does that sound good to you? I think that sounds simply divine.

Yours,

L.

I put down my pen and sit up, dressed in ratty sweatpants and an old T-shirt. I have completed my only task for the day. Henry has been deciding how I spend every single hour for the last two weeks. I grab my laptop and take it to my bed. Scrolling through my Facebook feed, I see people I went to high school with posting about their husbands and kids, and people I went to undergrad with posting about professional accomplishments. I slam the laptop shut and shove it under my pillow, as if to muffle everyone else's noise. I think about going out for a walk, but I have nowhere in mind to go. I think about cleaning

24

my apartment, but I've done that so thoroughly several times in the last few weeks there's nothing left to clean. I pull out my laptop again, open a new window, and search "bdsm spanking porn good story hot."

Dear Sir,

Well, I'm a real dummy. I confessed my sexual thoughts on day one, and now I have to think of something new to tell you. You did order me to share a new thought every day. Here's one: I wanna be your pet. Hmm, no, that's too similar to yesterday. I could tell you about my day. Is that what you want to hear? If only you hadn't ordered me to be so chaste in your absence, I could fill these pages with fun stories for you. Instead, I spent the day with Sasha. I hadn't seen her in a while because she's been so busy. Her boyfriend is working on the election; he got hired on a local campaign and keeps talking about how this election is going to be a "game changer." He uses that phrase like five, six times a conversation. I'm not going to tell you which candidate it is, but he is handsome and charismatic and absolutely dumb as shit with mediocre politics, just like Sasha's boyfriend. I have no plans to support his party, and neither does Sasha. Is that honest enough? Or is that kind of boring? Okay: When I see my best friend's boyfriend, I can't imagine how anyone in the world, least of all her, could ever imagine fucking him.

I can imagine fucking you though.

Sincerely,

L.

I am, explicitly, not a writer. I am well read because I was a lonely kid, went to a liberal arts school, and work at a bookstore. I made efforts at being a writer during my undergrad because it seemed like a logical choice given my major. There was teaching, of course, but being responsible for a future generation of minds terrified me. Then again so did any semblance of real journalism; asking people difficult questions, prodding and pursuing controversial stories, taking a stance that would be read and consumed and judged by the public seemed anxiety-inducing to me. At my internship during undergrad at the *Hogtown Weekly*, a.k.a. *The Hog*, the city's alt-weekly, I found a comfortable beat spotlighting local underground artists, interviewing them about their process and work. I liked the part of the job where I got to share niche things with the public, although when I thought too hard about my work being read by a large audience, I would get anxious, afraid of being judged. Writing to Henry is different, of course, only because with him being judged is the point.

Sometimes at my internship I helped the real reporters with their stories, transcribing long interviews or organizing research, and I enjoyed the safety of hiding behind their work. The editor I worked with most, a louche hipster named Malcolm, once called me his girl Friday, which of course made me incredibly horny. Then my internship ended, and the paper said they didn't have the resources to offer me a real job, and I got hired at the bookstore, and, well. I don't put any of this in my journal entries to Henry. My career anxieties feel like a different sort of private, banal and unerotic.

Dear Sir,
Today Sasha and I went to a protest at city hall to show solidarity with the taxi-driver union against the lack of legislation for

rideshare companies and how this is negatively affecting already exploited workers, but get this . . . I wasn't wearing any panties. Pretty naughty, huh?

Sincerely,

L.

Dear Sir,

Wow, you've been gone a whole week. I'm getting a little antsy. At first I thought it would be super hot not being allowed to touch myself or cum at all while you were away, but it's really hard! I also haven't been on any dates or sexted anyone because I am trying to be good at my job and this assignment and not be such a dirty slut all the time. That's my honest thought for today. Come home soon! I miss you.

L.

Dear Sir,

I know you are having fun in Peru, but I sent you an email today anyway asking if I could please, please touch myself. I mean, by the time you're reading this diary, you definitely will know about the email. You haven't responded yet, probably because you're so busy travelling and seeing the sights, and, let's be real, getting laid. I hope to hear from you, even if it's just a short message!

L.

Dear Sir,

Okay, so you still haven't responded to my email, so I sent you a Facebook message too. Ha ha, I can be such an insatiable little brat ;). I don't know how I'm going to read a little winky face out loud to you when we play later, but I'm sure we'll figure out a way. I miss you.

L.

Dear Sir,

I've accepted you probably don't have much in the way of Wi-Fi/computer access on your trip, and I should probably be leaving you alone since I'll be seeing you in a few days, but . . . I made myself cum today. And it felt soooo good. Worth whatever punishment you decide to give me, even though I'll probably regret saying that later.
L.

Dear Sir,

You come home today!!! My honest thought is that I've missed you more than I originally thought I would and I'm very, very excited to see you.
Lucy

5

My phone buzzes, and I jump up from the couch where I've been trying and failing to read for the past hour. Henry has been home for five days, and I haven't heard from him yet. I figured he would need a couple days to settle in once he came back, but Violet has already been posting pictures to her Instagram out partying with friends, smiling wide in a low-cut shirt. "Great being back with these bitches," she captioned one. I swiped through the photos of her trip with Henry, a series of beautifully staged shots, each tagged #wanderlust.

But the text is not from Henry.

You still haven't told me what days you're coming home for Thanksgiving, my mom wrote. I ignore it.

I try to go back to my book, a slim French midcentury novella in which the protagonist is having lots of sex, but I can't focus. I pick up my phone again, open Instagram. Violet's grinning face fills the screen. I close Instagram, pick up my book, remember that I can't focus, put the book down again, pick up my phone, my thumb hovering over Instagram. *No, dummy, you tried that already.* I decide to call my best friend.

"It's 2015," Sasha answers the phone. "Who uses their phone to call people?"

"Let's do something," I say.

"I can't hang out today. I have to work later."

"No, not like that." I look around the room, willing the words to come. I need a distraction, something noble that will brush my own petty problems aside. I don't want to sit around waiting for a guy to call. I should be out there, living my life and saving the world, so when the guy calls, he'll be impressed with how important and altruistic I am. "The election. We should be out there pounding the pavement for whichever politician wants to ban cars and eat the rich or whatever."

"Ugh, the dumb election. You know I don't love the dude Ryan is working for. And I don't think it would look good if I volunteered on the other candidate's campaign."

This is not the answer I needed to hear. Sasha always seems to have at least a dozen causes. "Tell Ryan he's being the literal patriarchy right now."

She laughs. "You can tell him yourself, except he's never home. He's working stupid-long hours. He's convinced that if his candidate wins, he'll be hired full time. I haven't seen him this passionate about anything since *The Newsroom* was on the air."

"So isn't there *any* system we can shake up this week?"

"You can work on a campaign without me, you know. And if you're really looking for something new to do, I started volunteering with this cool program at the library twice a week. We help kids with reading. The application takes a while because they do background checks to make sure no weird pedophiles are signing up, but I can be a reference for you—"

I don't hear the end of her sentence because my phone buzzes again and I pull it away from my ear to look at the screen. I see Henry's name above what looks like a novel.

"Listen, Sash, I gotta go, but I'll call you later?" I hang up.

Henry's text message is long. My eyes blur as I try to absorb what he's telling me. He is sorry he took his time getting back to me, he says, but he's been thinking a lot about us and what I need. This whole business of him telling me what to do all day has become emotionally draining and is distracting him from the relationship that counts in his life, with his girlfriend. He says he hopes I understand that he will no longer be able to offer me that going forward. Frowny-face emoji.

"But *you're* the one that made me send you a list every morning!" I say to no one in my big empty room.

I text him back, *I didn't mean to be emotionally draining.*

He says he knows. He thinks I'm a wonderful person with a lot to give to the world, and this has nothing to do with me personally.

I text him, *K.* I go to bed. It's 3 p.m.

The first time I remember the rules really starting to change was in eighth grade. I always assumed it would happen right at the beginning of middle school or high school, something with a clear boundary indicating that childhood was behind us and we were starting a new phase of our lives with new priorities, but it was a dull, amorphous progress, like waiting for sea monkeys to hatch.

My childhood friend Kenzie was the first to get boobs. She had always had a softness to her, a gentle layer of baby fat that gave her a cherubic look, with rosy cheeks and fine ringlets. But between seventh and eighth grade, something changed. She started straightening her hair until it was as flat as straw, her crispy split ends accentuated by the recent blond streaks. ("She uses an actual iron to get that effect," Alyssa whispered to me in geography class one day. "More effective than a ceramic straightener even.") Her skin hid under a thick layer of foundation. She wore mascara that made her eyelashes into spikey instruments of war. Her lips were permanently sticky with MAC Lipglass, which cost way more than everyone else's Caboodles gunk. I assumed the swell of her chest must be a padded bra, like the ones my mom had been buying for me while I insisted on sticking with my cotton undershirts, but in the change room before gym class I saw them, held up by the pinkest of bras from La Senza, gentle stretch marks sprawling out from the lace trim towards her torso like her own body could barely contain their size. I didn't realize they could even get that big at our age.

"Are you staring at my boobs?" she said, bringing me back to the change room. She said it loudly enough that a dozen other pubescent heads turned to look, first at her, then at me. "What are you, Lucy, some kind of lesbo?"

I heard snickers of disbelief while the other girls looked at me accusingly, protecting their own half-undressed chests with their arms as if they were next. Kenzie didn't cover up. She stood there, hands on her matching pink-cotton-and-lace-underwear hips, as if daring me to keep looking.

"No, I—" I stammered. "Obviously I wasn't. Ew." I don't know if that locker room had ever been as quiet. "I was looking at . . . your necklace. It's so weird, you wear it every day, but I've never really paid attention to it until right now. It's so pretty." It was bullshit. Kenzie would see straight through my lie and double down on calling me a lesbo and all the other girls would join in and laugh and I would have to change schools, although there was no way my mom was going to let me ride the city bus on my own, which I would need to take to get to the next closest middle school.

But Kenzie surprised me. Her hand went straight to her collarbone, fingers gently brushing the necklace, and she beamed. "My dad brought it back for me from a work trip," she said. "He had to get it custom made at the store because my name is so uncommon."

"It's super pretty," said Steph R.

"Is it real gold?" asked Larissa. I gently exhaled and resumed changing into my gym clothes while the rest of the room mercifully resumed their chatter. We would be doing volleyball in class that day. I hated volleyball.

Studying felt safe. I was ahead in all my classes but tried not to show it. It was no longer cool to be smart the way it had been in earlier grades when it was impressive to come to school with fully formed facts ready about Ancient Rome or marsupials, picked up from *National Geographic Kids* in the library. Now, I made a strict rule for myself to raise my hand for only one out of four questions our teacher asked, regardless of how many answers I knew. I had made the mistake of knowing too much about geography the first week back to school—I had gotten really into playing a Carmen Sandiego computer game that summer—and after I correctly answered the sixth question in a row, Mrs. Marisol said, "Why don't we hear from someone else this time?" My face burned as I put my hand down. I turned to Alyssa, sitting next to me, for reassurance that I had done nothing wrong, but she just stared at her notebook. I had thought the goal in school was to get as many answers right as possible; it was a system that had worked for me so far. Instead it seemed that everyone, including Mrs. Marisol, had privately agreed there was now a new way to do things.

Still, nobody could stop me studying alone in my bedroom. Maybe it was inappropriate to show off how smart I was, but I could still get good grades. This is what Bill Gates said, I thought to myself as I spent another weeknight alone in my room, reading ahead in a science textbook: "Be nice to nerds. Chances are you'll end up working for them." Everybody makes fun of the nerds in high school, but then they go off to get good jobs as computer hackers or millionaires or whatever, and all the bullies end up pumping gas or watering lawns. It was a fantasy I didn't believe, even at thirteen, before I read about labour rights in undergrad, but it seemed to be the thing I was supposed to want—to grow up rich and successful at the expense of any kid who had ever rolled their eyes at me. I had an image of myself lounging by a pool behind a giant mansion, drinking some fancy fruity drink out of a straw. Alyssa and Kenzie were there, fanning me with palm fronds. *This is what you're supposed to want.* I had been reading the same line in my textbook for over an hour, absorbing none of it, the fantasy ringing hollow in my head. Was sitting on a lawn chair by a pool without a book supposed to be appealing to me? Suddenly, the positions in my head switched. Alyssa and Kenzie were in the lawn chairs, and I was the one with the palm frond, fanning them while they whispered and pointed at me, wearing matching nameplate necklaces. I imagined Kenzie ordering me to get more drinks, and I said, "Yes, miss," and a tremor went through my body. I sneezed, which brought me back to the present. I sat up straight and slammed my textbook shut, looking over my shoulder as if someone was watching me, seeing into my thoughts. I went to take a shower for the second time that day.

"Why don't you invite the girls for a sleepover?" my mother asked over dinner one night. She had made baked chicken with asparagus and garlic mashed potatoes.

"What girls?" I asked. My mom referred to "the girls" often, but usually she was talking about her own friends. There were "the girls" from her university days, who she made a point of going away with at least one weekend a year, and "the girls" in her book club, who were mostly other moms from the PTA years prior, and "the girls" from work, a group of professionals who had fought seriously to be seen not as girls but as women and who got together every Thursday night to drink white wine and gossip. She never remarried after my dad died, though she had a few boyfriends over the years, none of whom stuck around long enough for me to meet. She claimed she was the youngest person ever to be promoted to vice president of e-commerce for the province-wide grocery-store chain where she worked, although I don't know how she actually confirmed that record. Her own mother never worked.

"I ran into Alyssa's mom at the bank yesterday," she said. "Have you seen her at all since soccer ended?"

"Yeah, Mom, I see her every day at school." I wondered what it would be like to have a friend whose full name, address, family, and blood type weren't already known to my mother. I had gone to the same school since kindergarten, with the same people I played recreational sports or took piano lessons with, whose older siblings had babysat me, whose parents sat on the same councils or committees as each other planning spring-fling fundraisers and bake sales. Most of the parents in the community had grown up with each other too; my mom was an outlier. My family had moved here from the East Coast when I was a baby because of my dad's work. My mom started at an entry-level position in the grocery store's headquarters and worked her way up. She was also one of the few non-white people in our neighbourhood, although she blended in well enough. She kept my dad's Scandinavian last name, Selberg, which was a lot more inconspicuous than Gambhir, her Punjabi maiden name. She bought her clothes from what she called the "high-end" mall stores, Banana Republic and Club Monaco. Her hair had been processed blond for so long that I almost forgot it was naturally darker than mine, and she stripped off her facial hair using a little pot of wax that she heated over the kitchen stove every Sunday night, until she was just like every other mom.

"You haven't gone out once this school year," she said. "You haven't had anyone over. You can tell me what's going on."

"I'm fine, Mom," I said, mostly meaning it. I never thought of myself as happy, but I was content as I could be in the circumstances. I liked watching two *Seinfeld* reruns after dinner and then retreating to my room to read or study until I was ready to fall asleep. It's not even that I loved school that much. I promised myself I only had to study lots now so I could get good grades and get into university in Montreal or Vancouver or Toronto or maybe even the States, where my real life could begin.

"Well, I told Alyssa's mom you were having a sleepover party next weekend and that Alyssa was invited. Kenzie and Steph D. too. I called their moms earlier today."

"Mom," I said in disbelief. "Are you serious? Nobody makes plans through their parents anymore. We're in middle school. And nobody calls them 'sleepover parties.' It's called 'hanging out' and 'crashing,' and you don't plan these things a week in advance, they just happen."

"I thought it would be nice," she said. "We can rent movies. I'll get lots of snacks. My parents never let me have friends over. They never even let me go to sleepover parties. And we can go shopping beforehand to get you something nice to wear." She reached out and thumbed the polyester dress I had thrifted from Value Village that summer, which I believed gave me a cool eclectic vintage look but really just sat misshapen on my body, trapping in the sweaty odours of that warm autumn day.

I pushed my chair back from the table and stood up. "Could you ask me before you go and completely ruin my life?" I said, and before she could accuse me of being dramatic, I slammed my chair back into the table and stormed off towards my room, my dinner unfinished.

Kenzie was the last to arrive to the sleepover party, which I assured the girls was just "hanging out or whatever." It was surreal seeing her again in the entrance to my house; she had been over all the time when we were kids, but now she seemed a million times taller, plunking her monogrammed TNA gym bag on the ground. (Where had she got that? We didn't even have an Aritzia in town.) She slid off her

UGGs. They were the real UGGs too, the ones that cost three hundred dollars and had the label on the back and felt like clouds and only came in camel and were ugly as sin and completely impractical for Canadian winters but were for some reason the outdoor footwear coveted by every girl in my grade. Kenzie was the only eighth grader to have a real pair; most settled for the grape or forest-green knock-offs. My mother offered to buy me a pair last time we were at the mall, but I begged her instead for a pair of hot-pink Doc Martens, which were half the price. She scoffed and asked if I really wanted to be one of "those girls."

I wondered if, in a bigger city, Kenzie would still be considered popular. She didn't look like the girls in the teen magazines my mom subscribed me to, angular reality-TV starlets with long blond extensions, pink velour track-suits, and chihuahua accessories. But Kenzie had a natural confidence that everything she was doing was exactly what she should be doing, as well as exactly what everyone else should be doing. And though I thought the sleepover was stupid, I was grateful she had shown up to give whatever was happening that night some legitimacy.

After pizza (Kenzie refused to eat the crust because she wasn't "into carbs right now," and Alyssa and Steph D. followed suit while I tried to hide that I had already had two slices), after watching *Bring It On* ("God that's, like, so our lives," said Alyssa; no school we knew of had a cheerleading squad), we set up our sleeping bags in the living room, sprawled out like a cross with our pillows at the intersection. Mom had decorated the room with streamers, which I had quickly torn down and shoved under the couch before anyone had shown up. Kenzie lay on her stomach on her sleeping bag, dressed in a floral tank top and matching shorts, propping herself up on her elbows. The rest of us mimicked her position on our own sleeping bags.

"Are we sure Anita's asleep?" Kenzie said. Hearing her refer to my mom so intimately jarred me.

"Uh, I guess so?" I said. "She's a light sleeper though, so we should probably be pretty quiet."

"Perfect," said Kenzie. She pushed herself up and reached into her TNA bag near the head of her sleeping bag and pulled out a bottle of amber liquid. "It's called Fireball. My brother got it for me. It tastes really good, not like beer at all."

"Is that . . . alcohol?" I asked, dropping my voice to a whisper. I looked around at Alyssa and Steph D., but they seemed untroubled. Excited even. Kenzie screwed the top off the bottle and took a swig. I had never had booze before.

"Don't worry," she said. "My brother isn't going to tell anyone." She passed the bottle to Alyssa, who took an equally large swig.

I didn't know what would happen to a person when they got drunk. I didn't know what would happen to me. On TV, characters seemed transformed from their regular selves, unaware of their actions, free from consequences until the next morning. The thought terrified and thrilled me. Would I know what I was doing? Would I be like a person possessed—completely out of control, at the mercy of a little voice in my head brought on by the Fireball—and do something really stupid like strip down naked, run out into traffic, and end up in jail? People did stuff like that when drunk. I'd read the news.

Alyssa was next to me with her arm outstretched, passing me the bottle, and I realized they were all waiting for me. "I don't know," I said. "My mom's right upstairs. We could get in trouble."

"Come on," Alyssa said. "We'll be quiet. She'll never know."

"It won't be fun if you're the only one sober," Kenzie said. "I've done this before. It'll be fine. Don't you trust me?"

She was sitting cross-legged on her sleeping bag in her pyjamas, but sitting up straight, she had an authority to her. She seemed to have figured out eighth grade in a way that I hadn't yet: how to drink, how to have boobs, how to simply live without fear. In that moment, I wanted to believe everything she had told and would ever tell me. I took a sip. It tasted pretty good, like cinnamon hearts.

"That's not gonna do anything," Kenzie said. "You have to drink a lot really fast if you want to feel the effects." I took a larger swig, winced as it burned down my throat, and passed the bottle on to Steph D., who squealed and clapped her hands, and Alyssa quickly mimicked her. I sat up a little straighter at their approval.

We passed the bottle around the circle three more times before deciding to play truth or dare. Kenzie asked Steph D. who her crush was, and Steph D. named Richard, a boy from our class we had all known since kindergarten. We all burst out into giggles—it was so funny, why was it so funny, I couldn't stop laughing at how funny everything was—and Alyssa said, "He is pretty hot." I didn't know boys our age could be hot. I still associated Richard with the time in second grade when he threw up at our class Halloween party after eating too much candy. I shuddered. *Don't think about vomit right now.*

"Alyssa, truth or dare?" Steph D. asked.

Alyssa started to giggle, and the rest of us joined in— everything about the game continued to be the funniest thing in the world, my friends were so funny, my best friends, I was light and happy with my best friends and nothing bad would ever happen to us while we were safe on our sleeping bags—and then she said, "I don't know. Dare, I guess."

"I dare you to . . . hmmmm." Steph D. looked around the room for inspiration. "Get on your hands and knees and bark like a dog."

"Ew, that's so gay," Kenzie said. I flushed. I knew we weren't supposed to be using *gay* as an insult, but it seemed like the wrong time to correct anyone, least of all Kenzie. Steph D. looked embarrassed too, self-conscious that her dare had been criticized.

"I think it'd be funny," she said, picking a piece of lint from her PJ bottoms.

"How is that even a dare? You should dare me to drink more Fireball," Alyssa said. Her words were starting to slur. How long did it take to get drunk? I realized I had no idea what time it was, how long we had been sitting there. Nothing mattered anymore, nothing except the taste of cinnamon hearts and playing the game. I looked at Steph D., who was still focused on her PJs, looking like she had done something wrong.

"I'll do it," I announced, the words out of my mouth before I realized what I was saying.

"You'll drink more Fireball?" Alyssa asked.

"I'll be the dog."

"Ew. Why?" Kenzie asked.

I sat tall, rolling my shoulders back. "I'm not afraid of a dare," I said. "I'll do whatever."

There was a moment of silence, and Alyssa looked to Kenzie as if to find out what her reaction should be. Kenzie burst out laughing.

"You're so funny," she said. "I forgot how funny you could be." The other girls started giggling again too, and I joined them, a safe, warm laughter.

I crawled onto my arms and knees and let out a little yap. Kenzie started laughing again. "You're so good at that," she said. "You sound just like Smarties. Do it again."

I yapped twice more, then stuck out my tongue and started to pant. I was making Kenzie laugh harder than I had ever seen her laugh, and it felt good. She jumped to her feet. "Wag your tail!" she commanded, adopting the condescending voice I had heard her use when talking to her family's golden lab. I did as she commanded, and Steph D. clapped her hands. "Good girl, good Smarties!" Kenzie said, and I wiggled my butt even harder. Right then I knew I had to keep making her laugh, to keep that smile on her face as she looked down at me, to know I was doing a good job, the best job, everything that was expected of me, everything I needed to be doing.

"I have an idea," said Kenzie, and she turned and started walking out of the room. She stopped, looked over her shoulder at me expectantly, and ordered, "Heel girl!" before continuing. I crawled after her. Alyssa and Steph D. jumped to their feet and followed.

Kenzie brought us to the kitchen, where she grabbed a cereal bowl from the cupboard and filled it up with water. She placed it on the floor by her feet. "Drink, girl!"

I did as she commanded, lapping up water from the bowl, my hips still in the air. "Keep wagging that tail!" she said, and I obliged, listening to another chorus of giggles above me. "Good Smarties! Good girrrrrrl." That last word fell out of her mouth a long drawl, and she crouched down to tenderly scratch me behind the ears. Her hands smelled delicious, like apricot body lotion and something else, something indescribably and uniquely Kenzie. I wasn't able to smell her for long because Kenzie pushed my face farther into the bowl until my whole jaw was submerged, the tip of my nose feeling the cool wetness, and I was unable to do anything but follow orders and make Kenzie happy. "Keep drinking," she said. "And keep that tail wagging, girl." I lapped away at the water. I wondered if I could finish the whole bowl from that position. I bet Kenzie would be impressed if I could.

"What the hell is going on here?" My mother's voice stopped us cold. Kenzie released her hand from the back of my head. I started to raise my head, water dripping down my face, but I couldn't bring myself to look at my mother, or to make eye contact with anyone at all.

"Mrs. Selberg!" said Kenzie, her voice honeyed. "We were just playing this game. It's something everyone is doing at school. We're so sorry if we woke you. We definitely didn't realize how loud we were—"

"Have you been drinking? Where did you get that?"

Still on all fours, I allowed myself to turn my head to see what she was talking about. Steph D. was holding the bottle of Fireball. It was half empty. The bottle swayed in Steph D.'s fist. No, not the bottle. My vision.

The sleepover party was over after that. Mom split us all up; Steph D. and Alyssa stayed in the living room, their sleeping bags moved to either side of the coffee table. Kenzie got my bed. I had to sleep in my mom's room, listening to her reproaches as I climbed under the covers of her big bed, tears stinging my eyes.

"I don't know what kind of sick game you were playing, or what on earth would possess you to debase yourself," she was saying as I put the pillow over my ears, my body turned away from hers, shame like I had never felt coursing through my body. She was still going off as I fell asleep, the alcohol knocking me into a heavy slumber.

By the time I woke up the next morning, Mom had already driven the other girls home, an hour before they were scheduled to be picked up, and I somehow felt even worse than I had the night before. A hangover? No, guilt. No, both. Mom met me in the bathroom with a glass of water and a Tylenol as I kneeled over the toilet, retching up the cinnamon-scented contents of my stomach. Later, I came down to the kitchen, where a pot of herbal tea and dry toast were waiting for me. Mom was wiping down the counters. I started to speak—I expected she would want to talk about last night—but when she heard me enter the room, she made eye contact with me, frowned, shook her head, and left the room. We didn't speak for the rest of the day.

I was mostly ignored at school the next day too. I learned that my mom had told Alyssa, Kenzie, and Steph D.'s moms that we had been drinking, and they had all been grounded. They—and their friends, and by extension most of the grade—seemed to take it out on me, as if I were the one who tattled. The silent treatment I could handle; I never cared much about being popular, but the shame felt new. I didn't speak to anyone except when I was called on in class until, walking down the hall to third period, I was stopped by a voice behind me.

"Hey, Lucy!" A pink-polished hand touched my arm. I jerked my head up. Kenzie had a serious expression. I opened my mouth to speak, to apologize—though I wasn't sure what for—but she spoke first. "Don't tell anyone, okay? About the dog thing. I mean it." She looked in my eyes when she said this and took off down the hall before I could respond. Watching the back of her UGGs, it struck me in that moment that she could feel the shame too.

6

"I'm a good person, right?" It's two nights after the last text from Henry, and I'm lying on the floor of Sasha and Ryan's living room. Her pug, Nigel, is curled up next to me snoring, and Sasha is rolling a joint. Nigel originally belonged to her older sister Juliana, who moved abroad for work. A strict vegan, Sasha let everyone know that she was against pugs on principle ("The way they're bred, it's not natural"), but she took to Nigel like she did to her bong.

"Of course you are," says Sasha, her eyes on the papers in front of her. "Why wouldn't you be?" The best part of Ryan working all the time is I can have Sasha to myself, hanging out the way we used to when we lived together, before friendship required coordinating schedules. Sasha, mercifully, has never pushed for me and Ryan to get along. I have refrained from telling her how annoying I find him, and she has never weighed in on what I've told her about Henry. We have a tacit understanding not to impugn choices made in the pursuit of intimacy.

"If I really were a good person, I wouldn't be so self-involved," I say. "I'd be, like, volunteering with kids and stuff, like you do."

"You go to protests all the time."

"Yeah, but I only do that out of guilt that I'm a bad person. That and you make it look so cool." My phone buzzes. I have a new Tinder message from this guy I've been trying to develop a sexting rapport with. His message, a response to one of mine, says, *What did u have in mind lol.* I text back, *I don't know, I've been a pretty bad girl lately.*

"The only reason anybody does anything nice is because they don't want to be thought of as a bad person," Sasha says. "Everyone's motives are dirty if you dig deep enough. You can't think about it too hard, or your head will explode."

"But if I'm so good, why is it so hard to find someone who loves me?" I say pathetically.

"I love you. And Nigel loves you." I roll over and poke Nigel in her pudgy side. Nigel is a girl, but Sasha decided that a dog with an old-man face deserved an old-man name. Gender is a construct anyway, she says, and that goes double for dogs.

"I love you and Nigel too, but a lady has *needs* that you can't really meet." My phone buzzes with a new Tinder message: *its ok everyone has bad days, i'll still fuck u.* "You don't get it. You have a boyfriend."

"Yeah, because all your problems in life magically go away once you're in a relationship," Sasha says. "Shit's not always easy here, you know."

"At least you have a partner on your side to manage those problems," I say. I pick up Nigel and give her a squeeze. "And this little baby. Your perfect domestic family life." Sasha looks up sharply as I say this, almost confused, but she softens when she sees Nigel's squashed fuzzy face.

"Perfect and domestic, my ass," she says. "It's like you haven't even read that Silvia Federici interview I sent you."

"I'm being a brat," I admit. "I'm just lonely and horny and tired of all my boyfriends having girlfriends."

47

"It's fine." Sasha licks the paper sealing the joint. "Look, do you want to, like, go for a walk and smoke this and find somewhere to play pinball?"

"God yes," I say, getting to my feet. As we put on our boots, Nigel starts her ritual freak-out, barking and losing her mind as we go out the door, scared we're leaving her forever.

7

I sit behind the cash at Prologues, staring out the window at two dogs humping in the park across the street. I barely notice when Nora comes up beside me, plopping down a stack of recently unboxed Knausgaards.

"What are you thinking about, sweet daydreamer?" she asks.

"Two dogs humping."

"Huh. You know, I think you may just be the voice of a generation."

She follows my gaze and nods at the scene.

"I'm just holding a mirror up to society, man."

"Speaking of . . . " She starts printing off price labels.

"Speaking of what? My genius? My gift for seeing the world around me with startling accuracy?"

"Speaking of humping. How's your love life?" I look around to see if anyone can hear. Sex is so embarrassing the second you stop having it.

"I love a lot of things. I love . . . Sasha and tacos and books by women who would probably find me annoying if they met me. Those are my love life."

"You know what I mean. I haven't seen your phone light up in a while. This one of your little sex games?"

She is referring to the time Henry ordered me to text him a detailed description of a different sexual fantasy every hour of an eight-hour shift but refused to reply to any of them till late that night. It was blissful torture, coming up with increasingly perverted scenarios. By the fourth hour, I couldn't handle it anymore, so I asked Nora to help, and we flipped through Harlequins copying the corniest passages and changing the names and tenses. She thought the whole thing was a riot.

"Nah, I've decided I'm done with men."

"Good for you! I experimented with women a lot in my twenties. You think you're going to hang out for good on the isle of Lesbos?"

"It's not like that. And I'm sure there was something offensive in what you said. I just can't be bothered to figure it out yet."

"Everything's offensive to your generation."

"Well, I am the voice of it. I have to rep them well." I let out a long sigh and start helping Nora unbox books. "So maybe you're right. Maybe all I want is for somebody to tell me what to do all the time and take care of me and tell me when I'm good and help me when I'm bad, and maybe it isn't even about sex because maybe I've wanted this ever since I saw *Secretary*, or maybe since I was a secretly horny four-year-old and I watched *Beauty and the Beast* and the Beast told Belle she could go anywhere she wanted in the palace except for the west wing or wherever the rose is, and maybe I watched that movie four hundred times and thought, 'I want someone to give me a palace and then forbid me to go into half of it,' and maybe that's messed up, and maybe *I'm* messed up, but now that I've acknowledged it, it's all good, right?"

"Oh, honey. So you're a pervert. Big deal. All the best people are. Those dogs in the park are."

"It's ruining my life. You said as much last month."

"You were having hot sex with a guy, and now it's over, and you're sad. Anyone would be."

"We never even did have sex. Not in the traditional penis-in-vagina way."

"I am aware of how sex works, yes."

"He tied me up, spanked me, ordered me around, and fingered me, but we never had sex. And I don't even care that we never had actual sex! I was fine with all the other stuff. Isn't that warped? I can't even follow through on being a pervert."

Nora makes a small noise in assent and is quiet for a moment as she considers my words. "Have you ever tried ayahuasca?"

"That's your solution for everything." I refocus on the task at hand and grab a pile of books to be shelved. "How are you doing, anyway? Why don't we ever talk about your problems?"

"Justine is with her father this week. I have no problems."

My phone buzzes, and I jump, dropping the books I was holding. There's a text from my mom. *Sale on peplum dresses at Banana Republic. Want one for Christmas? Will be good to have when you start going on interviews for real jobs.* There's a link to the Banana Republic webstore. I ignore it.

"Look," Nora continues as she helps me pick up the books, "you need someone to tell you what to do? I'll tell you what to do. Stop flopping around. You got rejected. That bites, I get that, and I'm sorry. But you either have to give yourself time to feel your feelings or get back to work. That's an order."

"I don't get it. Are you role-playing as my lover or my mom right now?"

51

"First off, honey, the fact that you can't tell the difference means you have a lot in your life you need to sort out. Secondly, I'm neither. I'm your pal Nora. I care about you, and I might not know much, but I do know that you seem to be having a strong reaction to a guy whose dick was never even inside you."

"Fine, I'll get back to work."

"I said you need to feel your feelings. Look, take the rest of the day off. I'm serious. I'll be fine here on my own. Go write in your journal, take a yoga class, drink a glass of wine and cry with your girlfriends, find a real therapist."

"But you're the realest therapist I know!"

"You're a hoot. Now get out of this store. I'm hereby banning you for the rest of the day."

"I don't know if you have that power?"

"You're more than welcome to test me. But I wouldn't."

Reluctantly, I pick up my tote bag. An afternoon to myself would be lovely if it didn't entail being alone with my own thoughts. It's a beautiful fall day, and I find a bench in the park to sit on. The air is breezy and crisp. There are birds chirping and families with young children and dogs running around in the off-leash area and flowers doing whatever it is flowers do and all I want is to be tied up and slapped across the face. I close my eyes and breathe in slowly for five seconds through my nose and out through my mouth. I repeat this action three more times. I guess it feels nice and relaxing or whatever, but as soon as I stop focusing on my breath, I open my eyes and remember how big and vast the world can be and how utterly alone I am in the middle of it.

I remember what Nora said about writing in a journal and rifle through my tote bag for the notebook I bought for writing to Henry. I've been carrying it around with me in case there's a fire at my apartment when I'm not home and the firefighters who salvage my stuff recover it and read it and judge me, not in a hot way.

I reread the entries, feeling at first a sad longing for Henry and then horror at their contents. My thoughts are shallow and pathetic. I am shallow and pathetic. I felt flirty and playful and naughty when I wrote these entries; now I read them as desperate attempts to impress a guy who was ignoring me while he was in Peru with his pinup girlfriend.

I take my pen out of my bag and scribble over the pages, rendering them illegible. It's not enough. I rip out the pages and crinkle them up, then go further and tear them up into the tiniest little pieces. With the heel of my sneaker I scrape out a small hole in the soft soil in front of me and drop the scraps of paper inside before patting the dirt back on top. There.

I open the notebook to a clean page and pull out my pen again and start writing.

Dear Sir,

You gave me permission to trust you, and then you disappeared, and I'm not talking about to Peru. You hid behind a text message so you could retreat to your normal life with a partner who can validate that you're making the right choice, leaving me the sad loser alone with the shame of letting myself be vulnerable with you. It's like the top step disappeared from a staircase I got used to climbing every day, and all that's left in its place is a frowny-face emoji. Cordially, suck my dick, Sir.

Lucy

I barely finish writing that last sentence before I scratch out everything I just wrote and tear it up and bury the page. That my feelings don't even have the pretext of being part of some larger sex game somehow makes them that much worse. There is nobody here to give a shit about what I have to say. I just have to sit with my dumb stupid thoughts, a dumb stupid girl sitting in this dumb stupid park, alone and dumb and also stupid. To top it all off, I realize I'm crying. Crying! I'm all but throwing a temper tantrum over a guy Nora called a narc.

I shove the notebook into my tote bag with a dramatic flourish and pull out my phone. No new texts or notifications. I open Tinder and mechanically start swiping left, left, left, barely giving any of these guys a second thought. Eventually, a guy named Mitch gets my attention. He's twenty-nine with a solid build and those eyes that make a person look sleepy even when they're wide awake. Like James Spader in *Secretary*. Mitch seems like a standard guy; his pictures include him at a bar with his friends wearing sports jerseys, him at a wedding, him playing with his dog at a park. His bio says he's into "Good tunes, good food, and good times." He looks normal and wholesome, and his arm muscles seem as if they could be used to spank me something good. Maybe a Mitch is what I need right now. Mitch will solve my problems. I swipe right. We match instantly.

I can try to offer you good times, but I've been told I'm something of a bad girl, I message him. I don't expect a response right away. It's the middle of the afternoon, and Mitch is probably hard at work at his job of digital branding or front-end software development or whatever it is that normal people do. His reply comes almost immediately.

So ur definitely a bot. No way someone as hot as u opens with a message that exciting, comes his message.

It feels good to be called hot, especially by someone who is, well, mainstream attractive. Mitch looks like the kind of guy who would definitely have been popular in high school, maybe a jock who would always sit in the back of ninth-grade math, the one everyone took before the school started separating the gifted kids from the remedial students, goofing off and laughing and whispering with his friends about what a nerd I was for putting my hand up for every question.

Mitch and I trade a few more messages. He is at the office doing account management (account management, of course!) but asks if I am free to get a drink later tonight. I ask him to pick a place near his apartment, and we agree to meet at 8 p.m. Enough time for me to stop by the drugstore on my way home and buy a pack of Daisy razors to shave every inch of my body in the shower. I spritz on perfume that promises to make me smell like orchids and sex and carefully pluck my brows and the hairs on my upper lip. *Mom would be so proud of me,* I think as I dig an ingrown hair out of my otherwise smooth vulva. I drop my towel and spin around in front of the mirror, observing my polished and moisturized body. I look like I could be in a magazine. Not like *Vogue* or anything, but maybe a catalogue that sells higher-quality home goods.

I arrive at the bar at 7:55, think better of entering too early, and instead go to the corner store and flip through magazines. I return to the bar at 8:08. Mitch is sitting at a table at the back, a pint in front of him. He's picked a place I've never been to before, with exposed-brick walls and bare light bulbs hanging from the ceiling and a chalkboard with a list of fourteen-dollar cocktails. He sees me approach and stands up as I near his table, giving me one of those hugs in which his hand lingers for a couple extra seconds on my lower back.

"Sorry I'm late," I say breezily as I slide into my seat across from him. "I just had such a *killer* afternoon. You know how it is."

"That's all right," he says. "I literally just got here a second ago. Can I buy you a drink?"

"That would be lovely," I say. There is a pause where neither of us says anything.

"Um, what do you drink?"

I touch his arm and lean into him, letting my voice drop a bit. "Why don't you decide for me?"

"O . . . kay?" he says, clearly confused by my request, as if a girl has never asked him to take control in a subtle way while out in a public setting within the first few minutes of meeting before. He gets up anyway and goes to the bar, and I lean back casually against my seat, fidgeting and readjusting my posture as I try to adopt the perfect pose of nonchalant sexiness, finally deciding to just stick out my chest more. He returns a few minutes later with something frothy and pink with a little umbrella sticking out.

"What do you have for me?" I intone.

"A Sex on the Beach?" he says. I wince, which he clearly notices. "I'm sorry. I wasn't sure what you like, and I heard girls are into these drinks. I can get you something else if you like?"

"No." I lower my voice even more so it's barely louder than a sultry whisper. "If this is what you think I should have, then this is what I'm going to drink." My secret is that I actually like fruity cocktails that taste like punch, even though I'm surprised a place that seems to list aged bourbon or elderflower liqueur in everything they offer would serve this. The humiliation at the idea of drinking a prissy, juvenile beverage with a sleazy name at this guy's orders turns me on. I take a sip. "Mmmmm. Delicious."

"Hey, do you mind speaking a little louder? It's just, it's really hard to understand you when you whisper like that."

"Of course," I say at my normal volume, blushing. He looks at me like he expects me to keep talking, but suddenly I can't think of a single thing to say.

"So, you're uh, a writer?" he finally breaks the silence. "In your Tinder profile it says—"

"Oh, right, ha. Yeah, I've written a little bit before. A couple articles here and there. Mostly back in school. But uh, mostly I work at a bookstore. Prologues."

"Neat! I love reading. A lot of my friends make fun of me for being such a nerd. I'm on the second *Game of Thrones*. Have you read those?"

"I haven't. They sell really well at our store though."

"Oh man, you *gotta* check them out. I'm not even into historical literature, but these books, they're so awesome."

"Cool, yeah, I'll definitely look into it," I say, aware of how unconvincing I sound. I take another sip of my drink. More silence. I consider asking him about account management, but I can't bring myself to. "So you live nearby?"

"Yeah. My apartment is literally right up the street. I come here all the time. It's a good spot. They actually have a DJ here on weekends who—"

"Do you have roommates?"

"What?"

"Roommates," I repeat. "Do you have them?"

"Uh yeah, one. Carl. Good dude. We went to school together. He's actually away on a trip right now with his brother. They've gone—"

"So your place is empty?"

He looks around confused. "It should be." I look at my phone. It's 8:24. We've been here for sixteen whole minutes.

"Do you want to take me there right now?"

"You want to—what? Really? Now? You've barely touched your drink," he points out.

I take the straw out of my still-full glass and place it down on the table in front of me. I pick up my cocktail, put it to my lips, and drink directly from the glass, chugging the rest of the drink in one go. I place the now-empty glass back down and lick my lips.

"I'm done," I say.

He stares at me for a second and then jumps to his feet, grabbing his coat.

"You haven't finished *your* drink," I say coyly as he zips up his coat.

"Fuck my drink. Let's go back to my place."

He lives on the fifth floor of one of those fancy condo buildings, the kind with a doorman and everything. We make out in the elevator, and he squeezes my ass a little. *Oh hell yes.* We practically slip down the hall to his door, and I slide my hand up his shirt, tracing my fingernails across his back as he fumbles for his keys. As soon as he opens the door, we rush inside, and he flips on the light and slams the door shut, locking it behind him. We take off our coats and drop them by the closet. He directs me to the bedroom, and on the way, I spy the time on the microwave in the kitchen. It's now 8:39.

We're making out on his bed now. He's a surprisingly gentle kisser. I nibble his lip a little, hoping that will encourage him to get more aggressive, but he doesn't switch up his pace at all. A few minutes go by, and we're still just kissing on his bed. I guess it's on me to make the next move. I grab his hand and direct it under my shirt, up to my chest.

"You don't wear a bra?" he asks, his hand finally making contact with my small tits.

"No, Sir," I whisper. "I guess I'm a pretty bad girl."

"It's cool. Saves me from having to figure out the clasp thingy." He goes back to kissing me.

"Hey. Can you pull my hair a little?"

"Like this?" He gives it a gentle tug.

"Harder."

"I don't want to hurt you."

"Oh, I can handle way more. How about this: If it gets to be too hard, I'll say the word *red*."

He stops kissing me and looks at me, confused. "Why not just say 'stop?'"

"I don't know. 'Red' is just how it's done. Do you want to take off my top?"

He responds by pulling my T-shirt up. I raise my arms in compliance to help him, and then he takes off his own shirt. We resume kissing, and I roll onto my back, pulling him on top of me. He fumbles with the button on my jeans, and soon I'm kicking those off as well, along with my socks, until I'm underneath him in my underwear.

59

"Will you spank me?" I ask, and he nods, flipping me over onto my stomach with such ease I feel like I weigh eight pounds. It catches me off guard, and I let out a delighted giggle, ready for him to completely destroy me. He fondles my ass and raises his arm high. I close my eyes, bracing for him to strike.

Then he gently pats me on the bottom.

"Harder." I raise my hips a little to make it easier for him. His hand makes contact again, but it's so light I barely feel it. "Harder," I repeat. "Don't be scared to hurt me." A few more pats. I'm starting to get frustrated.

"Sit up," I say. "Like, sit up straight, with your legs over the edge of the bed." He does so, and I crawl over his lap, my panty-clad ass directly above his thighs, and I wiggle my hips a little to entice him. "Now you can really let me have it."

"Lucy," he says.

"Tell me I'm your little slut."

"Lucy," he says again, louder this time.

"What?"

"I'm really uncomfortable being this rough with you."

"Oh," and my butt stops wiggling. I hoist myself up, so I'm kneeling on the bed next to him, and fall back on my haunches. "Well, that's okay. I'm not really even into the pain thing as much. It's more the *idea* of being dominated, you know?"

"I . . . can't say that I do, no."

"Like, you don't even have to do anything." Am I drunk? I only had the one cocktail. Well, and a couple of shots before leaving my apartment to warm up, but those don't really count. "You can make me do your dishes in my underwear while you watch! Or do you have a broom somewhere? I can sweep."

"What are you talking about?"

"Or fine, you're not into the cleaning thing. I'll just suck your dick while you tell me what a good little slut I am."

"Lucy. Don't you think you're moving a little fast?"

This comment hits me like a slap to the face, and not in a sexy way. "I thought you were into it?"

"I was into the kissing you and undressing you and, I don't know, the normal stuff." He emphasizes the word *normal* as if to underscore what I'm not. "Even some of the hair pulling, I've been with girls who are into that. But you want to do my dishes? What the hell?"

Oh no. No no no. We aren't even remotely on the same page. For a second I am outside of myself, seeing the situation for what it is: a desperate attempt on my part to find a rebound without even confirming that he was into it. Then I'm back in my body, and back in it hard. I start to feel a deep, burning self-loathing, so similar and yet so different from the shame that usually excites me in the bedroom. This one is rooted in an anxiety that takes hold deep in my stomach and stings the backs of my eyes. "I'm . . . sorry," I whisper, not because I'm trying to seduce him this time but because I can't get the words out at a higher volume. "I guess I got a little carried away. I didn't mean to make you feel uncomfortable."

"Aw, no, don't cry," he says, and to my embarrassment I only then notice the tears coming down my cheeks. "It's not that bad. It was just a little much."

"I'm just having a day, and the last guy I was with was really into—not that I'm saying *you* have to be into that, or that you have to be into anything, or that even if you were that that's any excuse to push you into anything." I'm rambling now, the rumble in my stomach is getting worse, and I can feel the anxiety turn to panic. Crap. I haven't had a panic attack in months. I start hiccupping from crying too hard—because now I'm crying really hard—and it's getting more and more difficult to breathe. Maybe, hopefully, he'll just think I'm drunk. Mitch is standing up now in front of me, looking both deeply uncomfortable and concerned, unsure of what to do. He reaches his hand forward to touch my shoulder and then thinks better of it, dropping his arm down by his side again.

"Do you want me to . . . choke you now? Will that make you stop crying? If I choke you?"

I shake my head, unable to get any words out, the panic attack in full swing. Oh god. I have a sense of how this one's going to end.

"Tell me what you need. Please."

"A bag," I whisper.

"What?"

"Get me a bag. Something plastic. No holes. Hurry."

He runs out of the room, and I hear him rifling in the kitchen. He comes back seconds later holding a plastic bag from the grocery store, and I reach out, practically ripping it from his outstretched hands. I start heaving immediately, my puke a perfect Sex on the Beach pink. It takes about eight seconds for the contents of my stomach to finish emptying into the bag. The room is quiet. Mitch is sitting in front of me. I'm on the bed, holding a bag of my own vomit between my knees, still in my underwear. After a minute, he speaks.

"Do you want . . . Do you want me to get you a glass of water?"

"I think I just want to go home," I say quietly.

"I think that's a good idea."

Another quiet moment passes.

"I need to put my pants on," I say.

"Oh, um, right, uh, let me grab that," and he carefully takes hold of the handles of the plastic bag and carries it out of the room. As I get dressed, I can hear the toilet flush down the hall. He comes back and stands in the doorway, watching me put my shirt back on.

"I'm sorry," I say, looking at the floor.

"Hey, it's no big deal. We all have those days."

"Yeah," I say, but I think to myself, *Do we?*

I grab my coat, and he walks me to the door of his suite. I lean in to kiss him, but I immediately remember that my breath smells like puke. I can't bring myself to hug him either. So I stick out my hand, and he looks at it for a second and shakes it formally.

"Take care of yourself, Lucy," he says, and I don't respond. I take off through the hall, down the elevator, out the building, and hail a cab.

8

The next morning I brush my teeth three times but still can't get the residual taste of sick out of my mouth. Maybe it's psychosomatic at this point. Maybe everything about me is just fucking crazy.

I head to work early, arriving at the shop well before I need to open. As I lock the door behind me and turn off the alarm, I realize this is the first time I've been surrounded by something approximating silence in days. My thoughts are the last thing I want to be alone with; my eyes are still sticky with sleep. There is a patch of floor in front of me that looks smooth and inviting, warmly lit from the sunlight shimmering in through the window. I drop my tote bag and flop down, oblivious to the dirt as I rest my cheek on the faux-hardwood vinyl. I let my eyes close. I wonder how long I can forget about the world before I have to get back to reality.

The answer turns out to be approximately seventeen seconds. Someone is rapping on the window. There's a man outside, his greying ginger hair matching the scraggly beard on his face. I force myself up.

"We don't open for another twenty minutes!" I shout through the glass.

"Are you okay?" he responds. "You fell!"

"Oh," I reply. "Yeah, that—that was nothing."

"I can't understand you!" his voice comes muffled through the door. "Do you need an ambulance?"

"What? No, I'm fine!"

He cups his hand to his ear, straining to hear me. Reluctantly, I open the door.

"I said I'm fine. Thanks for your concern. I just . . . I dropped an earring. I was on the ground trying to find it."

"Your ears aren't pierced?" He points to my unblemished lobes. Great, I have fucking Javert coming to my rescue.

"It was actually a belly-button piercing," I say lamely, then hope he doesn't notice me wince at my own dumb excuse.

"So you open?"

"Not really, but you can come in if you don't mind me setting up." I push the door open to let him in mostly out of guilt.

"Thanks," he says and bends down to pick up a box by his feet I didn't notice before. "I'm looking to sell some books, actually."

"Oh, we aren't that kind of store."

"The library wouldn't take them."

"The library isn't that kind of store either. See, we're new books and—hold on, let me just get the lights and stuff." I head to the back of the store, where the lights are, straightening up a few shelves on my way. By the time I make my way back to the front, the man is standing by the checkout with his dusty box of books sitting on the counter.

"I carried this box all the way from my house, and it's pretty heavy. The least you can do is take a look." I'm suddenly aware of his height. He's big and burly and has a good seven inches on me. He has a faintly acrid smell to him, something like sweat or urine, and he is breathing heavily. His clothes appear not to have been washed in days. We are alone in the store, and the sidewalk outside is completely quiet. Pissing this man off seems like a very, very bad idea. "I'll take a look," I say, careful to keep my voice even. "But we really only focus on new books. There's a used bookstore on Bloor, like a ten-minute streetcar ride, and they could probably offer you a better deal than I could?" The book sitting on top of his box is a physics textbook from the eighties. "Maybe."

"I'm trying to do a good thing. I didn't want to throw these out. I could have just thrown them out, but it's bad for the environment, and I didn't want them to just *die*." His ability to talk about used books and still sound like a serial killer is impressive. I continue to humour him by rifling through the box. There are some old paperbacks with yellowing pages and torn covers that look like they were bought from a drugstore. A marked-up copy of *Atlas Shrugged*. An instruction manual for a VCR. I wish I had left the front door unlocked so another customer could come in and give me an excuse to end this interaction. Then, near the bottom of all his worthless garbage, is a stack of magazines. They're old, but in reasonably good condition, full-colour covers but mostly black and white inside. I flip through one and see a photo of a group of girls, not older than sixteen or seventeen, posing with instruments under the headline "ON TOUR WITH VIRGINIA AND THE WOOLFPACK." I look back at the cover, which features an eclectic collage of old photos. Blazoned across the top is the word *SMASH*.

"What's this?" I ask, holding up a copy.

"You've never heard of *Smash* magazine?" he asks. "What are they even teaching you kids in school these days?" His condescension is annoying, which is a nice change from his earlier intimidating demeanour.

"I'm twenty-five," I retort. "Is this, like, a music mag?"

"*Smash* was a *lifestyle*," he says. "It was everything *Rolling Stone* wished it could be. It was all the best music and writing coming out of LA. For a glorious eighteen months. Then it just disappeared."

I pull the other copies of the magazine out of the box, counting seven in total. "I'll give you twenty bucks for the pile," I say.

"Are you kidding me?" he booms, and for a second he's scary again. "These are collector's items."

I shrug, more petulantly than I mean to. "You can always cart them up to Bloor and try your luck there."

"Fine," he says. "But I better not come back here and see you selling them for a hundred dollars a copy."

"Nah." I grab my tote bag and reach for my wallet. "These aren't for the store. I told you, we only carry new books. This is for my personal collection."

"Do you want any of my other books? Buy them all, and I'll give you the box for free."

"I'll pass," I say dismissively, then, once again remembering his size, quickly add, "But thank you for letting me look." I hand him a twenty.

As soon as he leaves, I let out a breath of relief and also arousal, because being terrified always turns me on a little. Then I grab my new stack of magazines and start flipping through them. Immediately, I notice their quality. They're all dated from the seventies and are not only in good condition but seem pretty well put together: glossy covers and sophisticated layouts, different from the stapled zines I've collected. There are a few celebrities I recognize—interviews with Frank Zappa and Jimmy Page—but there are also bands I don't know of, with pictures of women on every other page. Beautiful women, with glamorous curls and glittery eyeshadow, but alongside the photographs are long interviews. The front woman of Virginia and the Woolfpack, a band I've never heard of, stares out defiantly through blond feathered hair, a proto-Cherie Currie with a snarl. A pull quote in large letters is next to her face: "The teachers at school said a girl would never make it in the music industry. So I dropped out of school."

And then there is the lifestyle content. An article about how to sneak out of your bedroom without your parents noticing. An advice column where a reader asks how to deal with falling in love with a teacher. A fashion story on the best style tips picked up at Hollywood High. And I realize this glamorous magazine focused on counterculture and rule breaking, filled with women and the envy of *Rolling Stone*, is a teen magazine. A teen girl magazine.

Sassy and *Rookie* I've heard of, with their riot grrrl features and DIY tutorials, but I'd never seen anything like this from the seventies. I flip to the masthead. A magazine like *Smash* must have been edited by someone really cool; I'm picturing a cross between Nora and Stevie Nicks. But there, listed as editor-in-chief in this issue and the rest of this pile, is a single, presumably male name: Chester Wright.

I spend the rest of the morning reading *Smash*, taking breaks only when customers come in and then doing the bare minimum to help so I can get back to reading. It's Nora's day off, and Danny comes in at noon. Danny is an aspiring experimental poet, nice enough and completely grating. He asked me out after his first shift, I politely declined, and he's been awkward around me ever since. I don't even notice him approach me an hour later, and when he taps me on the shoulder, I jump.

"Oh, um, sorry, Lucy," he says. "I just wanted to know if you were going to take your lunch break."

"What? Oh, right. Yeah totally. Thanks for reminding me." I slide off the stool behind the cash, where I've been sitting for most of the day, and gather the copies of *Smash* into my tote bag. After getting a slice of pizza from next door, I find a bench in the park to sit and eat. Pulling out my phone, I see I have three missed calls from Sasha.

Hey, at work, I text. *All good?*

She replies right away. *I'm just having the shittiest fucking day. Ryan and I got into an argument.*

Boo, dude, I'm sorry. I'm at work but maybe we can talk later.

It's fine. She is obviously not fine. She sends a quick follow up. *I'm running late for work myself. Bartending tonight.*

I'll come by after my shift.

The store is busy when I get back, but I leave Danny to handle the bulk of the customers while I go on the computer to see if there are more issues of *Smash* on eBay. There are only a few left; I'm able to buy them. I try searching for more information—a fan website maybe, a forum, an oral history in some indie magazine, *something*—but my search yields nothing.

"We got the new Mary Oliver in, did you see?" Danny asks.

"Neat," I say, my eyes on the screen. Danny never gets the hint that I don't feel like chatting.

"Of course, I've had the advance review copy for weeks," he continues. "I'm friends with someone at the publishing house. It's nice to really have some time to *sit* with a book before it hits the public, you know?"

"The publisher sent two review copies to the store. They're in the back somewhere. I think one is in the staff bathroom."

"She really ruminates on love in her latest, but it's not in an obvious way," he says. "Her work has inspired me lately, especially as I work on my newest cha—"

"I gotta leave early today," I cut him off before he can tell me about his chapbook. He's always working on a new self-published chapbook, and Marcella lets him sell them in the store though I don't think anyone has bought a copy. "You can cover me, can't you?"

"It's been sort of busy today, Lucy."

"And you're handling all those customers like a boss." I pick up my tote bag before he can say anything else. "I owe you big time, buddy."

The bar where Sasha works is on my way home. It's empty when I show up, still early in the day. She's alone at the bar slicing limes when I take a seat in front of her.

"Hey stranger," I say.

"Don't tell me you bailed on poor Danny again."

"I had a friend in crisis. And he was talking about Mary Oliver's ruminations on love. I only left like, an hour early."

"One of these days, he's going to learn to stick up for himself. And then where will you be?" She puts down her knife. "But I appreciate you coming. What're you drinking?"

"Oh, I couldn't possibly exploit my best friend's labour." Sasha scoffs. "But since I'm here. Can you make that martini thing you made for me last time? The one that tastes like a lemon drop?"

"I hope you realize you have the palate of a twelve-year-old." She starts mixing my drink. "There is alcohol out there that doesn't taste like candy."

"I'm making a feminist statement. I don't need some macho triple-distilled whiskey to get hammered." I watch her as she works with the precision of a surgeon, before plunking the fluorescent-yellow drink in front of me. She goes back to slicing her limes. I wait for her to speak first, to acknowledge the text messages she sent me this morning and to let herself be exposed in the way she only does when she's tired or drunk. "So Ryan . . . ?"

"Is being a prick." Angry Sasha is someone I'm used to dealing with; I've seen her get pissed off at corporations and politicians and strangers littering in the park, fuelled by a self-righteousness that pumps me up alongside her, that lets me trust that her worldview is the correct one and that anyone who wrongs her must be wrong, period.

"He's been working super hard on this campaign, and I support him, I do. But I don't see why that means I have to support his candidate." She spits out his name with disdain: "Callum Humphrey. Even his name is douchey. He sounds—"

"Like a Disney Channel villain," I finish for her.

"He's a potato of a candidate," she continues, "a flavourless spud. And I don't understand why Ryan is so invested in him. This morning he asked me if I wanted to go canvassing with the team, and I burst out laughing. I didn't mean to, but once I started, I couldn't stop. And so he got pissed and accused me of having purity politics, and then he had to go to work. What do you think? Am I being a bad girlfriend?"

"Of course not," I say, though I don't really know what being a good girlfriend entails. "You believe in stuff. And Ryan knows that. He loves you for that. He's just . . . I don't know, running on very little sleep."

"And look at what believing in stuff has gotten me." She waves an arm around at the bar. "The election is in two weeks, and I'm mixing drinks." This is new. Sasha complains about her job all the time—the obnoxious customers, the late hours—but she never doubts what she's doing with her life. She always has jobs that allow her to spend the rest of her time working on things that matter to her. I have been able to validate my own lack of professional progress by believing this.

"How's that workshop you're doing on Saturdays going? With the kids?"

She shrugs, but then smiles in spite of herself. "It's kind of . . . I don't know, it's kind of awesome? The kids fucking love me. I show up wearing blue eyeliner, and they, like, lose their minds."

"Yeah, because you're living proof that grownups don't have to be boring." She tells me about her favourite kids—she knows she's not supposed to have favourites; everyone claims they don't have favourites, but she knows they're lying—while I sip my drink, and it's not long before my glass is empty. It's barely midafternoon, and a wave of fatigue hits me.

"Go home," she says, noticing me yawn. "I'll be fine."

"Come over after your shift. I don't want you to be alone."

"I have to go home to Nigel. It's not like Ryan's going to take care of her."

"I don't want me to be alone." I pick up my empty glass and sip at the dregs, just to have somewhere to look that isn't at Sasha. I don't have to make eye contact with her to feel her concern. "What if I went to your place and brought Nigel back to mine? I'm a good babysitter."

"Lucy, that's like an hour out of your way." I say nothing. She sighs. "Okay. If you're really up for it. You still got my extra key? I'll meet you both at your place after work."

"Like the good ol' days," I nod, grabbing my bag, although which days I mean I'm not quite sure.

9

The day I met Sasha was also the day I left my hometown for good.

"Don't worry. The stores in Toronto will have the stuff we haven't been able to get here," my mom said as we set off. She seemed dead serious, but what in the world could be left to pack? Our minivan, which had always seemed excessive for just us, was stuffed so full of bags and boxes we couldn't see out the rear window. Half my childhood bedroom was packed. Plus we had spent the previous weekend at Walmart getting far more than what was on the checklist the school provided. I had told her I didn't think we were even allowed to have toasters in our rooms, but she waved me off and added one to the cart. "I had one in my room," she said. "And I had to buy it myself. My parents didn't help me out at all."

We spent a full day unloading the van and the final trip shopping for more supplies my mom was sure I would need. As we carried the last of the shopping bags into my dorm room, I barely even noticed that my roommate had moved in her stuff. Her side of the room was sparse: lavender sheets on the thin bed, a garbage bag full of clothes that had yet to be hung up, two suitcases still zipped up on the floor. Mom didn't acknowledge the signs of life on the other side of the room; she was too busy organizing my sweaters by colour in the closet.

"They don't give you enough space in these things. I'm positive my room at school had more space," she said as

I pulled books out of one of the boxes. "But that's okay. Those storage bins I got you with the wheels—we'll put your winter stuff in there, and—oh, hello."

A new figure had appeared in the doorway. She was dressed fairly plainly, in an old T-shirt and jeans, but on her feet she had hot-pink Doc Martens. She was compactly built, like a slightly too-tall gymnast, but her frizzy curls flared out, aggressively taking up space. She walked to the side of the room with the unpacked suitcases, but her gaze was on my half, as she seemed to be absorbing the sheer volume of stuff. I smiled sheepishly at her.

"You must be the roommate!" Mom said, putting one last hanger in my closet and turning with a hand outstretched. "Sasha Oliver?"

"Oliveira," the girl corrected her, politely returning the handshake.

"I'm Anita. This is my daughter, Lucy." I raised my hand in a limp wave, then returned to unpacking my books. "Are we in your way at all? Do you need help unpacking the rest of your things?"

Sasha shoved one of her suitcases closer to the wall with her foot. "I think I got it covered. Thank you though."

"Well." Mom eyed Sasha's lack of luggage. I could mentally write the speech she'd give me later. *That girl seems underprepared for university. She better not expect to use your stuff all semester.* "Anything you need, you can just ask Lucy here." Mom went back to unpacking one of the Walmart bags and started organizing office supplies on my desk. "You're probably so excited for frosh week. Did they tell you what group you're going to be in? We got our welcome packets when we signed in downstairs. If you forgot to get yours yet you can probably still get one. Lucy's on the Orange Squad. That'll be fun. I wonder what activities they'll make you do. When I did my frosh week, we didn't have teams or squads, but they did make us learn all these silly songs for the campfire. And—oh, damn. Lucy, we forgot to bring Ziploc baggies. And tampons!" She looked at her phone. "It's getting late. I'll keep the hotel room for another night, and we can go shopping again tomorrow."

"I can buy my own tampons," I said, trying to keep my voice down as if Sasha wouldn't be able to hear me from a few feet away on the bed. She conspicuously started unzipping one of her suitcases, as if to give us some privacy, though I could see a gentle smirk forming on her face. I turned back to my mom. "I'm going to be busy tomorrow. The frosh kickoff party is tonight."

"I guess there's no rush for the tampons. Your cycle doesn't start for two more weeks." (I looked again at Sasha, who was still keeping her eyes on the suitcase.) "Are you sure you don't need more help unpacking?"

"I can help her," Sasha said, and we both turned to look at her. I felt in awe of the casualness with which she approached a day that had, for us, represented so much planning and fretting. "It'll be fun. I brought extra tampons."

"See, Mom? I'm taken care of."

Mom squared her jaw. She looked around the room, as if searching for an excuse to stay, and started blinking rapidly.

Sasha jumped up. "You know what? I gotta pee," she said, exiting the room and leaving my mom and me alone.

"Mom," I said. "You're going to have to go at some point. I'll be fine." As much as I was ready for her to leave, I was scared to be on my own. I realized I had no idea where

I was supposed to take the trash out. What if I never figured it out and garbage kept piling up in my room and I spent my entire college career never knowing what to do with it? My mom always knew what to do with the trash. "I can figure things out from here."

Mom nodded silently. "Make sure you get your own tampons. I don't trust that girl to have the same flow as you."

"I will get some tampons. This week. I promise."

She sighed deeply and then pulled me into a tight hug. "I love you, baby girl. So much."

"I love you too, Mom." I hugged her back. We stood there quietly for a moment embracing. I let go first.

She stepped back, taking my face in her hands. "Look at you, so grown up already." She studied my face and kissed my temple. "You should pluck your eye-brows. They're getting bushy. What bag did we put the wax in?"

"Mother!"

The door opened, Sasha returning to the room. I walked my mom out into the hall, hugging her goodbye again, promising to call. And then she was gone.

Sasha had her suitcase open on her bed and was shoving T-shirts into one of the dresser drawers. She looked up at me when I came in and smiled.

"I like your boots," I said.

"These?" she looked at her Doc Martens. "They were my sister's. In the nineties. They're kinda old school, but they're comfy as shit."

"So," I hoped my voice had a casualness to it that would let Sasha know I was on her level, that I was cool and ready to live on my own. "Are you going to the frosh mixer tonight?"

Sasha snorted. "In a word, no. It's not really my thing."

"You're just going to not go? Are we allowed to just skip things?"

"Is that a serious question?" Sasha asked, and her tone wasn't accusatory. She seemed to be trying to suss out if I was being sincere or not. "You're eighteen, aren't you? An adult? It's university. We're here to go to class, and even that isn't mandatory. You can do whatever you want."

It seemed so obvious when she said it, and yet I hadn't considered the idea of options. I couldn't even decide where I was supposed to put my toaster. "What are you going to do tonight?"

She shrugged. "There are some bands playing at the Mod Club. It might be lame, but I can get in without an ID. One of my sisters is dating the doorman, and they're pretty chill as long as I don't drink too much. You can come, if that's your thing."

I fidgeted with the cord of the toaster. "I don't think I really know what my thing is."

Sasha studied me for a moment, and I wasn't sure what I was expected to do. I became hyper aware of the cord as I rolled it between my fingers. Finally, mercifully, she stepped towards me and took the toaster out of my hands. "Isn't that the point of all this? To figure that out?" She placed the toaster on the windowsill, equally between our two beds. "There. I think that's a good spot."

Sasha couldn't believe I had grown up only a few hours away but had never spent any time in Toronto. "I think we

made a pit stop on the way home when I visited Marine-
land with my cousins as a kid," I said, to which she grunted,
"I still can't believe that place is allowed to operate." She
had grown up just on the outskirts of the city with three
older sisters who seemed to have provided her unlimited
templates of how to dress, how to act, what to believe in.
She knew the best bars that weren't overcrowded with
other students and which boutiques it was okay to shop-
lift from as a political statement. Her parents were both
professors—they taught biochemistry or chemical biology
or something—which meant she got her tuition covered,
but she had decided to stay away from the sciences and
study philosophy. "It's the only real thing that it makes
sense to major in, when you think about it," she explained,
and I didn't understand what she meant but nodded
in agreement.

Sasha made me realize how much there was for me to
know outside of books. I came to school not knowing what
I wanted to do or be but thought if I had a foundation of
reading, I would be equipped to figure that out later. Sasha
had already figured out her opinions on everything. She
would give long rants about Palestine or labour unions or
men who interrupt women too much at parties. She wasn't
playing at being smart, the way I felt I was. She genuinely
seemed to understand the world.

I blew off the frosh mixer to go with her into the West
End. While I was sorting through my boxes, trying to
figure out what to wear, she pulled a wrinkled blue dress
out of her suitcase. "This colour would look great on you."
I was a couple inches taller than her, and the dress was
almost indecently short, but Sasha took one look at me

and said, "Damn, girl," with such nonchalant approval that I decided, yes, I belonged in this dress.

"Why are you being so nice to me?" I asked after we found seats on the back of the streetcar.

She blinked. "Why wouldn't I be nice to you? We're going to be spending the year together." She leaned her head against the window as the streetcar lurched ahead. "Besides," she added quietly, looking out the window, "I'm new here, too."

She was comfortable dancing in public, even before she had anything to drink. I watched her from the sidelines, drinking a rum and Diet Coke, chewing on my straw. We were in a bar with a DJ and a dance floor, and they weren't playing Top 40 hits; they were playing tracks I'd heard in the record collection I inherited from my father—Talking Heads and New Order—and a bunch of stuff I didn't recognize. I started bobbing my head to one of the songs, when Sasha said, "Come on, I love this one!" and pulled me onto the dance floor. She spun me around, and I felt the skirt of my already-too-short dress flare up and immediately tried to push it back down, but I had one hand in Sasha's and the other was holding my drink.

"My dress is flying up!" I shouted over the music. "Everyone will see my underwear!"

"Who gives a shit?" she shouted back, but she let go of my hand, taking a step back. I looked around the room at people wrapped up in their own business—dancing, flirting, checking their cell phones in the corner—and downed the rest of my drink, grabbing Sasha's hand again. She let out a hoot and then spun me, and again, three times in quick succession, and I started laughing out of pure pleasure.

Later on, I went to get another drink, and she started dancing with a guy. She had her arms wrapped casually around his neck with her hips against him, his hands pulling her close as he kind of swayed side to side. I took a seat near the bar. Sasha and the guy started to make out. I wondered if they were going to hook up. I wondered if she would put a sock on our door. I wondered where I was going to sleep that night.

I went to the bathroom to fix my makeup, even though everything I was wearing that night was borrowed from Sasha and all I had of my own was a Dr. Pepper Lip Smacker, which I applied three times, smearing the pigment of the lipstick underneath. I studied my reflection under the harsh lights. My eyes were more bloodshot than I expected, my eyeliner was smeared in a way I hoped was chic, my bangs were matted to my forehead with sweat, and there were dark stains on the armpits of the dress Sasha had loaned me. My mom wouldn't approve of any of this. I could imagine the lecture she'd give me about washing and ironing the dress before returning it. I shook my head, willing my thoughts to leave. My flip phone stayed closed in my purse on silent so I could ignore the inevitable texts.

The bathroom door swung open, and Sasha appeared. She was sweating profusely too, but on her it looked like a glow. She smiled at me.

"Y'all good in here?" She headed into the nearest bathroom stall and closed the door behind her. I heard the stream of urine and wondered if I was supposed to keep talking to her while she peed.

"I'm fine," I said. "So, uh. Should I find somewhere else to sleep tonight? Or are you going to his place?" Hopefully my voice sounded dispassionate, the voice of a girl who partied regularly and knew the drill when her friend wanted to get laid.

"What?" The toilet flushed. Sasha came out and joined me at the sink, washing her hands. "Wait, that guy out there? No, I was just messing around. You know how it is."

I nodded, my mouth set in a line, trying not to reveal the relief I felt.

She hit the button on the hand dryer with her elbow, then, when nothing happened, wiped her wet hands on her skirt. "I'll see you back out there, 'kay?" I grabbed the door before it closed behind her and followed her back out.

Sasha helped me clear my boxes aside when we got back to the dorm. "So you don't trip over anything when you gotta piss in the middle of the night." When I came back from the communal bathroom after my three-step skin-care routine and changing into my pyjamas in the stall, she was passed out on top of her sheets in her underwear, snoring softly.

I turned off the lights and crawled into my own bed, placing my toiletries bag on my bedside table and piling my clothes from the night on a chair. I picked up my phone. I had missed seventeen texts from my mother. I typed out a quick message. *Sorry for not texting, having so much fun doing frosh stuff!!!! Safe in bed, thanks for everything today. Love you.* I hit send, then turned off my phone.

"I had fun tonight," I said softly, not even knowing if Sasha could hear me. "You know, you're not like the other girls I know."

"That's internalized misogyny meant to pit women against each other by devaluing traditional feminine activities," she mumbled, half asleep, rolling over in her narrow bed. "But thank you."

10

I sit cross-legged on my bed, Nigel snoring on my lap, having tired herself out running around my small apartment twice and yapping at every corner in the room. I'm on my laptop once again trying to find something, anything, about *Smash* magazine. Google brings me lots about Smash Mouth and a magazine called *Smashing* about web design. I'm surprised I haven't heard of *Smash* before. I have hundreds of back issues of zines from university, when I made music zines and hung out at small-press fairs every weekend. I have piles of *The Hog*. I have subscriptions to every dumb literary magazine that's generally only read by its own contributors, which I buy out of some sense of responsibility to a community and also because I'd like to maybe one day submit to them.

I close Google, open the *New York Times* website—another publication I subscribe to out of obligation but guiltily never read—and search through their archives. Two articles spring up: one from early 1977, when *Smash* magazine launched, and another announcing it was shutting down. It was notable enough. New magazines don't get mentions in the biggest national newspaper, but the first article says *Smash* was owned by a major publisher called Sanderson. According to Wikipedia, in the mid-seventies Sanderson was fairly large, but mostly focused on trade magazines, car and motorcycle and gun publications, super mainstream macho stuff. A teen and (hopefully?) feminist magazine seems out of place with their other titles. I flip to the masthead, and sure enough, stamped at the bottom are the words "Published by Sanderson Inc."

My eyes flick up the masthead, and the list of names is short, with few actual editorial staff. Flipping through the magazine, I see the same bylines over and over, a hundred pages worth of writing from just a handful of people. There's an interview with an art rock band, an androgynous looking quartet of two men and two women, by someone named Jennifer Flounder. A few pages later her byline appears under another interview, this time with an anonymous woman, titled, "She Had a Nose Job. She Doesn't Regret It." I think of how ahead of its time it was to write about a woman refusing to apologize for taking control of her body like that. The last quarter of the magazine is dedicated to party reporting, grainy black-and-white pictures from the Whisky a Go Go of a drag show called the Cycle Sluts, some grinning waifish girls on the Sunset Strip in glittery short shorts and tall boots, punctuated by paragraphs describing in detail how crowds danced to rock bands until their legs ached; how parties were still going at four, five, six in the morning; how it seemed like all the freaks and dreamers and renegades in the city forged spaces to call their own, and *Smash* was there to chronicle it.

There's a story here. I mean, there has to be. I want to know how and why Sanderson decided it was worth investing in this world. Never in my life have I published anything longer than a few thousand words, but I imagine myself putting together the story of this flash of history, igniting a renaissance of love for a cult magazine. There could be an anthology release of all the issues, and I could write the introduction. Some cool up-and-coming indie filmmaker (a woman, of course) would direct the adaptation. I would work firmly behind the scenes, avoiding the stresses and trappings of celebrity while staying humble, but I would be recognized by those in the know as a tastemaker and a vital voice in feminist archival work.

This would never actually happen. I have no idea how to begin writing a piece of that breadth. But I want, more than anything else in this moment, to have an excuse to talk to somebody who worked in that world. To truly know what it was like to live like that.

I google Jennifer Flounder. There are a few results: Facebook pages that don't give away too much. There's a website for a speech therapist in Ohio. I click through, and on her About page it mentions that she grew up in California and started her career as a journalist. She looks about the right age. She'd be a little young when *Smash* was publishing, but not *that* young. There's a phone number for her office on the website. It's not late by Sunset-Strip-in-LA standards, but probably pushing it by working-professional-in-Ohio hours.

By the time Sasha lets herself in with her spare key, I've fallen asleep while sitting up on my bed, laptop still open in front of me. She enters gently, but Nigel wakes up and starts barking her tiny, adorable, annoying head off. "Shut up, fucker," I hear Sasha's soft voice say. Nigel stops yapping, and I turn on my bedside lamp, giving Sasha some light as she takes off her shoes and hangs up her coat.

"SHUT THAT GODDAMN DOG UP!" comes a voice on the other side of the wall. "IT'S ONE IN THE MORNING!"

"CHILL THE FUCK OUT, MR. FILLIPELLI. I HEARD YOU YANKING IT TO *THE GOLDEN GIRLS* LAST WEEK," I yell back in response, and he goes silent. I feel a quick pang of guilt for shaming him. *The Golden Girls* is a sexy show.

"I'm so sorry," Sasha says, standing in the doorway of the bathroom, her mouth full of toothpaste.

"Oh, it's fine. The walls are so thin in this place. Everyone is involved in everyone else's business." Nigel has settled down again and curls up at the foot of the bed. Sasha finishes brushing her teeth and changes into the pyjama bottoms and T-shirt she keeps in the bottom drawer of my dresser.

"It's kinda nice," she says, as I push over to one side of the bed and she slides in next to me. "Sometimes it feels like Ryan and I are so far removed from everything in the East End."

"How is that going? The Ryan of it all?"

"I cannot wait until this stupid election for jerks is done. It's fine. It's fine! It really is. Couples fight and shit."

I nod sagely like I know exactly what she means, like I have lots of experience in healthy long-term relationships. She scratches Nigel behind the ear.

"I think he looks down on me," she says quietly.

"But . . . you're so much cooler than him," I say, which is true. Everyone is cooler than Ryan.

"I think he imagined we'd be, like, some political power couple, working together in the same office." I could not imagine Ryan actually wanting a partner who was as or more successful than him. But I know that he cares about optics, and I can envision him wanting a traditional politician's wife, someone who knows when and how to prop him up.

"My biggest dream in life is to be a bartender. He thinks that's pathetic. I know he does."

"Sasha, you're not pathetic." She doesn't react to this.

"Hey, seriously, listen to me. You are not pathetic."

"Yeah, well," she says quietly, almost to herself, and then she turns over away from me, and neither of us says anything else before we fall asleep.

Dear Sir,

It's a dumb trade-off that in order to build a life with someone you inevitably give up parts of yourself. How often does it work that you meet another person you like and they like you and you're attracted to them and share their values and you're sexually compatible and you live in the same city and want similar things and neither of you already has a burlesque-dancing girlfriend? There is, like, zero overlap in the Venn diagram of people I want to spank me and people I am interested in holding a prolonged conversation with. My best friend thought she'd found everything in one person, but lately she seems more miserable than not. She says relationships are work, which is also what Nora says, and my mom says, and women's magazines say, like it's this universally agreed-upon truth that every way in which we try to make living a little more bearable is just another form of labour. The worst part is, thinking about the intersection of relationships and jobs makes me horny. That's, like, the whole setup to Secretary. *But nobody is ever referring to getting fucked at the office when they talk about relationships and work. Unfortunately.*

Lucy

11

Sasha is gone by the time I wake up the next morning. There's a note on my bedside table. "Hey girl, thanks for letting me and Nigel crash. Decided to meet up with Ryan for breakfast. Let's hang for real soon xx." The breeziness of it is troubling; Sasha would never throw in a double *x* unless she was trying really, really hard to sound casual, in which case her mind is probably racing a mile a minute. *Xx* means she's going to act like things are fine the next time we talk, and I won't say anything, and she won't bring up Ryan again until their next fight. In the light of day, the life she's built with him is seductively normal and stable.

I sit up in bed, still tired, and realize there is nothing stopping me from lying back down. And then all the events of the last few days hit me. Henry. Mitch. I threw up in front of him. I managed to humiliate myself in front of two completely different men in two completely different ways. I pull the covers over my head and force myself to take a deep breath. I can't. The panic is going to come back if I don't do something.

I pull the covers back down and reach for the laptop on my bedside table, open a new window, and go to my favourite porn site. I click through to find the video I'm looking for, not having any saved bookmarks. While it's loading, I open the bottom drawer of my nightstand, pull out my vibrating back massager, and plug it in. I'm about to press play on the video when I hesitate.

"Sasha?" I shyly call out. "You for sure gone? You're not secretly still in the bathroom, are you?"

Silence. Great. That means the next few minutes will be between me, my computer, and, unless I'm sufficiently quiet, Mr. Fillipelli next door. I press play.

In between pop-up ads of hot singles in my area, a video plays in which three twenty-something school girls are caught cheating in class and have to be punished by their teacher, also a woman. "We can't have three bad little girls roaming the halls of Pecker Academy," says the teacher, and I catch myself mouthing the words along with the video, I've seen this one so many times. She leans the first girl over the desk and pulls out a ruler, flipping her skirt up to reveal a black lacy thong underneath. This is when I turn on the vibrator.

Not even five minutes later, my body is heaving in orgasm. Everything bad I've ever felt in the history of the universe goes away as my body fills with lightness and glitter. Then the orgasm passes, and the video is still playing, suddenly so loud in my empty apartment, and I am aware again that I am alone, a sad pervert. I switch off my vibrator and reach over to my computer, shutting down the window that has the video playing. Jennifer Flounder's website, which was open underneath, now fills the screen. *Oh right,* I think.

I wipe down my vibrator, wash my hands, shower, clean away the sticky grossness of my morning routine. Then I make coffee and sit down at the Ikea dining-room table that triples as a kitchen counter and desk, and set up my laptop in front of me. Jennifer Flounder, the *Smash* contributor turned speech therapist. It's a Wednesday morning, so she should be at work. I take a deep breath, then dial the number.

"Speak Up Speech Therapy, this is Bev. How may I help you?" comes a chipper voice at the other end.

"Hi, um, I'm looking for Jennifer Flounder?" I say, trying and failing to sound more confident than I am.

"She's in a meeting right now. Can I take a message?" says Bev.

"I'm not exactly sure. I'm a writer, a journalist, trying to do research for a piece, and I am not even a hundred percent sure she's who I want to talk to."

"You're writing an article on speech therapy?"

"No, actually it's about another job she had. Or a job someone named Jennifer Flounder had. This is the only contact information I could find." Now she will of course hang up on me.

"What did you say your name was?"

"I didn't. It's Lucy. Selberg. Lucy Selberg."

"And you're a newspaper reporter?"

"Not exactly. I'm a writer. I freelance. For alt-weeklies and stuff. Like, do you know the *Hogtown Weekly*? It's actually a big deal in Canada, where I live. *The Hog*. It's sometimes called that."

"You're calling from Canada," Bev says, sounding skeptical, like everything I've told her so far is a lie. "What is it exactly you're trying to find out?"

I hesitate. I was really hoping to charm Jennifer Flounder before asking about her past, but now I feel incapable of holding a conversation with anyone. "I'm trying to find out if she's the same Jennifer Flounder who worked at *Smash* magazine in Los Angeles in 1977."

A beat passes. The other end is so quiet. "Hello?" I say shyly after a few seconds.

"Why don't you give me your contact info, and I'll take down a memo for her."

I spell out my email address and then thank Bev profusely for helping me.

"You're not really a journalist, are you?" she asks.

"I am! I mean, I used to have a zine. That's like a—it's a thing with writing. And I have written for *The Hog*. It's a big deal—"

"In Canada, right," says Bev. "Is there anything else I can do for you today?"

"No, thank you, Bev. You've been a big help and I—"

"Uh huh. Listen, this is a very busy time of day for us. If Ms. Flounder wants to get in touch with you, that's up to her. Good day."

I spend as much time as I can rereading the issues of *Smash* that I have. The articles are entertaining even now, and even to someone outside both the target demographic and the era. There is a photo shoot on "Oriental style," an article on what to do if an "evil chick" is trying to steal your man. There are digs at male chauvinists, but also at women deemed sexually prudish. *It was a different era,* I tell myself. *You can't hold an artifact up to today's standards, especially when the good outweighs the bad.* There is an advice column where readers can mail in their questions. "I feel I'm unable to live the groovy life that I hear about in your pages," says a writer named "Stuck in Nebraska." "My teachers are strict. My parents are stricter. I haven't found anyone like me. How can I be free when everyone is trying to keep me locked up?"

"Dear Stuck," the response begins. "I wish I could tell you the squares disappear when you reach adulthood, but you'll always have people who want you to conform. The good news is true freedom is like true foxiness: it starts as a state of mind. No one can force you to change your thoughts, even if they might try. Keep your soul and heart and head free, and you can bear it until the external forces catch up with you." The letter is signed "Love, Aunt Smashing."

Some of the pieces run a bit more teen beat. There is one interview with heartthrob Jack Franklin, a name I recognize because he was in the news recently, having died from a brain aneurysm. He showed up in movies I watched in the nineties, playing the dad or the teacher. His career had peaked decades earlier—first, playing the teenage son on *The Warlocks Next Door*, a 1960s sitcom about a suburban family with magical powers. In the 1970s he played the lead in *The Greasers*, a movie about dreamboat outlaws. He had no major roles after that.

When he died, my mom called me, crying. I didn't understand why she cared about a washed-up B-list actor, but this one seemed to have affected her. "We saw *The Greasers* on our first date," she said. "Your father and I."

"Oh," I said with the same awkwardness that emerged every time she brought up my father, which wasn't often. I was still in diapers when he got sick, and he died so soon after that my grief manifested less like loss than an insatiable curiosity. I could guess at certain mannerisms he'd had based on how they played out in my uncles and grandparents when we visited Nova Scotia, but he was a complete stranger to me.

"He looked so much like him," she continued on the phone. "Jack Franklin. So handsome. *The Greasers* came out when I was in high school, but I wasn't allowed to go see it. And then years later I met your father at a party, and he took me to a midnight screening, and it felt like such freedom."

"Oh," I think I said again, before realizing I was running late for work and ending the call.

The interview in *Smash* features Franklin in his early thirties, around the time *The Greasers* came out. I study his handsome face and perfectly styled thick brown hair looking for similarities to the pictures I have of my father. He seems like just another stranger. The accompanying interview seems uncharacteristically dull by the magazine's standards. He's asked about his favourite place to get a meal (the Hamburger Hamlet on Sunset), what he looks for in a girl (someone who "doesn't take herself too seriously"). I imagine my parents on their first date, my mother young and fresh-faced and my father appearing, even in my mind, blurred at the edges. They feel like characters in a movie, with the female lead so far removed from my mother as I know her now. I skim the rest of the interview, turn the page, and reread the feature on Virginia and the Woolfpack.

12

The following Sunday, I wake up and fumble to turn off my alarm, which is also my phone, and then pick up my phone, which is also a computer, and open my emails to check for new messages, like I do every morning. Today there is one from a jflounder@speakuptherapy.com. My heart skips.

Lucy,
My receptionist told me you were calling around my place of
work asking questions about SMASH. What is this about?
J.

I read the email five times, trying to figure out what to make of it. That she wrote out *Smash* in all caps, the way it's written on the cover of the magazine, means that she must have some familiarity with it. That means she is definitely the Jennifer Flounder from the masthead. The brevity of her message concerns me. She could just be a concise emailer, but what if I've annoyed her? What if she doesn't want people calling her at work asking her about her creative past? What if I'm dragging something up? What if she hates me?

Part of being a journalist, I've been told, means not taking everything personally, but part of being Lucy means everything is personal, all the time, unless I'm convinced otherwise. I've decided I've already ruined this woman's day because I am an incompetent idiot trying to play dress-up as a reporter and—for what? *What is your end game, Lucy?* All I need is for someone to tell me what to do. Tell me what to do, and I will be okay.

A minute goes by as I stare at my screen, then five. I take a deep breath and start composing an email to Jennifer.

> *Hello Ms. Flounder,*
> *I hope my message didn't catch you off guard. I am a writer based in Toronto, but I'm coming to you out of my own personal curiosity more than anything. A collector recently introduced me to* Smash *magazine, and I am fascinated by it, especially because I had never heard about it before and there is so little information on the internet about it. I looked up your name after reading it on the masthead, which led me to your website; my sincerest apologies if it was inappropriate to contact you there. I was wondering if you would be willing to chat about your experiences working at* Smash *(that is, if you are the right Jennifer Flounder) because I am curious about how this incredible magazine came to be.*
> *Best,*
> *Lucy Selberg*
> *PS: You can read some of my writing here:*

I include a link to an interview I did with some graffiti artists for *The Hog* last year and hit send before I can overthink it. Immediately, I start to cringe. The flattery is thick; I wonder if I am either too apologetic or not apologetic enough. And is it Ms. Flounder or Dr. Flounder? What do speech therapists use? Should I have called her doctor to play it safe? Would it have been patronizing if she wasn't a doctor and I called her one?

The ding of a notification. I have a new email from Jennifer Flounder.

Hello Lucy,

Thanks for your interest. Yes, that's me. I am happy to talk to you, though I don't know how much help I can be. My number is below. Call me anytime outside of business hours, I should be home.

Sincerely,

Jen

Jen. Jen! I cannot believe minutes ago I was devolving into panic over Jen, my new friend whom I am on a nickname basis with. Jen is happy to talk with me!

My shift starts at noon, and Nora's already there when I arrive, blasting Siouxsie and the Banshees. I asked her on our previous shift if she had heard of *Smash* magazine, but it was new to her too.

"What should I even ask Jen Flounder?" I say to Nora.

"I'm sure she'll just be happy to have someone interested in her earlier life. She was part of something cool, and now she lives in Ohio. You're giving her a chance to get nostalgic, relive the time before she had to worry about her job or her kids."

"If you say so," I say, and then I think to add, "Do you wish I asked you more about your life? Like, in the eighties?"

Nora lets out a laugh, so rough and quick it sounds like she's choking.

"What do you want to know, sweet pea?"

"What did you do back then?"

She shrugs. "Not as much coke as you'd expect, but not no coke either. I listened to some bands that hipsters might still think are cool today and a whole lot more that people have forgotten about, rightly so."

"I bet you dressed amazingly."

"Are you implying I don't now?" She gestures to her outfit. She is wearing a slouchy sweater over a leather miniskirt—which I object to on vegetarian levels but have to admit looks great on her—and boots zipped up over her knees. Nora's boots always go a little farther than they need to.

"You know what I mean. Now you dress awesomely in a 2010s way. Before you got to dress awesomely in a 1980s way."

"Do you want to hear a secret?"

"Do you and I even have any secrets left?" I say. Nora spins around in her spot and walks away. "Did I—did I offend you?" I call after her. She's back a second later with a book from the music section.

"Found it!" She's holding up a copy of *Spit on My Face: A History of Toronto Punk in the 1970s.*

"I hate that book. Just because of its name. It sounds like it should be something sexy. Very misleading."

Nora flips through the book. "I know it's in here somewhere." She stops at a black-and-white picture halfway through. "Aha!" She turns the book to me. I examine the photo. It's not the best quality. A freckled girl who can't be older than sixteen is staring at the camera; her face is in a snarl that looks adorable on her young features. It looks like she was studying a picture of Sid Vicious and is doing her best imitation. I can't tell if her greasy hair is pulled back in a messy ponytail, or if it's simply a short spiky haircut gelled back. She's wearing an old plaid shirt, and sticking out of the breast pocket is what appears to be a dirty fork.

"What am I supposed to be looking at? Were forks the hottest fashion accessory of the punk underground or something?"

"Look closer. Do you recognize that girl?"

"Nora, is this *you*?"

"Read the caption, honey."

I have to squint to read the small print. *Nora Goldstein, bassist, Meatrat, 1979.*

"You were in a punk band?"

"I could barely play my instrument. Some guys thought it would be cool to have a girl in the band, so they gave me an old bass guitar and told me what to strum. But we were kind of the shit, in the local scene."

"I keep forgetting how many lives you've lived. I'm so jealous of you."

"I'm jealous of *you*. It's all just beginning for you. You have so many lives left to live."

"All I do is sell books and jerk off."

"The dream."

"And you started way younger than I did. I must be a decade older than you were when this picture was taken."

"I was sixteen and living with my boyfriend." She pulls the book out of my hand and studies the photo of her younger self for a second. "My mom and I were fighting a lot. I couldn't stand the guy she was dating. So I left." She says this so matter-of-factly. I've never heard Nora talk about her mother before, and I'm not sure if I'm supposed to say something, but she starts flipping through the book and continues talking. "Keane was seven years older than me, dropped out of university after finishing half a philosophy degree, playing in a band, of course. He lived in a big house on Spadina Crescent with about half a dozen other people. It's hard to say exactly how many lived there. People were always coming and going."

"So you just . . . moved out when you were sixteen? That was that?"

"Oh no. I was gone just for the summer. My mom wasn't a bad person. Not that I buy into that bunk that all parents have their kids' interests at heart. My best friend Cindy's mom was a heroin addict and stole from her daughter to support her habit. Who does that? Who steals from their daughter? It's supposed to be the other way around. I stole from my mom all the time, like a normal kid." I nod, like I am the type of person who can understand and relate to teenage rebellion. "But my mom wasn't like that at all." She shakes her head. "Her boyfriend truly sucked, though. Straight-up awful."

"He didn't, like . . ."

"Didn't what?"

"Didn't, like, you know . . ."

"Honey, no one knows what you're saying right now. Just say it."

"He didn't, like, touch you, did he?"

"Jesus, honey, no." She slams the book shut. She lets out a sound like a laugh, but there is no humour to it. "No, no, no. Nothing like that. He sucked in an above-board way, legally speaking. He cursed me out a lot, and he could get a little aggressive with my mother, not violently, but in a way I didn't like." I look away, embarrassed that my mind went to a salacious place. "Don't get me wrong,

I dealt with enough handsy guys," Nora continues. I was living with my boyfriend in a rooming house filled with aspiring rock stars and going to sweaty shows. You get your ass grabbed. It happened. But it meant freedom from everything else terrible about the world."

"I'm so sorry that happened to you," I say, relieved to use a familiar script to comfort. "None of that was your fault. I am always here to talk about your trauma—" and Nora surprises me by laughing again, this time loudly and generously.

"Trauma? Sweetheart, please. Those were some of the best months of my life. There were no rules, for worse but mostly better. I'd rather deal with those boys than parents or cops or other broken systems. It wasn't a utopia; that's fine. But what are the alternatives?"

"It sounds like men were having a better time than the women."

"I could take care of myself. A guy grabbed me, I'd smack him one. Or I'd tell my boyfriend, and Keane would get real ticked on my behalf." She says this last part almost proudly, like it was an accomplishment to have a boyfriend willing to fight for her honour.

"But that's patriarchy! Men thinking they're entitled to your body in any regard is part of a rape culture that—"

"That's the same rationale used by women I knew who would judge your little weekend S&M practices. Were those boys pricks? Sure! I'm not defending them," she says, seeing me open my mouth to respond. "I'm talking about kids, you know. Teenagers, maybe a little older. They don't know shit from wild honey. And it's not like it's so easy being a boy all the time. They were always being goaded on by other guys to get some. My mom's boyfriend, he was an adult man, and he was terrorizing his girlfriend and her daughter. *That*'s messed up."

"But," my voice is softer and higher pitched now, the way it gets when I can sense a conflict arising that I want to avoid at all costs but can't keep myself from talking, "if Justine's narc boyfriend grabbed her—"

"—I'd smack him one." She sees the look of upset I have on my face, the edges of her voice soften as she continues. "And men can't get away with the bullshit they used to, and that's a good thing. Your generation is changing that. I'm on your side." She pauses, swallows, considers her next words. "I'm just saying, maybe thinking of every negative interaction with a male as *traumatic* isn't necessarily as helpful to the girl-power cause as some of your peers think it is. We're not all victims, you know."

Nora is wrong. I know she is wrong. Her ideas, right now, are not the good ones, and I know that if I can't make her understand that she was a victim and that she should feel bad about what happened to her, then I will be failing women, Nora included, and then I will not be able to call myself a feminist. But when I open my mouth, I do not find the right words. So I'm silent, while Nora reflects on her experiences, her early life, who she is and who she was, outside any of the theory I've read or arguments I've digested.

"And I did go home, eventually." She's not looking at me. She's flipped back to the picture of herself, the teenage girl with the dirty fork. She's talking to herself; I may as well not be there. "My mother eventually broke up with her boyfriend, and I came back for my senior year, and we never talked about it. She could be awful at times. But she was trying her best. Most of us really are just trying our best."

Dear Sir,

Here's an honest thought for you: Sometimes something happens, and I know right away that I'm overreacting. Like I'm watching myself in a movie, and there's a separation between what my mind thinks and what I actually feel. You know in horror movies when the character hears a spooky noise, and she goes to investigate, and you think, Get out of there, you idiot! Run for safety, call the police!*? I wonder if anyone else watching these movies who also thinks those things (because I do! I do think those things!) simultaneously thinks,* Go, explore those sounds. Satisfy your curiosity. You need to know what it is. You need to know how bad it can get. *Sometimes that's what it's like when I start to let my thoughts wander. Somebody says something, makes a sound that could be totally benign, or it could be that they hate me. It could just be the house settling, or it could be a serial killer in the attic. And I think,* Okay, time to take a step back, go to a place where you feel safe, and explore these things from a distance. *But then my impulses also say,* No, you need to explore this right now, you need to dive in headfirst, forget about the flashlight, forget about backup, you need to go in now. *My brain is like the attic in a horror movie, and I have no choice but to explore it. Will anybody be surprised when they find my corpse?*

Love,

L.

13

One day during second year of undergrad, Sasha convinced me to go to a meeting for something called "Whale Poaching Rally."

"So it's a rally *for* whale poaching?" I said, after seeing the poster in one of the hallways.

She rolled her eyes. "Obviously not." She studied the poster. "At least, I think obviously not."

"I just feel they could have made this sign a lot clearer," I said. Whale poaching seemed like the kind of thing I would be against. I had stopped eating meat a few months prior, joining Sasha in her decade of vegetarianism. "But is whale poaching even a problem here? Like, are they doing this in Lake Ontario?"

I had been adapting comfortably to the academic part of university. Outside of the required literature classes for my major, I took Intro to Philosophy and Women's Studies 101, the latter including a seminar in which students were encouraged to debate and discuss the texts we read. I had never given much thought to whether prisons were obsolete or if we had enough female CEOs. Most of the texts we read seemed to contradict each other—the curriculum was "designed" that way, our professor explained—but I couldn't help agreeing most with whomever we were reading at the time, so confident was everyone else in their thinking, like they had figured it all out, and I needed to trust them, the way I trusted Sasha.

My grades stayed high, unlike Sasha's, whose GPA was just good enough to keep her off academic probation. She claimed she didn't care about stuff like that, that the world was bigger than what you could learn in a classroom, but I often heard her loud voice from her bedroom in the apartment we shared, arguing with her parents on the phone about her future. Two of her older sisters had their PhDs. The third was in law school. She loved her family but would shrug off their "bourgeois priorities" if I asked whether she was okay when she emerged misty eyed from her room after one of their heated arguments.

Which is why I was confused when she brought me to the planning meeting for the whale-poaching rally one winter afternoon.

Sasha's activism was laser focused in a way her academic career wasn't, and I had seen her scoff at some of the more untenable organizations on campus. "Some people just want to pretend as radicals," she had complained to me, and I agreed with her even though I wondered if that's what I had been doing.

We were the first to arrive, except for two upperclassmen already in the room. A tall, sandy-haired boy was sitting on the desk at the front of the empty classroom, reading over some photocopied literature and eating a tuna-fish sandwich.

"Ryan!" Sasha said, in a voice I had never heard from her before, an octave higher than her usual register. The boy looked up from his paper.

"Sash! You made it!" He put down the papers he was reading and pulled her in for a hug.

"This is my roommate, Lucy," she said. "Ryan is in my ethics class."

"Are you a philosophy major too?" I asked, politely shaking his extended hand.

"Minor. I'm in poli-sci." He didn't ask me what I was studying.

After introducing us to his friend Grant, he explained the idea behind this meeting.

"Have you seen that new documentary *The Cove*? It's nasty what the Japanese are getting away with."

Sasha and I sat on two student desks opposite Ryan, our legs dangling over the edge.

"Don't you think it's a little imperialistic, though, focusing on the practices of other countries when we have so many unsustainable forms of farming here?" I asked, parroting a thought I had heard Sasha express only a week before. I assumed she would agree with me. Instead, she kicked my foot, hard.

Ryan just laughed. "You sound like my housemate, Elliot. Two of you would get along. He doesn't like thinking about global issues either."

"That's not what I'm saying—" I started, but I was cut off by Grant this time.

"It's five after," he said, looking at his phone. "Do you think anyone else is going to show up, or should we get started?"

"Students are getting so apathetic these days," Ryan said wistfully, and I snorted. Sasha kicked me again.

The meeting lasted maybe fifteen minutes, during which Ryan summed up in detail the documentary he had seen. We were joined by a couple of freshmen halfway through who looked like they had wandered into the room by mistake and were too polite to leave. At the end,

Grant passed around a sign-up sheet for a mailing list. Sasha jumped to her feet and put her name down first. "Thank you so much for coming out, Sash," said Ryan pompously, hugging her again before we left. "It's so nice seeing people really care about the issues."

I put down my defunct Hotmail address, smiled, and then left the room with Sasha. Neither of us spoke for a minute as we walked down the hall.

"I know it's dumb," she said, her eyes staring straight ahead.

I let out a laugh. "Listen, if you'd told me the whale-poaching guy was hot—"

"It's just, he *likes* that I'm so passionate about shit, you know?" Her voice was louder than it needed to be, with the gravitas she usually reserved for her well-rehearsed political rants. "Most of these guys I bone are nice enough, but I know how they see me. The cute little activist who gets all riled up about things. It's like a fetish for them. They don't say it, but you can tell. I can tell."

We kept walking. I didn't know what to say to this. I couldn't imagine anyoné thinking Sasha was a joke.

"Do you think it's actually going to happen?" I asked softly. "This rally?"

"Jesus Christ I hope not," and she burst out laughing. She looked at me, and I laughed too, feeling a sense of relief knowing that we were going to do absolutely nothing that day to stop Japanese whale poachers.

14

I call Jennifer Flounder as soon as I get home. I don't give myself enough time to think about it, because I know if I do, I will psych myself out.

She picks up right away. Her voice is softer than I was expecting, a little weathered. She reminds me of my grandma. I put on my best professional-lady voice, the same one I use to deal with uptight rich customers who come into the store, the voice that says I know exactly what I'm doing.

"Jennifer Flounder?" I ask. "Hi, this is Lucy Selberg calling from, um, Canada. I just wanted to confirm that now was a good time to talk?"

"It is," she says.

"Excellent," I continue. I take a risk and ask her if I can record our call, telling her it would be useful to my research if I could have a reference tool. *She knows you're full of shit*, I think; *she knows you have no idea what you're doing.* She says, "Sure," like she doesn't care much either way.

There is so much I want to ask her, about *Smash*, about her career, about life in LA in the seventies, about the writing and the parties and the music. "So how did you end up in Ohio?"

"My husband grew up here," she says. I give her a second to elaborate, but she doesn't continue.

"Where did you meet him?" I ask.

"When I was living in LA."

"Was he a journalist as well?"

She scoffs. "Nah. He was a waiter. Wanted to be an actor. They all do, really."

I ask her what happened, if he ended up working as an actor, when did they move to Ohio, three rapid-fire questions to prompt a longer answer.

"His mom got sick, so we decided to move back here. And then we just got . . . comfortable, I guess." She pauses again, and this time I don't try to fill the silence. I wait one second, two, three, until it almost gets so uncomfortable I can't bear it, but then she continues. "I was sick of Southern California. I loved it. I loved it with all my heart, I still do. But the sunshine sucks you in. It tricks you. You believe anything is possible, and then the next thing you know . . ." she trails off. Her candidness throws me. I wait for her to finish the thought, but she's quiet again.

"Is Flounder your maiden name?" I say.

"It is. I was single when I worked at the magazine, or as single as you could be in Chester's world. I kept my name when I got married."

"Was that common?"

"A little bit more in my community. I knew a lot of women who did that. Some kind of statement."

"What do you mean by community? Like, feminism? You were involved with that, right? The feminist movement?" I sit up a little straighter, galvanized by my own excitement.

"You could say that, yes. I'm not sure if there was one 'feminist movement' singular, but there were communities. It was really taking off in California at that time. Mostly up north in the state, but it was exciting where we were too. We thought we were going to change the world."

"Well you did, kinda," I say. "Second-wave feminism did."
She laughs. "Yeah, we did, except when we didn't.
You win these victories, abortion rights, accessible birth
control. The men loved that, at least the ones I spent time
with. Sexual liberation was great for them."

"You sound just like this friend I have," I start to say,
and for a second I'm tempted to bring up what Nora said
earlier today about victimhood, but I want Jennifer to keep
talking about her own life.

Here's what I learned about Jennifer Flounder:
She was born in Pasadena in 1956. Studied English at
UCLA with the hopes of becoming a journalist. She got
her first internship at a women's fashion magazine in the
city the summer after her freshman year, when she was
just eighteen. Back then, the internship thing was new
but actually meant something, as people still believed
there were futures in media jobs. I listen enviously
while also thinking about early chapters of *The Bell Jar*,
wondering how Jennifer's own experiences compared.
Jennifer wasn't doing anything fancy at this magazine,
mostly just writing copy to go with fashion editorials. It
was fluffy stuff. One of the other interns was a hardcore
feminist who spoke about changing the system from
the inside. She introduced Jennifer to radical second-
wave writers: Shulamith Firestone, Valerie Solanas.
This other intern was Jennifer's Sasha. They joked
about what life would be like once the matriarchy took
over. Jennifer tells me that working at a fashion magazine in the seventies was bleak, simple work, but that
she took the atmosphere for granted. "If I knew then
what I know now about how brutal men in publishing

can be, I would have appreciated that time more," she says ominously.

"What do you mean by that?"

"Well, about Chester and the general vibe at *Smash*," she says. I tell her I don't know anything about *Smash* except what I've read in the magazine. I explain about the customer at the bookstore, the back issues, how I'm waiting for more from eBay but otherwise can barely find anything about it. I was reluctant to tell her this part at first; I wanted to make it seem like I was a fan to flatter her into opening up, but it's become clear that she doesn't revere the time she spent working at the magazine and that my ignorance about it is a virtue.

"Look," she says, and her voice is still soft but she sounds exhausted, fed up. Not angry, just very tired. "*Smash* was no better or no worse than any other scene at the time. We believed our own mythology. That we were better than the establishment. But magazine men'll get fresh with you the same as any fella, and then call you uptight when you don't give in." She starts to say something else, hesitates, stops, and then adds, "*That's* why I moved to Ohio."

"And things are better there?"

"Things are better everywhere, I think, than they were forty years ago. That moment in time gave us a lot. Women's liberation, or at least our attempts at it. The music. It was a mess, but it felt beautiful. I just never want to go back."

"I appreciate your frankness," I say, and I mean it. "How did you meet Chester?"

She replies with a throaty laugh. "Chester, that bastard." Her casual cursing is jarring against her gentle voice. "I met

him at an industry party! A launch for some other magazine—I think *Vogue* was doing a California-themed issue.
One of my girlfriends invited me. He had just gotten the
job editing *Smash* and was feeling high and mighty. Tried
to hit on me, actually. I wasn't having it, at least not then.
He thought I was a model, or that was just the line he used
on me. I told him I was a writer, and he didn't believe me;
the next day, I found his contact info from some mutual
friends and mailed him some clips. It was a cheeky move,
I suppose, but he hired me anyway. Couldn't offer me
much of a pay raise, but he let me do what I wanted."

"What do you mean, at least not then?"

"Pardon me?"

"You said he tried to hit on you and you weren't having it
then," I say, less confidently this time. The opening intrigues
me, but I'm trying to think of a delicate way to approach
the subject. Did she and Chester have a relationship?

"Oh, I had seen his type before. Fellas like him were
all over Southern California, and probably the rest of the
country too. Too drunk on their own brilliance to even
realize there was a world around them. The difference
of course being that he had a magazine to run. That's all
I have to say about him."

I ask her about Sanderson. She doesn't know why or
how they decided to publish a teen magazine; she wasn't
really interested in questioning a good thing at the time.
Most of the other magazines were published in New York,
and the ones that did share an office with *Smash* generally kept to themselves. *Smash* was in its own little world
of music and rebellion and glitter, a flash in the pan that
burned bright and burned out quick.

"Am I really the first person to talk to you about all this?" I ask.

"You have to understand, we didn't care much about things like legacies back then," she says. "Maybe Chester did. But for most of us, we were happy to have a job, and we were too caught up in the moment. There was very little supervision to what we were doing. You can see that in the product we published. None of us was thinking about promotion, or archiving work. I don't even have any copies saved. We were around for a year, and then we weren't, and we all moved on with our lives."

"But don't you miss any part of it?"

"I miss being young, sure. And I miss California, even though I visit a few times a year. I miss the Sunset Strip, and I miss all the free records I got through work. I don't miss the parties. We were heavily encouraged to go to them, like they were a job requirement. You met a lot of pricks at those parties—photographers, rock stars, shitty actors who thought they were God's gift to women. And we were expected to flirt to keep the magazine in their good graces so they would want to work with us. Chester always said we weren't big enough to piss them off. Do you want to know the fastest way to suck the fun out of sex, drugs, and rock and roll? Make it mandatory."

"You keep referring to these men. Do you remember anything specifically? Stories, or . . ." My voice is weak. I hate how weak my voice is. Jennifer's voice is soft, but she hasn't once sounded weak.

She lets out an exhale, thinking. "It's a blur, really. There was this actor who came to one of our wrap parties. His career was just starting. I think the only reason he was there was because he was friends with one of the photographers and likely was trying to get a spot in the magazine himself. He kept making a big deal about buying me drinks, except it was open bar—Chester made sure these things always had an open bar—so it was mostly just him flagging down the bartender for me. I drank the first one and started dumping the rest in some plant pot. It didn't seem like a good idea to just turn them down."

"So an actor kept pushing drinks on you all night?"

"I'm not finished," she says. "He wanted me to go back with him to his hotel room. I told him I had a boyfriend, probably a lie, I can't remember. He was more pathetic than intimidating, a sloppy drunk who had the worst breath. That's the part I remember the most."

"Do you remember who the actor was?"

"I'd really rather not get into specifics," she says, and I reply that I understand, before making a mental note to ask again later. She pauses for a moment, then continues, "I was bored at that party. I had been to so many at that point. So I go out to hail a cab, and Chester stops me. He joked around at first, 'Leaving so soon?' He made it sound like it wasn't a big deal. He was good at that. He even agreed with me that the party was bogus! He said that's why I should stay, that the party needed me to keep going. He didn't force me to stay or anything. But I didn't know how to say no to that."

"And the actor?"

"He was still there. Still wouldn't leave me alone. Chester said I was doing a good job keeping him happy, that if I kept this up, I could be the one to profile him, as if that was some kind of honour. One of the younger girls—there were a lot of younger girls who hung around—she came to me in the bathroom and told me I was so lucky that the actor had picked me. She had been trying to get his attention and wasn't used to getting turned down. Everyone kept calling me lucky, but they didn't have to smell his breath."

"What happened after that?"

"Nothing, really. He got me another drink, then jammed his tongue down my throat. I let him. I've kissed many men at parties; it was no big deal, except they usually didn't taste so bad. I was busy thinking about what my move would be if he tried to get me to leave with him. But he was on a lot of stuff that night. He passed out of his own accord, and I was off the hook. When it came time to interview him for the magazine, I let someone else do it."

"That sounds like a lot, what you went through." I hope that I sound sensitive enough as I say this, like Barbara Walters or Oprah. I don't want to trigger her.

"That was working at *Smash*. You had to hope those kinds of people would self-destruct before they destroyed those around them, and then you showed up to the office the next morning waiting for your next assignment."

"Do you miss having a creative outlet?" I say.

"My whole life was a creative outlet," she answers. "*Smash* was just what we happened to put together when we weren't too burned-out. And now I have my work, my marriage, my kids. I paint sometimes. Those are my outlets."

"But don't you miss—" I start to ask before she cuts me off.

"I think you're trying to paint a portrait here of someone who had a glamorous life and gave it all up," she says. "And I get it. I was a writer too. You have to find an angle. But I don't miss it any more than I miss the bridge club

115

I was a part of the first six months after I moved to Ohio. It was a nice moment, but the world has changed so much. You mentioned you're in your early twenties? You can't even imagine what it was like to be a woman in the seventies. I'm not trying to sound patronizing, but you can't."

"I understand," I say, even though the question I was going to ask before she cut me off had nothing to do with that. *But don't you miss Chester,* I want to ask. I rearrange my question. "Do you keep in touch with anyone else from that time?"

"I lost touch with mostly everybody when I went back to school for speech therapy. I email with a couple of the writers and one of the photographers. Buck Swinton. He does mostly commercial stuff now. I can try to find his number for you, if you'd like."

"But you don't keep in touch with Chester," I ask, more of a statement than a question.

"Honestly, I don't think many people from those days do. He sort of faded away. It happened so suddenly, us shutting down. But those things always do. We were given about two days' notice before we were locked out of the offices. The explanation they gave us was that the publisher's wife, Sanderson's wife, was religious and some of the stuff we were doing offended her. Chester announced that he would be going on a bender and anyone who would like to join him could. I don't know if anyone took him up on that offer. That's my last memory of him."

"But you don't know if he . . ." I start. There's a moment of silence; I want Jennifer to anticipate what I'm trying to say next, as I don't have any way to ask tactfully. Instead, I just say it. "He's still alive, right?"

"Oh!" she says. "Very much so, last I checked. It's been a few years since I heard anything, but friends of friends will always mention when they see him around LA. I'm positive he still lives there. I can't imagine him anywhere else."

I have so many more questions for her, but I hear someone calling her name in the background, and she excuses herself, offering to talk again later if I need any more information. I thank her profusely for her time, and we both hang up.

The *Smash* project feels real now. I have conducted a genuine interview with a genuine human being. I now need someone to guide me on what to do next. I need an editor.

At *The Hog*, my editor, Malcolm, used to intimidate the hell out of me, but he always made my writing better. He quit to freelance full time, writing for a mix of newspapers and magazines that would actually impress my mom, as well as niche literary websites, where he would write long, intricate film reviews that quoted philosophers or old complicated texts like they were no big deal. The way people talked about him at the office, I always assumed he would end up in New York with a book deal. We're Facebook friends, though it seems he hasn't touched his profile in years. Still, I shoot him a quick message.

Hope you're well. Have a favour to ask. I started researching this story idea. I'm not even sure if it is anything. It's not right for The Hog. I don't know who it's right for or if there's even anything there. I love your writing and think what you've been doing lately is really smart. Would I be able to run my idea by you, and you tell me if it's even worth anything? Sorry for bothering you.

I hit send, wince at my awkwardness, and switch my tab over to go back to transcribing my interview with Jennifer. A minute later, I see I have a notification in the other tab where I left Facebook open. Malcolm has written back already.

Lucy! So good to hear from you. I'd love to hear more about what you're working on. How about we get a drink. You free now?

I wasn't expecting much beyond maybe a lukewarm response a week from now offering to look at my idea. His words flatter. It's already 9 p.m., and I do work tomorrow. But I don't want to let this opportunity slide in case Malcolm loses interest. I message him back, asking what neighbourhood he's in, and type out my phone number.

15

"Fuck, there's a lot of potential there," Malcolm is telling me at a bar in Parkdale. There's a pitcher of beer between us. I'm not much of a beer drinker and was worried I wouldn't be able to keep up with him when he ordered it, but he convinced me it was a way better deal than buying our own pints. I feel a strange sense of pride being at a bar where they would kick you out if you tried to order a Sex on the Beach. I decide, yes, I can be a beer drinker for tonight.

"But do you think there's anything actually there? I've interviewed Jennifer Flounder, and I can probably talk to her again. She was super open with me. And I have ordered a bunch of issues off eBay. But I can't figure out what the story is. A cool little magazine existed for a year; then it didn't. Big deal. Thousands did."

"You said this wasn't just a cool little magazine. This was a cool teen magazine published by Sanderson. They had money. So find out why they decided to invest in this. Find out why they hired, from what you're telling me, a bunch of artists and burnouts and gave them complete creative control. And sure, it may not be a story that runs on the cover of the *New York Times Magazine*." Malcolm doesn't need to remind me that he has written for the *New York Times Magazine* on three separate occasions. "But I can see this being somewhere smaller. Maybe even in print."

"Totally," I say, sipping my beer, even though the idea of writing for a magazine that people can go into a store and spend real money on feels as likely as me taking control during sex. But Malcolm seems to believe it's possible, and I like the idea of believing what he does.

"You need to find a way to get in touch with Chester next." "I wouldn't even know how to begin doing that. There are, like, a thousand C. Wrights in the LA phone book." "Or at least some people who read the magazine when it was around. And stop overthinking what it all means at this stage! You tapped into something cool. You should run with it."

"Thank you," I say, and he gives a dismissive wave of his hand, so I repeat myself. "No seriously, Malcolm, thank you. I appreciate this."

He's looking straight into my eyes when he says, "For someone who can be such a funny writer, you have a serious way about you, you know?" I blush. He called me funny. Malcolm thinks I'm funny. "I like it. It's endearing," he adds, and I blush harder, averting my gaze. I take another sip of my beer and realize my glass is empty. The whole pitcher is empty. He suggests ordering another. I'm already feeling a little buzzed, but we're having such a good time. I smile and nod as the waitress comes back. I decide not to take it all so seriously.

An hour later, I'm on Malcolm's couch in his one-bedroom apartment around the corner from the bar, making out with him. He has his hand on my thigh, inching towards my crotch.

"For the record," I whisper into his ear as he works his hand down my tights and against my panties, "this isn't why I messaged you. I really did want to talk about my writing."

"Sure," he laughs, choosing that moment to press his thumb against the exact right spot so I shiver against him. "I know your type. Butter me up with flattery, then casually suggest we go back to my place."

"Pretty sure you were the one who suggested this."

"I seem to recall you were complaining about how gross the bathrooms at the bar were. I was simply being a hero."

"Okay, veto on the bathroom talk now," I say, connecting my lips to his. He kisses me back hard and bites my lip, one hand still working in my panties, the other threaded through my hair, gripping the back of my head. This is good. This is very good. I grab the lapel of his shirt and pull him against me. After a few more seconds he stops kissing me, and I panic for a moment, wondering if I've done something wrong, but he motions with his eyebrows to the bedroom. I nod in response. In a move that almost finishes me right then and there, he stands up while sliding his hands under my hips, hoisting me up with him. I gasp as I wrap my legs tightly around him, my hands holding on to his broad shoulders. He takes me to the bedroom and drops me down on the bed, and I sprawl out on my back. He crawls on top of me, and his expression has morphed into intensity, almost anger, and I realize how easy it would be for him to murder me right now, which makes my nipples harden, which seems like an evolutionary flaw I don't have time to consider right now. His jaw, sprinkled with stubble, looks so angular and strong from this vantage point. I reach out to touch it, but he intercepts my wrist with his hand and pins it above my head.

"Do you like being in charge?" I say.

"I do, baby. I do very much."

"Fuck, it's so hot when you call me that." He cuts me off with a kiss, nibbling the bottom of my lip in the process. He then takes the hem of my dress and slides it up my body, revealing my stomach and naked chest. I rise as he does so, allowing him to take it off. "Do you like to be called any names?" I think about how long it's been since I called anyone Sir.

"You can call me Daddy," he says.

I stop moving beneath him. *Daddy?* I've never been asked to call someone that. I didn't even realize people did that outside of Lana Del Rey songs. My own father died two decades ago. Malcolm must know this. I mentioned it over drinks, I think.

"I don't like, have daddy issues, if that's what you think." How could someone who barely knew their father have daddy issues? "Mommy issues, maybe. But it's not like that."

"What?" He relaxes his grip, looks in my eyes. I worry that I've hurt his feelings, made him self-conscious, but he looks wolfish and amused. "Do you think I think you're an actual baby when I call you that?" I shake my head, looking up at him. "Don't let your need to overthink everything stop you from having a good time."

"Okay," I say, and then I shyly add the word "Daddy," testing it out, and as soon as I say it, visions of actual fathers disappear and are replaced with Malcolm, just Malcolm, and his long, taut body, his big hands, his dark curls, that razor-sharp jawline, Malcolm leaning over me, dominating me, controlling me. "Daddy," I say again drunkenly, and I never want to call him anything else. We keep kissing, our tongues entwining, the beer on his breath not uninviting, commingling with the taste of him. I want him inside me. I press my thigh up between his legs, trying to feel the stiffness there. "Fuck me, Daddy," I whisper, the words slurring even more.

"Maybe we should hit pause," he says, relaxing his grip on my hands and sitting up, adjusting himself so he's no longer on top of me.

"What?" My stomach churns exactly the way it did before I puked at Mitch's place a few weeks ago. *Now you've done it, Lucy. You pushed it too far. You fucked it up. Why do you always do this?* "Were you not having a good time?"

"Baby, I'm having an incredible time." He wraps one of his arms against my naked back, pulling me against him and lying back on the bed so I'm curled up on his chest. He's still fully dressed, and I'm half-naked, wearing only my panties with my tights twisted around my thighs. "But you're wasted."

"Oh," I giggle, realizing that, yes, I did have way more beer than I meant to, but only because Malcolm kept ordering it. "I thought I did something wrong."

"Not at all, sweetheart." He kisses my forehead, and my stomach flutters. I've never been called sweetheart before, not in a romantic context. Nora calls me sweetheart all the time, but that doesn't count. She's, like, someone's *mom*. I decide I like it a whole lot. It makes me feel fuckable and cherished, or maybe like a 1950s housewife, a whole new level of perversion. I curl into him a little more. It's enough to just lie there with him. No, that's not it. It's enough for him to just lie there with me, this hot, smart, dominating man who calls me sweetheart and enjoys my company and who respects active consent so much he won't fuck me when I'm drunk even though I really, really want him to.

"Do you know how long I've had a crush on you?"

"Really?" I say, genuine disbelief in my voice because I've seen the girls he goes out with. Blasé, stylish girls with job titles like model/DJ, who seem to have no origin story, at least not one befitting a human.

"Oh yeah. Right from the beginning."

I knew who Malcolm was from his writing before we met for the first time. I was still a student, and I went to the launch party of some literary magazine that was eighty-seven pages long and cost ten dollars. I was there alone because Sasha had a class that night, and she encouraged me to go—"You need to network, future superstar!"—and I imagined it being a sexy 1920s Parisian literary salon instead of a half-empty pub filled with people in snow boots and puffy winter coats, drinking pints and talking to one another with a familiarity I wasn't afforded. I flipped through copies of the magazine set up at a small table, then went to the bathroom to kill time, then flipped through the magazines again even though I had already bought a copy, and then stood by the bar, drinking glasses of water from the pitcher because I had spent all my money on the ten-dollar magazine. A tall skinny white man with wire-frame glasses and a weak chin came over and offered to buy me a drink. His slumped shoulders and shaggy hair made me think he was in his midtwenties, but as I studied his face in the dim light I saw soft wrinkles around his eyes and greying at the temples of his hair; I asked him how old he was, and he said thirty-eight, an adult age that truly terrified me, and I politely excused myself to go back to the bathroom. When I came out, I scanned the room, looking for someone to talk to, and there was Malcolm, handsome and older than me but not, like, *old*. He smiled so warmly, a million fucking brilliant teeth, and said, "I don't mean to cramp your style, because you have this mysterious loner thing going on and I can respect that, but you're more than welcome to join my friends and me." I responded gratefully, and the way that he gently touched my elbow and steered me towards his circle of friends was so casual and cool and in control that I had to remind myself I wasn't here to flirt—that I didn't even know how to flirt— I was here to network.

"I remember that. I told you I wanted to be a writer, and you told me to send you some pitches at *The Hog*." A thought enters my head. "Did you just do that because you wanted to sleep with me?"

He laughs, and I feel his chest move as he does. "I was attracted to you, but you were *so* nervous just being in that room, even without the older guys hitting on you. I asked you to send me your writing because I thought you were smart. I still think you're smart."

"I can string a few coherent words together with minimal typos, I guess."

"Stop that. Do you know how many people send me pitches that are utterly unusable? Listen to me and believe me when I say you have talent."

"Yes, Daddy," I reply, still drunk enough to mix up the roles I'm supposed to be playing. I lie back down into his chest. He wraps his other arm around me and holds me tight.

I don't realize I've fallen asleep until a few hours later, when my beer-filled bladder wakes me up. Malcolm is still holding me. I had forgotten what it was like just to be touched without being hurt. I carefully snake my way out from between his arms and make my way to the bathroom. I check my phone when I'm back in the room. It's 2 a.m. I look around for my dress before finding it crumpled in a heap on the floor and sneak out to the living room where I left my bag.

"Going somewhere?" a deep voice startles me as I finish getting dressed. That's the thing about Malcolm's voice; it's way deeper than you'd expect given his lanky frame. Like Edward Snowden's. I spin around and see him leaning in the door frame of his bedroom, still wearing the clothes he had on earlier, wrinkled from sleep.

"It's 2 a.m. on a Monday morning, and I have to work tomorrow," I say, pulling up my tights.

"You're more than welcome to spend the night here."

"It's tempting." I mean it. His bed is the most inviting place in the world right now. But if he can take things slow, then so can I. For the first time in my life I decide to show some restraint, even though the very word *restraint* makes me very horny. "But I really think I have to go."

He nods. "Let me call you an Uber." He turns back into his bedroom, asking for my address over his shoulder.

I'm alone in the living room, which also seems to function as an office. He has a real desk, one that looks like it didn't even come from Ikea, with a MacBook and a Moleskine notebook and a stack of glossy magazines, a copy of *New York Times Magazine* from last year sitting on top, and I realize they must be magazines he's published in. There is a short stack of thick, curling papers at the corner of his desk under a coffee cup holding pens. I look closer, squinting in the dim light, and see that they're certificates—National Magazine Awards—unframed, coffee stained, and collecting dust. I'm tempted to look through them, feeling drunk and brazen, but then Malcolm returns, phone in hand. "Kim will be here in a blue Prius in four minutes." "Thank you." I walk over and kiss him. "I had a fun night." "I did too." He wraps his hands around my waist and pulls me tighter. "Will I get to see you again?" "God, I hope so," I say, kissing him. We get so caught up in making out that it takes the vibrating of his cell phone announcing Kim's arrival to tear us apart. "Has it been four minutes already?"

"Sleep well." He kisses my forehead, and I run out of his apartment and step into the car.

16

I'm exhausted by the time I get home, but I know I won't be able to sleep until I make myself cum. Instinctively, I reach for my computer to find a video, but then I decide I don't need it tonight.

The first time I googled "pornography," I was alone in my dorm using the new laptop my mom had bought me, and I realized that for once I was truly unsupervised. I clicked a link and watched a perfectly perfunctory video of a well-endowed heterosexual couple getting it on, but then I started to click on tags and subjects in the search bar and discovered fetishes I didn't know existed. I watched beautiful women sit on balloons until they popped and animations about men who were pulled in by tentacles—content that did absolutely nothing for me sexually—but I was rapt at the idea that just below the surface of polite society were depraved perverts into kinks I couldn't make sense of. My searches always ended up at BDSM sites, to which I would dutifully masturbate.

The more time I spent watching hardcore bondage videos, the more terrified I was at the idea of pursuing sex in real life. In high school, I hadn't cared about hitting the same milestones as everyone else. I firmly believed that my time to shine was in university; and then there I was, and I realized even the nerds were getting laid while I focused on my classes.

Sasha told me not to worry about it. "Virginity is a construct," she said, but sex was all I could think about.

I came home from my Shakespeare seminar during my final year, completely exhausted from an all-nighter I had pulled to finish an essay. I had picked up poster board and rainbow-coloured Sharpies, ready to make a sign for a protest I promised Sasha I'd go to with her that evening. She came home just as I was putting on the finishing touches.

"I have my sign for the rally tonight." In large letters, I had written, "We Belong Here." Sasha frowned.

"What's wrong with it?" I said, scanning it for a spelling mistake. "It means we women belong in the street. We're taking back the night, right?"

"Take Back the Night was last week. You bailed 'cause you had class, remember? We're doing Idle No More tonight. A white girl can't hold a sign that says 'We Belong Here' at a rally for Indigenous rights."

"I'm biracial," I mumbled, putting the sign down.

"You're a settler," Sasha pointed out.

"Well, maybe I can change it," I said, picking up a Sharpie. "Turn the *W* into a *Th*. Make it 'They Belong Here.'"

"That's even worse!" she said. "That's othering. You can't do that on stolen land."

"Fine." I tore the poster in half, flinging both sides on the floor. "I won't bring a fucking sign. I won't use my oppressive voice to talk over the oppressed so that everyone there can know I'm one of the good ones."

"Hey," Sasha said softly, picking up the poster pieces. Her voice seemed affectedly calm; I wasn't one to lose my temper, especially around her. Getting visibly angry usually meant inviting discomfort, which I avoided at all costs. "Why don't you take it easy tonight? I think you're a little burned-out." I didn't say anything. "I'm serious, Luce," she continued. "Audre Lorde says self-care is an act of political warfare. You can use one of my bamboo-shoot face masks."

I nodded, grateful she was giving me permission to stay home and rest. After I heard the front door close, I opened my laptop and clicked play on a video called "PUNISHED SLUTS GET PUNISHED."

One weekend, Sasha brought me to a house party at Ryan's place in Bloordale. It was one of those houses occupied by a rotating cast of students, with a pyramid of empty beer cans that doubled as decor. I recognized Ryan's housemate Elliot from campus, though I couldn't remember ever having a conversation with him. He was tall and skinny, with the softness and pasty complexion of someone who spends a lot of time inside, but he wasn't bad looking. He asked if I wanted to play foosball with some of his friends. He said I looked like I could "kick some serious foos-ass." I had heard him use the line on another girl, who brushed him off, but he had nice eyes, so I laughed at the joke as if it was funny.

We won the game, and every time our side scored a point, he would high-five me, his hands big and warm, and he would hook his fingers into mine, letting them linger a little bit before resuming the game. After, he asked if he could "get me a drink," and I watched him fiddle with the keg for five minutes before realizing it was empty and cracking open a tepid can of beer for me. When he asked if I wanted to see his bedroom, it was a move so obvious I snorted but still felt my body crackle with nerves.

I excused myself to go to the bathroom and then found Sasha and pulled her aside.

"I think I'm going to have sex," I told her, trying to keep my voice low but failing over the chatter and music.

"What? Here? Now?" she asked. I nodded. "Are you sure?"

"Yes. I think so. With Elliot. Upstairs."

"Okay. I'll be down here. If you change your mind and he gets pushy, kick him in the nuts and come find me, okay?"

"Okay." I turned to leave, then stopped. "What if—what if I'm not good at it?"

"Have you seen your ass in that dress? That nerd's about to have the best night of his life."

I smiled nervously, then turned to leave, but Sasha put a hand on my arm. "Hey," she said, and I stopped. She pulled me in for a hug. "I love you, okay?" she said into my ear. She released the hug and gave me a playful smack on the butt. "Go get 'em. And I'm serious. He gives you trouble, give him the ol' nut kick."

Elliot's room had a desk with an expensive-looking computer setup, a mattress on the floor, a few stacks of books, and an overflowing laundry hamper. He started kissing me as soon as I entered the room, one hand on the small of my back, the other holding the back of my head. I wasn't sure what to do with my hands. I put them on his back near his shoulders, counted to three in my head, then moved them down his back and counted to three again. Elliot didn't seem to notice if my moves were mechanical. He sat on the mattress and pulled me down next to him, all the while his tongue refusing to leave mine. *This is good,* I thought. *I'll let him do all the work, and I won't have to figure out anything except for where to put my hands after the next three seconds.*

His hand went to the hem of my cotton dress, and I raised my hips so he could pull it up my body and over my head until I was in nothing but my bra and tights. The most undressed I had ever been in front of a man. I put my hands back on his shoulders and mentally counted to three again. He put his hand on one of my breasts, though through the padding of my bra I could barely feel it. I wondered if he would care that my tits were so much smaller than they appeared under clothing. Counted to three. Moved my hands. His other hand went down the front of my tights, made its way beneath my underwear, and started rapidly fingering a part of my vulva nowhere near my clit. In porn, the woman would be moaning by now. I wondered if he noticed I wasn't moaning, if he could tell I was inexperienced. I let out a loud moan. Elliot paused and looked at me, and for a second I thought maybe it was too much, but then he resumed the task at hand with much more enthusiasm. He pulled my tights and underwear down with one hand (*Did I shave too much or not enough down there? Will he notice?*) and jammed two fingers inside my slightly damp vagina, rapidly pumping in and out. I squeezed my eyes shut, counted to three, moved my hands again. Should I be moaning more? I tried to remember what women in porn would be doing in this situation. I didn't even realize when Elliot's fingers stopped.

"Are you okay?" he asked me gently, and I let myself open my eyes. He was bent over me, looking concerned. I started thinking of excuses or explanations in my head that would account for my nerves, but instead I spewed out something worse than vomit: the truth.

"I'm a virgin," I said, closing my eyes again.

Elliot started to laugh. "Very funny," he said. I felt him push himself up to a sitting position on the mattress, but I didn't move, my eyes still shut. "You're serious. How did that happen?"

"I don't know!" I said, grabbing a pillow and holding it against my chest. "I just got busy with homework, I guess."

"Do you want . . ." he started and paused, as if trying to pick his words carefully. "Do you want to be here right now?"

"I do!" I opened my eyes to look up at him, never releasing the pillow. "I really do! I just want to get it over and done with. Can't you just do it?"

I truly did not want him to stop. Because if he did, then I would never have sex. I would be even older the next time I tried to do this, and whoever that guy was would be even more incredulous about my virginity, and so on and so on until I died a virgin. It had to happen right now, and I needed Elliot to understand that it had to happen right now. "Please, Elliot. Just do me a solid and take my virginity?"

He exhaled, got up, headed for the door. It wasn't going to happen. It was never going to happen. I hoped more than anything that I wouldn't start crying right then. But Elliot didn't leave. Instead, he turned off the light so the room dimmed and we were lit from the soft glow of an outdoor street lamp muted by the sheet he had hung up as a curtain. I lay back on the mattress, kicking my bunched-up tights off my feet but leaving my bra on. I watched him silently as he undressed and rolled a condom over his erect penis. (*You did this,* I thought. *You made it hard. You have that power.*) Then he climbed on top of me and maneuvered a little, one hand firm on the mattress by my head, the other on the base of his cock, and I knew he had entered me by the way he closed his eyes, letting a little gasp escape his throat.

As he pumped in and out of me I felt a little pressure, but none of the pain I was warned about in teen magazine articles about having sex for the first time. I leaned back and waited for the waves of pleasure to start. They never came. As Elliot's breathing became more pronounced, I exaggerated my own to mimic his. Some time passed— maybe five minutes, maybe an hour—before he shuddered, collapsed on top of me, and then rolled off onto the bed. The mattress.

"Wow." He pulled me into him so we were spooning, his cock deflating against me. "That was really good. Are you sure that was your first time?" I pulled myself out from his embrace and silently picked my dress up off the floor, putting it back on before returning to the bed and letting him hold me as we both fell asleep. He would become my boyfriend after that. It seemed like the thing to do.

17

The morning after my date with Malcolm, there is a thick brown envelope jammed in the mail slot in my building's lobby. My eBay order. I take it back inside and tear it open. A pile of *Smash* magazines tumble out. I retrieve the ones I already own and put them in order, flipping through each one, tracing my fingers over them, feeling the completeness of my collection.

The new issues are similar in format to the ones I've already read. Brightly coloured ads for Wrigley's Spearmint and a raspberry-coloured Volkswagen stick out. There must have been meetings where this major publisher sat down with Don Draper types to sell ad space in a magazine for proto-hipsters. Three decades later, they could fit an Urban Outfitters advertorial. There are profiles with artists and musicians, a quiz to gauge how "far-out" you rate, and a column where a psychic interprets readers' dreams. I leave my apartment to get coffee from the shop next door, then come back, sit cross-legged on my bed, and flip through each issue, wondering what it must have been like behind the scenes producing each one. The masthead doesn't change much between issues; there's Chester's name at the top and Jennifer's a few lines below it. I notice something I hadn't before. Aside from Jennifer's name and a couple of contributing writers and interns, I can barely find any women on the masthead. I start skimming the bylines on articles and features, but again, they're mostly dudes.

I think about the story Jennifer told me, about the pushy actor and how Chester enabled him. It was obviously gross behaviour. But again, I remind myself, it was a different era, and it's not like anything really bad happened. *Smash* seems like a boys' club behind the scenes, but it still counts for something that they dedicated so many pages to speaking to teen girls as if they were actually human. So maybe Chester was a little chaotic; I can't imagine the editor of such a magazine putting a woman in actual harm's way.

My phone buzzes. It's Malcolm. *I had a great time last night. When can I see you again?*

I wonder if I should wait a while before responding, play it cool, as if cool were ever a way I knew how to be. I type an immediate response, *Hopefully sooner rather than later*, and hit send. I hesitate for a second and then type out a follow-up: *Daddy.* Hold my breath. He replies right away with a *:)*.

On the streetcar to work, I pull out my notebook.

Dear Loser,
Guess what? I found a new person who answers to Sir. So I don't need you or this dumb notebook anymore. Here is an honest thought for you: I am very happy right now. It's a long-as-hell time since you or anyone else made me feel this way.

My mind feels pleasantly blank when I stare at the page and then I snap to, filled with a juvenile giddiness at the thought of kissing Malcolm, at transcribing the rest of my Jennifer Flounder interview, at reading all my new magazines.

I'm working alone for the first few hours today and relish the freedom, spending most of this time texting with

Malcolm. He wants to hear more about what turns me on, and I oblige in full detail. I don't let Nora see me with my phone in my hand when she shows up. I double down on doing my job when all I want is to text with Malcolm. *You're doing nothing wrong,* I tell myself. *You have nothing to hide from Nora, because there is nothing wrong about half hooking up with your old coworker slash maybe-boss last night and now calling him Daddy.* I don't tell Nora about Malcolm because I don't have it in me to explain all the ways in which I am not wrong, which I clearly am not. During the first free moment we have, unsure how long I will be able to keep the look of horny contentment off my face if she asks how I am doing, I immediately ask her if her daughter Justine is still dating the narc.

"Do you know about this thing called steampunk?" she says. "It's not quite science fiction, it's not quite Victorian, but *man* is it full of nerds. And there are conventions for it."

"Have they been going to a lot of those?" I ask.

"There's one coming up," she says. "Justine and Randall—that's his name, can you believe it? Randall!— they bought tickets, and she's more excited for this than she is for any high-school dance, including the semi-formal. She asked if I could help with the cosplay element. Apparently that's just a fancy way to say costume."

"So what are you going to do?" I ask.

"What do you think? I'm helping her with the cosplay element," she says. "We thrifted a dress from the Salvation Army last week. It's not really steampunky, but there's a lot of room to play with it. We bought this charcoal dye, the type I used to dye her clothes when she was in her goth phase last year, which was totally different than steampunk, by the way. I already had the right records for that. To give the dress that poufy flair, I did this thing with chicken wire and tulle, and the real pièce de résistance is we went to the army surplus store to get these goggles and—why are you looking at me like that?"

"You love it. You totally love it. You love steampunk."

"Shut your mouth. I'm just an excellent mother."

"An excellent mother would have stopped with buying her kid a dress and handing her a bottle of dye. You are getting into this. Come on. Chicken wire? Army goggles? Nora, this is your *thing* now."

She shrugs. "I'm not going to lie and say I haven't been enjoying parts of it, maybe. It's nice to see my kid happy. Shut up."

"No, Nora, I love it too. This is my new favourite thing."

My phone buzzes with an incoming text. I reach out to grab it, but not before Nora looks down at the screen, one eyebrow raised. A message from Malcolm appears on my lock screen. *I can't wait to tear off your fucking panties,* it says. I really should learn how to change my lock-screen settings.

"Someone new?" Nora asks.

"An old coworker I've recently started seeing," I say, not elaborating that "recently" means yesterday. I turn my phone off silent and put it facedown on the counter. "We're having fun."

"Show me."

"Show you . . . the fun we're having?"

"Oy. Show me his face."

I pull up Facebook on the computer and find his profile.

"Oh, he's a looker." We scroll through his profile pictures, and I'm proud of myself for not picking up the phone again and responding to his text. Malcolm, unlike Henry, knows his angles. "Fully approve of the panty tearing."

I spin around and wrap my arms around Nora's waist, resting my head on her shoulders.

"And what is this about?"

"Nothing. You're a good mother and a good coworker and a good friend and I'm in a good mood today, and I just wanted to—I don't know. I'm just happy to know you, Nora."

"Shit. This dick must be spectacular." Then she wraps her arms around me and hugs me back.

What I experience over the next couple of weeks is, I think, total happiness, or at least a simulacrum close enough that I don't feel the need to sort out the difference. Sex with Malcolm brings me waves of pleasure. Not the act itself, of course, because I tell him the first time we sleep together that it's really hard for me to orgasm without a vibrator, and he says that it's "so hot to be with a woman who knows her body like that" before suggesting I just go down on him. I know Nora won't understand this part, that the thrill I get is from being wanted, not needing to justify my perversions with someone who doesn't already have a burlesque-dancing girlfriend. Maybe this is enough; maybe true happiness comes with having someone hot answering your texts.

Elliot used to put effort into trying to make me cum. He would make his way down between my legs and lick me clean. Sasha had described the experience of getting head as "fucking transcendent." It was a perfectly pleasant experience, and if Elliot wasn't a pro at what he was doing, he at least had the foresight to ask, "How does that feel? Is there anything else you want?" But I didn't know how to answer those questions. There was nothing he could do with his tongue that could make me escape the constant buzzing in my head. It was overwhelming to try to accept the pleasure he wanted to give me. He was so nice; everything about him was nice. Nice couldn't make me cum. I wanted him to tie me down, to shove my panties in my mouth, to grab my thighs and spread them apart so firmly that his hands would leave bruises, to attack my clit so ferociously I couldn't think, couldn't answer his questions, couldn't do anything but feel the sensations I imagined the women in the porn I was watching felt every time they fucked. But I also knew that was a kind of pleasure reserved for a different kind of woman, and I had no way of knowing how Elliot would react if I brought these desires to him, and I didn't want to risk giving up the little bit of physical affection I had been allowed.

Sometimes I would ask him to take me from behind. (I could never bring myself to call the position "doggy style," a term so degrading I was scared at the extent to which it turned me on.) I would arch my back dramatically, getting my hips as high and my head as low they could go, thrusting backwards to match his rhythm, willing our thighs to slap so hard they hurt. I would touch myself with one hand and turn my head to the side, and we were so low to the ground on that mattress that I had a detailed topography of every crumb, every dust bunny, every layer of grime on his floor, and the filth of it all turned me on. What kind of nasty slut gets pounded on the floor of some guy's apartment? Without being able to see Elliot I was able to imagine him as any random man, some guy off the street who would never think to pause while eating me out to ask how it felt. This was the sex with Elliot that I enjoyed the most. When he got accepted into grad school across the country, I found relief in having an excuse to break up with him; we could both be blameless.

When Malcom fucks me, I don't cum, but I also don't think. Later, when I'm alone in my bedroom, I touch myself until I cum to the thought of not thinking.

On election night Malcolm plays a livestream on his laptop, but we get distracted smoking a joint and making out. He asks me if I know what would be *really* hot? And then orders me on my knees, and I take him in my mouth while he watches as the last ridings are announced. He boos as our handsome new prime minister's face fills the screen, and then cums, and after I swallow and get up to join him on the couch, he shakes his head.

"At least the Tories are gone?" I offer.

"He has this special feminist street cred, but he's just another emblem of our capitalist patriarchy," he says, watching the screen. I nod in agreement, then cuddle into him. He pulls out his phone to call me an Uber—he has to work early the next morning, he says—but I tell him it's fine, I'd rather walk.

I pull out my cell phone when I'm outside and see I have a stack of missed calls from Sasha. It's unseasonably warm for a late-October evening. I call her back.

"This world is bullshit," she answers.

"Hey now," I say. "We already knew that. I imagine Ryan's gotta be happy with these results."

"Oh, Ryan's ecstatic," she says dryly. Callum Humphrey won his seat, which isn't surprising. Sasha had already expected this, and, she tells me, it's not like he was the worst possible candidate running in that riding, and she was easily ready to be happy for Ryan.

The after-party was at a pub, and Ryan texted Sasha to go on ahead without him; he would be late, coming from campaign headquarters. Sasha hated going to these things alone, making small talk with Ryan's coworkers. As usual, she hung around the bar and joked with the cater waiters.

Callum Humphrey is there. He greets Sasha warmly, and she is surprised; she's met him twice before, but she knows he meets a lot of people and doesn't expect him to remember her. He has a politician's face, dimpled chin and teeth aplenty, and he's so charismatic as he speaks to her without using her name that she wonders, *Maybe he doesn't remember me. Maybe he's just this charming with everyone.* She doesn't hate it though. She's open to being charmed. And when he asks her if she's excited about the new parliament forming, she answers honestly. She tells him she's a bartender. She says she wants to be optimistic about the future, but labour rights are important to her, and she hopes they don't get brushed aside in the name of superficial changes. Callum Humphrey agrees with her, and maybe he's just being a politician again, but she really is grateful that he seems to be listening to her, that he is taking her seriously. Then he asks if she's taking drink orders or if he has to go up to the bar.

"He thought I was working the event!" she practically shouts into the phone.

"Isn't that a compliment? He didn't think you were a bourgeois partygoer!"

"He's an asshole."

"Oh, completely," I agree. "I'm sorry you had to deal with that."

That wasn't all, she continues. Ryan shows up, and he's having the time of his life. He and Callum Humphrey even do that weird handshake that preppy men do when they're letting loose, where each grips the other's hands and then they lean in to pat each other on the back without actually getting too close. And Sasha gives him space to do all this, because she understands he is technically at work. But when he gets a free moment, she pulls him aside and tells him what happened. "He thought I was a bartender!" she tells him, only for him to get confused and say, "You *are* a bartender!" He realizes immediately this is the wrong thing to say and tries to back it up, pointing out that Sasha *is* wearing all black, just like the rest of the staff, and isn't it a good thing that Callum Humphrey was willing to give so much time to the help, and really, wasn't this a whole funny misunderstanding for them to laugh about later? But Sasha was pissed, and she left in a huff.

"So are you more pissed that this Callum guy didn't realize you were there as a guest or that your boyfriend didn't back you up?"

"Yes! Both! I don't know. *Am* I overreacting?"

"I think your feelings are valid," I say because it's a good thing to say when you have nothing else.

"You're right. They both suck. I wouldn't give a shit if I didn't believe that Ryan was always looking down on me for my work. It's like, that's the worst part. I went there to support him! And I still can't be recognized as an equal."

"Do you want to come over?"

"It's late, and I'm already in bed. My plan is to be asleep by the time Ryan gets home. But I'm off work tomorrow night, and I just don't think I'm in the mood to see him."

"So come over then. Bring Nigel. You can let yourself in when I'm at work. Fuck up my Netflix queue. I have Wednesday morning off anyway, so we can stay up late." We settle on our plans, and I hang up, content that my life is finally together enough that I can help my friend with hers.

18

Sasha is there the next day when I come home from work, slumped on the couch, with my laptop propped open on the coffee table in front of her pumping the sounds of a slasher movie. "So we can agree to never discuss your computer's search history, yeah?" she calls out, eyes not moving from the screen. Nigel is gently snoring at her feet.

I don't respond. Instead, I put down my keys and coat and go stand in between her and the laptop. She looks up at me, eyebrows furrowed like she suddenly just realized something is blocking her view.

"What's in the bag?" She gestures to the brown paper bag I'm holding.

"Tequila."

"Tequila?"

"Tequila. And," I pull out the produce bag that I threw in with the haul from the liquor store, "limes."

"Limes?"

"Limes. Tequila and limes."

"What's that for?"

"The limes are to follow the tequila, and the tequila is to precede going out to a bar tonight," I explain. "Well, I guess the tequila precedes the lime, and the lime precedes the bar, if you care about semantics."

"Why are we doing tequila shots?"

"Because the booze at bars is way too expensive when you're not there working to hook me up."

145

"And why are we going to a bar?"

"To take advantage of our fleeting youth."

"I only care about youths fleeing from Freddy Krueger," she says. "And it's hard to do that with you in the way."

"Sasha, come on," I close the laptop and sit on the couch next to her. "When was the last time we had fun? Like, real fun? When was the last time you went somewhere that wasn't to work?"

"Ugh, Lucy. It's a Tuesday night, and I'm dressed so blah."

"So, your first problem solves your second. It's Tuesday night. No one will give a shit about how we're dressed. And wherever we go, we'll have the place to ourselves."

"Fine," she says. "We'll carpe the stupid diem. But only because you already bought the limes, and I hate wasting produce."

We end up compromising. It's still early enough in the night when we start getting ready, so we do our tequila shots while watching another horror movie. Sasha turns off Freddy Krueger, because she knows I can't handle the concept of hell when I am inebriated, and puts on *Vertigo* instead. We've seen it before, but right now it feels like the funniest movie in the world.

"Everyone is so well-mannered and so *horny*," she says. "God, why don't they just fuuuuuuuck?"

"It's called suspense, and he is the master of it." The word *master*, of course, only serves to turn me on.

"Suspense is just horniness dressed up for Halloween." She looks down at me, lying on the floor, petting a sleeping Nigel. "Fuck it, let's go out."

Outside there are other people and sidewalks and traffic lights and all these rules we need to follow to be a part of society. Sasha starts listing bars nearby, and I think how each one brings in more rules, with IDs being checked at the door and coats hung on those little hooks under the table and it's so overwhelming and I just want to eat potatoes. "I just want to eat potatoes," I tell Sasha, so we postpone our bar plans and start our night at McDonald's for fries and coffee. It's one of those deluxe McDonald's with two storeys, and we find a seat on the nearly deserted second floor. The fluorescent lights and smell of caffeine have a sobering effect. Not literally sobering but I am suddenly reminded of being a body among seven billion others, at least five of whom are currently inside this McDonald's. The drunk kind of sober.

"Did you ever imagine this is what life would look like at twenty-five?" she asks.

"Eating McDonald's on a Tuesday night with my best friend after drinking tequila I bought myself just because I could? This was, like, my dream in high school."

"I'm not even offended he mistook me for a bartender!" It takes me a second to figure out what she's talking about. I focus on the fry in my hand. This part of the conversation we already had last night. Tonight is supposed to be the part where we move on, where Sasha is fun again. But she wants to keep talking. Fine. There is still time for Sasha to be fun again later tonight. "I never wanted to be defined by my job. I think I hated that he didn't seem to recognize me as Ryan's partner. Isn't that fucked?"

"Your feelings are valid," I say for good measure, hoping she doesn't realize it's all I have to say.

"And now, I can't imagine . . . I can't just throw away everything I have with Ryan and start over. Literally, this is what I have."

"But your relationship doesn't have to define you any more than your job does. It's okay to not know about either."

She dips a few fries in her little paper carton of ketchup but doesn't eat them.

"I love Ryan," she says firmly. "We fight sometimes, but I love him."

"I know." I decide not to add anything else. She eats her fries.

"Do you think you want kids?" she asks. I laugh, mostly at the randomness of the question, but Sasha is serious, sober even. "I'd fuck it up," I say. "Think about it. Every serial killer, every murderer in the history of forever, had a mother. And whenever something goes wrong, whenever somebody makes the news for some notorious reason, the first thing people look at is how they were raised. And a lot of times their moms were these nice, wholesome women who didn't know what they were getting into."

"So you're scared your kid would turn out to be a socio-path?" she asks.

"No, because at least if they're a sociopath I'm absolved of any responsibility. I'm scared my kid will be a nice normal human being who would stand a chance if they were being raised by anyone else, but that I would destroy them." I try to find the right way to express this, to make it make sense to Sasha. I focus on the carton of ketchup. "Like, you're this naturally nurturing person who could have a kid tomorrow and be great at it. But I'm scared that even if I try really hard to do it right, all my fears and anxieties will be projected onto them, and they'll internalize it, and it'll fuck them up, and not only will I have caused harm to another person, but they'll go forward and cause harm to other people, a giant chain reaction of pain that all started with me. I can't even ensure *I'm* a good person; how am I supposed to raise someone else?"

Sasha rests her hands on mine, to hold them steady. I hadn't realized how much I had been fidgeting, twisting my hands around each other like they were both trying to grip onto something.

"Wasn't tonight supposed to be about cheering me up?" she says with a small smile. "C'mon, Lucy. It won't work if you have a panic attack. Breathe. In. Out. Like you know how to."

I take a few deep breaths and slowly calm down a little. Sasha doesn't let go of my hands.

"I'm sorry."

"Don't be." She doesn't have to tell me that my feelings are valid. My feelings are always valid with Sasha.

"Why is it always so complicated?" I whine.

"Listen. We went about this all wrong. We're supposed to do the drunken late-night heart-to-heart *after* we go dancing. Release those endorphins. So let's go. You got me out of the house and medium dressed up. Let's leave this McDonald's. It's destroying us."

I nod decisively, and we stand up, still holding hands, and leave the fluorescent lights in our wake.

We end up at a mildly trendy bar that's too crowded to get into on weekends. Tonight, it's pretty sparse. There's a

DJ who looks barely old enough to drink, self-consciously
fiddling with his laptop, playing popular R&B songs. Sasha
lets out a whoop as he puts on an early song by a Toronto
rapper that seemed ubiquitous when we were living together,
one that I never deliberately listen to but somehow still know
all the words to. "Come on!" she says. "I haven't heard this
one in forever!" We put down our bags on one of the sticky
tables. We're the only ones dancing. Sasha closes her eyes
and raises her arms, spinning in a slow circle, out of sync
with the music but utterly content, and I join her, feeling
like I'm in a music video while looking like I'm at a kid's
bar mitzvah. We forget about Ryan, about work, about good
and bad and everything in between and dance until the bar
closes and it's time to go home.

Sasha flops on the bed and falls asleep almost as soon
as we get home. I brush my teeth and take off my makeup
and change into pyjamas, but I don't feel like sleeping.
I open up Facebook on my phone and idly scroll through
my newsfeed for a few minutes, stopping occasionally to
like a friend's selfie. I look up Henry's name and see he's
recently gone to a party that resembles a rave; in every
photo, he's with a different woman, mugging for the
camera. He's growing a beard, it seems. I decide it looks
terrible on him. Then I see what Malcolm is up to. He
doesn't update his Facebook much. He's much too smart
for social media. Except for Twitter, but he only uses that to
follow news outlets, politicians, and meme accounts. Still,
there are enough photos to click through, and I feel a sense
of calm just looking at his face. *This guy likes me,* I think.
This handsome man thinks I'm great. I send him a message, a
quick :), something for him to wake up to. It's been a full

day. This is the longest we've gone without seeing each other since we started hooking up a couple weeks ago.

I'm still pretty drunk. Opening my laptop, I see *Vertigo* is paused, and, in another tab, the Freddy Kreuger movie I refused to watch because I know at some point in the franchise Freddy goes to hell, and I don't have the bandwidth for that. It reminds me of a Looney Tunes cartoon. A few seconds of googling and I find the short, "Satan's Waitin'," from 1954. The whole thing is online. "The future is magic," I drunkenly whisper before clicking play, closing a pop-up, closing three ensuing pop-ups, and clicking play again. The cartoon unfolds on the screen almost exactly as I remember it.

Sylvester is chasing Tweety Bird over the roofs of tall buildings. As a kid, I was never sure which characters I was expected to root for in these cartoons. Tweety and the Road Runner were the obvious victims, the hunted, the innocent, but there was something so pathetic in the way the hunters kept trying. Wile E. Coyote and Sylvester were just doing as nature intended; Elmer Fudd got the proper hunting permits before he set out. And they would be punished, humiliated in the most dramatic ways. Not only were they the bad guys, but they were failures. I would sit uncomfortably on the couch, eating my chicken nuggets, trying to muster laughter for the cartoons that were catered to me, after all, with the crispy dead birds on my plate that I dipped into plum sauce. My vocabulary at seven years old was not sophisticated enough to explain the nuances of the situations, but I felt it, deep in my gut. *I am the bad guy.*

Sylvester is chasing Tweety, the perfect victim with his perfect lisp, and Sylvester falls off the roof, lands *splat* some dozen storeys below. His little cartoon spirit hobbles off, descending an escalator down to hell. Like, literal, actual, biblical Hell.

The gatekeeper to hell is a big red bulldog with heavy-lidded eyes. Dogs because . . . they're the natural enemies of cats? Just as cats are the natural enemies of tweety birds. So I guess cats just don't stand a chance in this world; they're condemned to hell for following the same instincts birds and dogs do. From the very beginning they're doomed. Sylvester stands trembling among the fire and brimstone.

The bulldog tells Sylvester that he's been a bad pussycat with a delivery that now happens to make me completely horny. Then he orders Sylvester to sit and wait until his other eight lives catch up. He laughs sadistically as Sylvester submissively slumps off to a bench and sits patiently, waiting for certain doom.

Back on earth, the still-living Sylvester decides he's going to do what he can to put off going to hell. I mean, not right away; he tries chasing Tweety Bird again, gets hit by a steamroller, and loses life number two, only to be taunted by the truly terrifying dog. The spirit of the dog-devil goads him into continuing to pursue Tweety, at one point physically pushing him in the bird's direction. Eventually he learns his lesson: he'll repress all his natural urges because he doesn't want to be tortured for eternity. He's so scared, alone, and unloved. But it's too late for him. He dies a ninth time and is sent to hell forever, and the credits roll while the cheerful Looney Tunes music plays onscreen.

I close my laptop. I thought watching the video would be reassuring, the way watching episodes of *Goosebumps* that terrified me as a kid are now no big deal. But the weight of the episode, of Sylvester's fate, bears down on me. It's dark in the apartment, and Sasha looks so peaceful sleeping, so I grab my bag and head to the bathroom. My bathtub is spacious; definitely the centrepiece in my minuscule apartment. It's big enough that I can sit in it, fully clothed, and stretch out my legs and take out my notebook. I'm only doing this because Malcolm isn't awake to text me back right now, I tell myself.

Dear Sir,

I was very good at math growing up. You don't know that because you don't know much about me, but also because it's not a fact I easily share. Math isn't something I associate with in my day job or aspirations. Math isn't sexy or romantic or poetic or revolutionary. Or maybe I just never thought it was because those are all qualities I have to work really hard at, and math always came easily to me.

It seemed like the most straightforward subject in school. Science and history were based on memorizing facts. English and art were too subjective; it seemed hard to fail at those, which meant it seemed hard to know if you were really succeeding, which is not appealing when your idea of virtue is wrapped up in approval and binaries. But math, at least at the most elementary levels, was based on learning a few tricks and rules and then applying those rules to problems involving numbers. There was always a right answer, and it seemed possible to find them out on my own without textbooks or punctuation marks. Just me, my brain, and my consciousness figuring out pure simple truths in the world. And it felt so right.

At least, it did in the beginning. When did I first start learning about division? Maybe second or third grade. The thing is, when they first teach you division in school, you don't learn about decimal points. You learn about remainders. So when you divide ten by three, the answer you get is three with a remainder of one. And then a little while later the decimals come in. You add zeroes to the divisor and continue doing the math until you get your final answer. So dividing ten by four, the answer is a neat two point five. But not every answer looks like that. Go back to ten divided by three. You get three with a remainder of one. Add a zero next to the one to make it a ten, and divide by three again. Three point three. Keep going. Three point three three. Again. Three point three three three. You could sit there dividing tens by threes for a million years, and you would never get to the halfway point.

I wasn't raised religious. My mother was Hindu growing up, but mostly lost the thread of her religion when she assimilated in Canada. I couldn't tell you one deity from the other. I think my dad's parents were Lutheran, though they never really practised. I grew up opening presents on Christmas, hunting eggs on Easter, and doing all those general Western Christian cultural things, but, you know, without all the Jesus stuff. Any of the actual religion I know, I picked up by osmosis.

I remember the name of the girl that fucked it all up for me: Stephanie Prince. Steph P., for short. Like me, Steph P. was a nerd. Good at school, never dreamed of breaking rules, read big fantasy books. I mostly ate lunch with the girls from my soccer team, because this was before Kenzie got boobs and stopped hanging out with me. But I spent a lot of time in the library, where Steph P. was, and we struck up a comfortable friendship. One day she asked me if I was a Christian. I said yes, sure, because I watched the Charlie Brown Christmas special every year and grew up excited over the idea of Santa Claus, and if you believed in Santa, you were Christian, right? So she asked me what church

my family went to, and I said, "Oh, we don't really do that,"
and she said, "Well where do you go on Christmas?" and I said
"Nova Scotia?" because that's where my cousins live. And she
said, "Wow, I don't know any Christian who doesn't go to church
on Christmas."

I went home and demanded to know why my mom hadn't
taught me about church and God growing up. She said, "We live
in a country where who you are and what you believe in don't
matter." I didn't understand how that was relevant. She went on.
"You celebrate all the normal things that everyone else does." This
seemed to be enough for her. I realized, if I was going to be okay,
I had to completely take care of myself.

I took a Bible out of the library and hid it in my room, under
my mattress next to my pink padlocked diary. I didn't know how
I would explain it to my mother. I didn't know where to start.
Were you supposed to read it from the beginning? Is that what
they did in church? I read the table of contents, or whatever the
Bible version of that is called, and saw there were sections on
"humiliation." I dug the idea of humiliation (as I did the idea of
serving "the heavenly Father"), but I didn't understand why. It
seemed to be the wrong takeaway from that section. I asked Steph
P. what the most important lesson the Bible can teach was. "Definitely accepting Christ into your heart," she said. I liked that
she had an easy, definitive answer. "What happens if you don't
accept Christ into your heart?" I wanted to know. "Well if you
don't follow the teachings of Christ," she says, "you go to hell."
I knew about hell already. Hell was everywhere. Hell was in my
Saturday-morning cartoons. Here's what I understood about it:
it was bad, and it was infinite. Infinite like what happens when
you divide ten by three, but you wouldn't be doing math forever.
You'd be tortured.

I couldn't fathom torture any more than I could fathom infinity. I tried to think of the worst thing I'd ever felt and decided it was definitely my nausea when I had the flu. But when that happened, I got to sleep in my comfortable bed and my mom brought me medicine. In hell, it would be that feeling of nausea all the time—I would constantly be on the verge of throwing up—but I would have no soft bed, no mother to take care of me. In fact, I would see no one I loved ever again. Billions and billions of years would pass, and I would not even be one percent of one percent of my way through.

And (this is where I really started to lose it) what if Steph P. was wrong about Christianity? She believed what she believed because her parents believed it, but parents are just human like the rest of us. Some of my classmates were Muslim, and my grandparents were Hindu, and our neighbours were Jewish. Who knows which rules are the right ones? And how many rules does a person have to break before they're condemned to hell? So many people are so confident they know what's going to happen, but nobody can really know. Not Steph P., not her parents, not my mom, not the Pope, not Albert Einstein, not any of the smartest or most spiritual people in the world. Maybe there is no hell. But what if there is? Statistically, no matter what religion I pick and no matter how I practise it, I am likely doing something wrong. I was a very, very practical kid. And that scared the shit out of me.

The only subsequent decision I could imagine would be to prepare myself for the worst-case scenario, which was, of course, an infinity of torture. The summer I was eleven, there was a heat wave. I went for long walks in jeans and long sleeves and a heavy hoodie during record temperatures. I would see how long I could go without talking to my mom or friends. How would I be able to handle a billion years in isolation if I couldn't spend an afternoon alone in my room with all the lights off, willing myself to defeat the boredom?

So my honest thought of the day is this: I still don't know. I don't know if I'm making the right choices. Some other people seem so confident in theirs, and I'm jealous, but how can anybody really know? And I'm so scared that no matter what I do, even if I try really hard, it's going to be the wrong thing. I'm going to screw it all up. I'm going to hell. And I'm not prepared.

Sincerely,
Lucy

I've been writing in the bathtub for hours, my wrist cramping and my heart racing. A dozen pages in my notebook are filled with my illegible handwriting, more than I've written in one sitting since I was at school. I force myself out of the bathtub and stretch, about a dozen knots seem to have formed in my back. According to the digital clock on my stove, it's almost 5 a.m. Sasha is in bed, snoring gently; Nigel is on the floor, considerably louder. I quietly peel back the covers and crawl into bed next to my best friend, falling asleep almost as soon as my head hits the pillow.

19

I end up having a vivid nightmare about Sylvester and the dog, and when I wake up the next morning it takes me a while to realize the sounds of growling and chewing aren't coming from my terrified subconscious but are happening in the corner of my apartment. It's just Nigel chewing on something she found. The room spins. The ground feels a million miles away. There's Gatorade in the fridge, I think. I planned for this. I planned for this hangover by stocking up on Gatorade in my favourite flavour, purple, and so it is fine that everything is spinning and my insides want to be on the outside and my head is pain, because I just need to make it to the fridge. I have finally succeeded in taking care of myself.

But when I roll up and out of bed and finally get my bearings, the floor of my apartment looks like a crime scene. There is shredded paper everywhere. No, not paper. Magazine scraps. I reach down to pick up a fragment by my foot and see the words *Contributing Editor: Jennifer Flou.* There's hardly a scrap bigger than this piece. My heart sinks into my stomach, which is already filled with contents it doesn't want to be there.

"NIGEL," I shout, or try to. My voice is a rasp. Nigel doesn't even look up from the issue she's gnawing on, the one I recognize as being the very first one I flipped through when the man at the store brought them in; a teenage model's face is currently being torn into. I'm across the room in a second flat, and I rip the magazine out of Nigel's tiny little jaws. She yaps shrilly and jumps up to try to retrieve it out of my hands.

"What's going on?" Sasha mumbles from the bed, her eyes still shut. "How early is it? Are you not hungover? I feel hungover."

Nigel seems to think we're playing a game; she goes back to the magazines on the floor, like we're caught up in the world's worst game of fetch. It takes a few tries before I can grab her, my hand still gripping the worthless sliver of magazine, unable to put it down. I stick Nigel in the bathroom and shut the door as she continues to yap, wanting to play. When I turn back to my room, Sasha is out of bed, pulling on her jeans.

"I'm sorry about that. Nigel hasn't been that destructive in years. Something about you brings out the puppy in her."

"So this is my fault?" I drop to my knees in front of the mess, rifling through the scraps all over the floor, trying to see if there's anything worth salvaging. My head pounds with a hangover, with lack of sleep, with the noise of the dog coming from the bathroom, with my project reduced to pieces on the floor.

"Hey," says Sasha gently. She comes to join me on the floor. "It's nobody's fault. She's a dog. She does dog things. We'll clean these up, and I'll replace them."

"You can't replace them. They're all I could find on eBay. There aren't any more left." I don't know if that's true, but it feels like it is in the moment. I was going to read them, and research them, and do . . . interviews or whatever it is reporters do, and then write some kind of article, I don't know what, and it was going to be really good somehow, and then I would be a real writer and my life would come together. That was the plan. I think. *Where is my purple Gatorade?* Nigel yaps again, and my head hurts so fucking much. I don't realize I'm crying until Sasha points it out. "Lucy, I'm sorry. Tell me what you need me to do to fix this."

And I know it's because I'm tired, I know that the magazines are just magazines, I know that the tears are ridiculous, and knowing this only makes more of them come, because every second that my feelings escalate, I'm taken a step further from the person I'm trying to be, and maybe it's the look on Sasha's face, a split second of concern that she doesn't know how to solve this problem, that makes me realize for the first time in my life, I don't want to be her either. "Why is it on me to suddenly figure out how to fix every mess?" I get up, wince as I get a head rush. "I still haven't slept off trying to fix the last one."

Sasha had started pushing the magazine bits into piles, but she stops to look up at me. "What mess did you need to solve last night?"

"You know." I wave my hand. "You're going through some shit right now. Things are messy. And then when they get back to normal—"

"So I'm the mess," she says quietly.

"Not *you*. The situation." She's blinking rapidly, and I wonder if she's about to start crying too. *When did Sasha get to be so sensitive?* "Sash, c'mon. I just mean how Ryan is making you act all sad and weird all the time."

She stops blinking, and I can see by the furrow of her eyebrow, the hardness of her eyes, that she isn't about to cry at all. She's pissed off. "I'm acting weird?" I open my mouth to correct her, but she cuts me off. "Jesus Christ, Luce, do you know how exhausting it is to be your friend?" I wasn't prepared for this, for her to admit what I've always wondered. *You're a burden, Lucy. Everybody thinks so.* The fridge is so close to me. It's probably the wrong time to get a purple Gatorade. The Gatorade was supposed to solve all my problems. "Every week since I met you, there's some new crisis where you need me to tell you what to do. And now I fill you in on a fraction of what's going on in my life and, yeah, maybe need some support, and you claim that it's making me *weird?* I'm sorry if my own problems get in the way of me solving yours."

I'm pissed off too now. I think. I'm feeling a lot of things, my drowsy body a corpse animated by the adrenaline of hurt and anger and defensiveness, an indistinguishable spark. "I've been showing up for you! I've been supporting you. And if I realized that I was such a burden to you all these years—" I don't get to finish my thought because a torrent of yaps comes from the bathroom. We both turn to look at the door. "I don't want my neighbour to be pissed at me."

She sighs, goes to the bathroom, and I focus intently on cleaning up the mess as I hear her open the door, pick Nigel up, talk to her in a soothing voice. "You're okay, baby girl," she says, and the barks subside, and I find, not for the first time in my life, I'm jealous of a dog.

"I should take her home," she says. I grunt in assent. Is this a fight? Is this what fighting is? Neither of us speaks as she packs up her stuff from the night before. It's the harshest we've been with one another, I think. It hurts to think. We've never had a reason to fight before. We've teased each other, joked. I guess we've disagreed on things, although that doesn't seem true. It's not that I always agree with what Sasha says. It's that I've trusted that she always knew what she was doing and I would be safe as long as I went along with her. Yet in my apartment, watching her pack up, frustrated with her job and her relationship—and with me—I realize I need her to leave, I need the bad feelings to go away, I need to purge, I need—

And then I am hunched over the toilet, heaving the contents of my stomach into porcelain.

"Lucy?" I hear Sasha behind me, Nigel whimpering in her arms, but I focus on the toilet. I heave again, but nothing comes out. "Are you having a panic attack?"

"Hangover," I say, which is probably true.

"I'll get some Gatorade," she says. "Purple?"

"Please just go." I flush the toilet, heave again.

"I'm not going to leave you like this. If you need—"

"I need some space. It's not—I just have a headache. Please."

I rest my forehead on the toilet seat and think about how many germs must live on it, how degrading it is to rest my head here, how I wish it didn't turn me on. I am prepared to argue with Sasha some more, to ask her to leave again, to accept the inevitable Gatorade she will bring me, but none of that happens. She just takes her things and leaves.

I trudge back to my nightstand and pick up my phone. It's 8:30 a.m. I sit on my bed, open my list of contacts, and hit the dial button. I hear it ring seven, eight times in a row, and decide I will hang up before it goes to voicemail, but I'm not quick enough.

"Did you butt dial me?" Malcolm answers.

"Are you not used to girls calling you intentionally?"

"It's the crack of dawn on a Wednesday, babe." *Babe.* He picked up my phone call, and he called me babe. Like he's my boyfriend or something. I allow myself a smile.

"I'm having a shitty morning. Do you want to come over?" I say and then tentatively add, "Babe."

"What, is this a booty call?"

I can't tell if he's annoyed with me. I don't want him to be annoyed with me. "You've probably got work. I'm sorry for bugging you." I mean this sincerely, but he laughs.

"I'm a writer. I don't start work for another six, seven hours at least. Tell you what. Text me your address. I can pick up coffee and be there in an hour."

Yes. This is what I need. Calling Malcolm was the right idea. Malcolm will not wallow in feelings all morning. Malcolm knows how to make a decision and stick to it. Malcolm will come over, and he will call me babe again and turn all my bad feelings into good feelings, and I won't have to think about Sasha or what she said or how I am a burden to her. Malcolm doesn't even need to know what's wrong. He will just make everything better.

I text him my address and then get to work brushing the sick out of my mouth, chugging a Gatorade with some Advil, showering. I slept in a pair of ratty flannel pants and an old Deerhunter T-shirt with stains at the pits. I change into a pair of black cotton panties, a slightly oversized black T-shirt that falls off my shoulder, and knee socks I found at the back of my sock drawer. I wash my face, then apply mascara and eyeliner, carefully smudging it just a little bit with my finger. I sweep the rest of the torn magazines into a plastic bag and have barely finished blow-drying my hair before there's a knock on my door. I quickly spritz some hairspray at my roots, then tousle it with my fingers.

"I'm sorry I'm still in my pyjamas," I answer the door. "It was a late night. I probably look like such a mess."

"You look fucking sexy," Malcolm says. He looks good too, standing in my doorway, tall and strong jawed, holding a tray of coffees and a paper bag. He came all this way just to see me. When I hug him, he smells like one of those sixty-dollar candles they sell on Roncesvalles: musk and soap and cigarette and leather from his jacket, which obviously I don't condone on animal-rights grounds, but which his shoulders fill out like a fucking champ.

He comes into my apartment, putting down the coffees and bag on my kitchen table, and shrugs off his coat, revealing the outline of his upper arms through his thin grey T-shirt. I follow him into the room and get two plates from the cupboard for the bagels, but as soon as I put them down, I'm distracted again. I hug him from behind, pressing my cheek against the space between his shoulder blades, feeling the warmth of him as he methodically puts the bagels onto the plates. Sasha makes being in a relationship sound like so much work, but being around Malcolm is easy. Not that I think we're in a relationship. He's just someone I've known for years, who I recently found out happens to like the same kind of sex I do, and now he's in my kitchen on a weekday morning bringing me breakfast like we're in a relationship. Which we're not. I wonder how he'd react if I asked him to role-play as my boyfriend, just during sex. Maybe I should get one of those scented candles.

"You feel nice," he says as I continue to hug him, my arms around his chest. He rubs his hands up and down my forearms, then entwines his fingers in mine so that we're holding hands. Like two people in a relationship, which we are not. He brings his hand down with mine, tracing it over his stomach, past his belt, until my hand is on his crotch, feeling his cock hardening under the thick layer of his jeans. I start rubbing him because it feels like it's the thing to do in that moment and because he did bring me bagels. He moans for a second and then gently pushes my hands aside, turns around, and kisses me softly before biting my bottom lip.

"I can*not* wait to fuck you again, sweetheart. But I'm so fucking starved right now. Eat first?"

I nod, relieved. I wasn't in the mood for sex anyway. He picks up the plates, and I grab the coffees, suggesting we go to the bed. He sits down on my bedspread, his legs over the edge, balancing one plate on his lap and putting the other on the nightstand. I hand him his coffee, then sit on the floor beside him cross-legged. I pick up my own bagel and rest my face against his thigh. When he asks me how my morning has been, I take this as permission to vent. He strokes my head affectionately with one hand, eating his bagel with the other, occasionally scratching me behind my ears as I tell him about Sasha coming over last night and a condensed version of the exchange we had this morning, the one that wasn't a fight but felt like one. I leave out the vomiting.

"Hm," he says when I finish. He's done his bagel. I still haven't touched mine. "It sounds like she was pretty uncool to you, after you let her crash here."

"But I started it! She came to me feeling terrible and vulnerable already, and I was supposed to make her feel better. That's what friends do."

"Well, I still say you didn't do anything wrong." He's still stroking my hair. It feels good, safe. Then he stops, grabs a bunch of my hair, grips it firmly. "But it sounds to me like you still feel the need to be punished. Isn't that why you called me?"

Is it? I know I called Malcolm to make myself feel better. And I suppose he has. I feel like I could stay here, sitting on the floor, resting my head on his thigh all day, although the word *punished* does make me very horny.

Malcolm takes my silence as a tacit agreement. "I know your type well, baby girl." I don't like being reminded that I am a type, that we're both here to play a role, one being reenacted in similar ways by other couples, not that I think we're a couple. Obviously, Malcolm isn't new to any of this, but when I picture him with other women—scratching them behind the ears, calling them sweetheart, bringing them coffee—I realize none of this is special. Being nice is just another type of foreplay for the sadism that comes next. And yet. Am I not just using him too? I've known him for years, yes, but he was an acquaintance until a few weeks ago. And now he's here, and he's sitting on my bed, and I'm not wearing any pants, and he smells so. Fucking. Good.

"I have been a pretty bad girl, Daddy." My shitty curtains do little to block out the oppressive sun in my apartment, and the words feel different in the light of day. It was the right call not to drink the coffee, I think. I'm still so tired—the headache at least subsided thanks to the

Advil—and the effect is dreamlike, so far away from real life that I can say whatever I want.

Malcolm puts aside his plate and empty coffee cup and orders me over his lap. It's comfortable there, his knees pressing into my middle, another safe position especially because I don't have to look at him. I press my face into the pillow, which is a bad idea because it's the one Sasha used last night and still smells like her. I breathe through my mouth. I do need to be punished. I need Malcolm to hurt me hard enough so that I stop focusing on the pillow and Sasha and how I'm a fucking burden to her. Of course I need to be punished, and of course Malcolm knew what I needed before I did. It reassures me that calling him over was the right move.

Malcolm raises my shirt up, clearing a path to my panty-clad ass. His hand, which he rubs over my butt, is still warm from the coffee cup he was gripping earlier. It feels soothing. Then he hits me.

The spanking starts off slow and deliberate. Each strike is hard, and he waits a few seconds before hitting me again. Those seconds feel endless, with a silence in the room so pervasive that as the sting of each slap dissipates there is enough time for me to reflect. *I am getting what I deserve.* The pain isn't so bad at first, but then he starts picking up the pace, spanking me over and over again in the same area, revisiting already tender spots with the palm of his hand until my legs start kicking, and I instinctively reach back to protect my bottom.

"Don't you dare try to cover up, sweetheart." He grabs my wrists and pins them to the small of my back, while continuing to spank me with his other hand. *Dumb slut*

167

can't even take a spanking right, I think, but I don't have long to sit with that thought because the hits are coming so quick now, too quick to think, bringing with them a blissful throbbing pain and Malcolm's hard cock pressing up into me.

"I think it's time we get these panties out of the way, don't you, baby?" I moan in response, turned on and humiliated and turned on even more by the humiliation. He grabs the waistband of my underwear, and I raise my hips slightly to allow him to slide them off of me, but instead, he pulls them up tight, revealing my naked bum cheeks to him while increasing my discomfort. I bury my face back into the pillow.

"I wish you could see how pathetic you look right now. Spread over my lap, ass turning a bright pink, can't even keep your panties on right." He reaches one hand underneath, into the space between his thigh and my crotch, and presses his fingers up against my cunt. "It seems like you're enjoying this. You disgusting pervert. Do you normally get so wet at being debased and humiliated like this?" I stay quiet, and he slaps me hard, much harder than before, so that I let out a high-pitched yelp that startles even me. "Answer me, slut."

"Yes, Sir," I whisper.

"Yes, Sir, what? Use complete sentences when you answer me."

"Yes, Sir, I get off on being debased and humiliated."

"Good girl." He lets go of my wrists, though I continue to hold them in place at the small of my back. He uses his free hand to stroke my hair gently, like he did when I was sitting on the floor earlier. "But I think we really need to drive in the lesson, so we can make sure it gets through that pretty little dumb brain of yours." He reaches out to grab something off the nightstand, but I don't turn my head in time to see. Then he hits me with something so hard I scream. My hairbrush. He grabbed my hairbrush, and he's using it to really hurt me.

I thought the earlier spanking was intense, but now he is letting loose an almost unbearable amount. It's harder than anything I've experienced, definitely harder than Henry's methodical approach with his paddle. Tears sting my eyes. He's going so quickly now I don't have time to recover from each spank before the next one rains down, no rush of endorphins following each surge of pain. I begin to seriously wonder how much more I can actually bear. Is it worth telling him to stop? Will he think that's part of the role-playing? Does he know about the traffic-light system? We never discussed a traffic-light system. I grit my teeth.

Finally, after several more minutes of prolonged intense spanking, he relents. His hand replaces the hairbrush, caressing my burning hot buttocks. I still don't dare get up. He gives me a moment to catch my breath and stop my wriggling.

"Now," he says. "I think ten more spanks will really drive the point home. I want you to count each one. Do you understand me?"

"Yes, Daddy." I wonder how on earth I am going to last for ten more, especially when I hear him pick up the hairbrush again. He whacks it hard against my butt, and a loud *crack* fills the room. I scream in pain, then dissolve into sobs. He doesn't move, and I wonder if he realizes he's gone too far, but then I realize he's waiting for me to count. "One," I croak out.

The next nine spanks are excruciating, but I get through them. By the end I'm a complete mess; I do say "Ten," but I'm crying so hard the words are barely audible. Still, he takes mercy on me and decides to count it. "Good girl," he says softly. "You took your punishment well." He helps me to my feet, then turns me around and pulls me back so I'm sitting on his lap. The contact against his rough jeans burns against my sore bottom, but it feels so good to be held. I bury my face in his shoulder and sob while he strokes my back. It was worth it, I think. This wouldn't feel so good if he hadn't hurt me so bad. He knows what he's doing; I just need to trust him. For a second I consider asking him if he knows about the traffic-light system, but I stop myself. There's no point in ruining the mood now. I raise my head from his shoulder, and a trail of snot extends from my nose, connecting to his shirt; I quickly wipe it away with the back of my hand before he can notice.

A loud rap on the wall behind the bed snaps me to attention, and I see the scene for what it is: a naked woman, covered in tears and snot and red handprints, sitting on the lap of her former coworker. If somebody didn't know I was making an empowered feminist choice, I could see how it would look bad.

"Everything okay in there?" a voice calls. "It sounds like you're having a brawl!"

"Shouldn't you be at work, Mr. Fillipelli?" I shout back, my voice still raspy from crying.

"I called in sick today!" he says. "I have a cold! I think it's going around! Does this have anything to do with the fight you and that girl had this morning?"

"I didn't have a fight then, and I'm not having a fight now! I've just been watching movies all day!"

"Pretty fucked-up movies if you ask me!"

Instead of responding, I get out of bed, amble across the floor to my desk, open my laptop, and blast the Cocteau Twins, picking a reverb-heavy song that's a lot louder than it sounds to drown out the noise. There's a message notification on my screen. Sasha, I think, but it turns out to be my mother. *Have you booked your flight out east for Xmas yet?* it reads. I'm sure I already explained to her the holidays are the busiest season at work. I x the window shut. I turn back around and see that Malcolm is standing up in front of my bed. He undoes his belt and pushes down his jeans, revealing a bulge in his boxer briefs. I stare at his crotch, then up at him. He nods and gestures to the space of floor in front of him. I take a few tentative steps and kneel in front of him, gazing up into his face. He reaches down and strokes my hair before cupping my jaw.

"This is how good girls say thank you after receiving a punishment. Ask nicely, pet."

"Please may I suck your cock?"

He slaps me across the face. "Is that how you address me?"

"Please may I suck your cock, *Daddy.*"

Frankly, I'm exhausted and would love to still cuddle, but I like Malcolm too much to ruin things by being uptight. If I could just learn to turn all my discomforts in life into kinks, I would have way more fun. *Just trust him,* I think.

I start the blow job slowly, spending lots of time on the, you know, general groin area (the balls, I mean the balls) and lick the shaft, but it doesn't seem to be quick enough for Malcolm. The second that my lips wrap around the tip, he grabs my hair and starts fucking my face, jamming his penis into the back of my throat again and again. I need to break for air, but he doesn't relent. I can't move my head with how hard he's moving it and obviously my mouth is too occupied to tell him to stop, and I raise my hands slowly, tentatively considering pushing him away. But the voice in the back of my head nags me. *Don't fuck it up,* it says. *You like him, remember? You like this guy and have fun with him and he's perverted in all the ways you are. You know better than anyone how hard it is to find someone to like all your deeply messed-up parts. Don't fuck this up.* I relax my jaw. I try to breathe through my nose. I think about other things, anything else. Work. That collection of Lucia Berlin short stories I've been meaning to start. My fight with Sasha. No, not that. *Why are you such a bitch? You're definitely going to hell. Hell. Hell. Hell. Infinite torture. Your mother was right about you.* Back to the blow job. Just focus on the blow job. I only have to put up with a few more minutes; then we can stop and cuddle; then I will be his good girl again; then he will take care of me, and I won't have to think about anything.

Finally, mercifully, he finishes, shooting a hot stream of bitter cum into my mouth, and I swallow, then reach for my coffee cup and take a lukewarm swig to wash the taste out of my mouth. Malcolm helps me up, and we crawl back into bed, lying on our sides with him spooning me from behind. We stay like this silently for a few minutes. It's nice. He pulls me tighter into him so my hips are pushed up tight against his, and I can feel his boner growing once again. I hope he doesn't want to go for another round. It would feel so good to just nap right now. My head throbs again. I should call Sasha.

"What are you thinking about?" he mumbles into my ear, biting my lobe.

"Sasha," I respond without thinking.

"I beg your pardon?" he asks.

"I'm sorry," I say quickly. "I'm having fun with you." *Please don't make Malcolm be mad at you. Not after he came all this way to take care of you. Please don't fuck this up, Lucy.* "She just . . . got in my head this morning."

He pulls me tighter. "I'm sorry she was so uncool to you."

"It's not that, it's just . . ." I let myself trail off. I don't want to badmouth Sasha to Malcolm, not because Sasha needs me to defend her, but because it feels disloyal to her. Complaining about the men I date to Nora feels different. Those are just stories to tell. But I know no matter what I have to say about Sasha, even if I only described her in positive terms, I can never detail a full-enough picture for Malcolm to understand her, or why I need her, or why I'm terrified when she needs me, or why I don't care who was wrong or right this morning. How I just need to be a worthy-enough person for her to love me, just like I need to be a worthy-enough person for Malcolm to bring me bagels and to hold me and to call me sweetheart. "That was really nice of you," I say. "Bringing me coffee. Coming over at a moment's notice. It felt really good, to have some-body do that for me." He's quiet, which I take as an indi-cation to keep talking. "I really like hanging out with you, you know." And he still doesn't respond. It takes me a few more seconds to realize he's fallen asleep.

20

I haven't heard from Sasha in a week. *I should call her,* I think. Then, *She should call me.* Then, *Maybe the reason she hasn't called is because she hates me and if I call her I'll make it worse. I should give her space.* Then, *Why is she being such a bitch?* Malcolm and I continue to spend every night we can together, and I let him be as rough as he wants, my pain tolerance increasing every time until it's like he can't hit me hard enough. I ask him while we're cuddling in bed after I've swallowed his cum why he hasn't moved to New York the way everyone at *The Hog* thought he would.

"Too expensive."

"But surely the jobs in New York pay more?" I push. "I mean, you've written for the *New York Times Magazine* three times now."

"Getting there is expensive. The visa application alone is a whole thing. Immigration lawyers cost thousands. I'm not some rich kid with family connections. I can't just buy my way into a better life."

I think about the National Magazine Awards I saw shoved disdainfully on his desk. Malcolm in Toronto doesn't make sense. He seems to belong in Brooklyn, or maybe Berlin, somewhere the ambitious people from Toronto always seem to end up. "Couldn't you—" I start, but he rolls on top of me, pinning me down and sticking his tongue down my throat.

"We're not talking about this anymore, sweetheart."

He pecks me again gently on the lips. I free an arm and pull him closer, willing him to fuck me again.

I pick up more shifts at the bookstore. Nora and Christopher are spending a week in Vermont to look at the foliage or, in Nora's words, do it without worrying about the kids hanging around and then watch American TV. This means I'm working with Danny way more than usual.

"Good morning, Lucy," he says when I show up for work after a particularly raucous night with Malcolm. Danny has an exceedingly polite way of speaking, making every interaction more formal than it needs to be. I always unintentionally end up matching his tone.

"Good morning to you, Danny." I go behind the checkout counter and take my usual seat on one of the hard metal barstools, immediately remembering a nebula of bruises on my tender ass and jumping back to my feet, pretending to adjust my tights. It was Halloween last night, and we watched *Secretary* sitting on Malcolm's couch, pausing occasionally when trick-or-treaters came by. I had put together a lazy cat costume, and once it was late enough that the last straggling trick-or-treater had left us alone, he spanked me and fucked me while leaving my cat ears on because, in his words, I looked "adorable in them."

"Is there anything new happening in your life?" Danny asks. It's our seventh day in a row working together, the seventh day in a row Danny has asked me this. If Nora were working, she wouldn't even need to ask. I'd have already launched into a play-by-play recounting of my fight with Sasha and latest hookup with Malcolm, asking her what she thought in the most honest terms and then flinching when she told me the truth. I give him one-word answers, focusing on my phone, while he describes a zombie-themed poetry reading he went to the night before. I get a text from Malcolm.

Send me a pic of your ass. I want to see my marks on you.

I smile to myself, angling my phone screen away from Danny.

"Will you watch the floor? I gotta go to the bathroom. Be there for a while. Lady stuff."

Danny starts to reply—probably to offer me a tampon—but I'm a blur on my way into the stockroom. Then in the bathroom, making the most of the shitty fluorescent lighting, I stick my ass out, holding up a copy of a children's book below to reflect the flash off my phone, a fucking Ansel Adams of butt selfies. My bruises have blended like watercolours, purples and blues, the handiwork of someone who took a tour of all my perversions and matched them with his own. After fifteen minutes or so—I can hear a rush of customers in the store, but Danny seems to have it under control—I manage the perfect picture to send to Malcolm.

Good girl, he replies. *I can't wait to add more tonight.*

When I get home from work, I decide to pull out all the stops. I blow-dry my hair to voluminous sex-doll levels. I put on an elaborate lingerie set with garters and stockings I bought ages ago but have never worn because I'm not sure how exactly I'm supposed to wash them. I shave and pluck absolutely every stray hair, an hour-long process that stings and waters my eyes and turns me on. And Malcolm appreciates all of it. When I show up to his

176

place, he says I look "absolutely stunning" and kisses me hard before even shutting the door behind us. He takes off my dress right away and says, "Hell yes," when he sees the set underneath.

What if this is what it's all supposed to lead to? This, right here, feeling like I've won the Nobel Prize the way this man looks at me. What if the pop songs and Hollywood films and other heterosexual propaganda were secretly right all along, and I am supposed to be constantly striving towards these moments of looking and being utterly fuckable for the right person, that this is the only way to ever feel loved or safe or at peace with who I am? I don't have time to consider this for long though, because soon Malcolm has me bent over the bed and is striking me with his leather belt, forcing me to count each hit.

After he's done hitting me, he flips me onto my back and has me shift up so that I'm on the bed. He grabs my wrists and pins them above my head, and then reaches for the belt he just beat me with to tie my wrists to the head of the bed. Being tied up is my favourite, the ultimate in surrendering control. Malcolm grabs my stockinged calves and pushes them up so my ankles are resting on his shoulders. The pose hurts, but if he notices me wince, he doesn't say anything. Instead, he enters me hard and begins thrusting in and out. Soon, I'm enjoying the feeling of his weight on top of me as he keeps control, and it's almost enough to make me forget about the straining in the muscles of my thighs. Almost.

He finishes with a small gasp of pleasure, gently closing his eyes. When he cums, his face looks so vulnerable and peaceful and boyish, the way the face of every man

I've been with looks, no matter how dominant they may act when they know they're being observed. It's a funny thing, how much of our lives is controlled by sex and how much of sex is controlled by this pursuit of a few seconds of giddy frisson. There's an advantage in not cumming, I tell myself. If I don't climax with him, then I never have to lose this feeling that I'm going to be okay that furls in the depths of my belly whenever I let someone else take over with making the decisions. I have all the power now. I'm able to make him lose control like this while still hanging on to my own, and I don't even need ropes or bondage gear to do it. I can get myself off later at home when I have my vibrator. It's what I always do.

Malcolm unties me, and we cuddle for a few minutes before I get up to go to the bathroom. I catch my appearance in the bathroom mirror. My hair is mussed and my makeup smeared, but in a way that looks completely striking. I don't look like a mess, at least not in the way I look the morning after a night of heavy partying and drinking. I look, well, beautiful. Like a model shot in soft focus, maybe behind a lens of Vaseline, and also you have to squint a little, but this is the most I've liked the way I look in a while. I tiptoe back out to the hall, grab my phone, take a selfie.

There's a new text from my mom on my phone—*Ran into Sharon's mom at the grocery store. Sharon's got a good job working as a PR consultant. Maybe that's something you can do? She's buying a house*—which I ignore.

I have a new notification from Instagram too. Sasha liked a photo I posted earlier today—a dead squirrel on the side of the road that I captioned "mood." Obviously liking someone's Instagram post when you're in a fight is a way of saying, "Hey, I really miss you, and I think we should talk." I start scrolling through her Instagram as I walk back to bed. Her latest post is a selfie we took together at the bar the night before our fight. I barely remember taking it and haven't seen it until now. It's a bad picture. The lighting is terrible, and we're both clearly drunk, flushed and sweaty from dancing and heavy lidded. My head is resting on hers, cheek against curls, as we both grin for the photo. There is no caption. I like the photo, then slide back into bed next to Malcolm, who turns over just as I close the app.

"What're you looking at?" he asks. I know I can't explain to him the politics of liking Sasha's Instagram post. Men never understand that sort of thing.

"I'm wondering if I should reach out to Sasha. Like, even just to see if she's okay."

"You're a very caring person," he says, though the way he expresses it sounds more like a criticism than a compliment. I place my phone facedown on his nightstand, cuddle into him, let him put his arm around me. "People are going to want to take advantage of your emotional labour."

"You don't even know her," I say, which is true. But he sounded so confident, and I realize I want the comfort of believing Malcolm is a person who knows what he's talking about. I rack my brain, trying to think of examples of Sasha possibly taking advantage of me. Crashing at my place when she had a fight with her boyfriend. Venting to me about her problems. When did friendship get rebranded as emotional labour? And then I think about all the times I've gone to her, stressed about school or my internships or work or sex. Sasha's words to me: *Do you know how exhausting it is to be your friend, Lucy?* I think of all the times I go to Nora, as well, when I'm at work. Does she feel the same way about me? Do I even know how to have friends, or do I just exploit them for emotional labour? No. Bad line of thinking. I curl into him, pressing my face into the inch of space where his chest meets the bed, willing myself to fall into that space, to lose myself there, to take a break indefinitely from being a person. His naked erection pushes against my thigh. A problem I know how to solve. He's still talking above me, something about how he's just trying to look out for me, but I wriggle in my position for there to be enough space to run my fingers up and down his shaft. This shuts him up. I take the whole thing in my hand and begin to methodically pump. Malcolm pushes on the top of my head, and I let his hand guide me, moving my body down farther until I can take him into my mouth. And I do the thing that I've become good at, focusing until the job is complete, our earlier conversation reduced to foreplay.

Dear Sir,

It's hard for me to remember the first panic attack I had, because I was so young. How do you even define a panic attack as a child? Panic and fear are two of the first emotions we feel. Waking up in a crib as a baby with a pain of hunger in your stomach, not knowing what it is or how it got there or how to fix it, not having the language to express yourself or to even think about the right words; all you can do is lie there on your tiny little back and scream your tiny little lungs out in the hope someone hears you and can figure out what's wrong. Most of the reasons babies cry have easy solutions: they need to be fed or changed or burped. But some babies are really sick. Some babies need more than anyone can give them. Some babies need medical care, emergency relief. Parents feel a kind of panic, I've been told, every time their babies cry, because what if their child is the rare exception, the one that needs more than a diaper change? What if there is something genuinely wrong with their child? I imagine what the baby is feeling in that moment mirrors what their mom or dad feels, but a million times worse. For them, a rumble of hunger in their bellies is just as terrifying as colic, as an earache, as a full diaper, as a playmate who disappears during a game of peekaboo.

The panic I felt as a baby never really went away. I would hear stories on the news of parents who abandoned their children, who had had enough. The older I got, the more I would hear about people who were publicly disgraced, who messed it all up for themselves, who stopped being worthy of being loved. Once-beloved comedians accused of taking a joke too far or politicians who couldn't keep it in their pants at the right time, good kids who wound up in the wrong crowd and went along with the group, even if they knew deep down what they were doing was wrong.

For all I say and complain about my mother, I know she loves me. I know she's not one of those mothers who will give up on her kid. This is actually one of the biggest sources of our fights; sometimes I wish she would back off, give me space, not try to help (because she really does think she's helping). I think everybody in their lives needs someone to love them unconditionally, at least one person. Even if they do something really wrong. My biggest secret, the most honest truth I can tell you is: I'm scared as hell of what will happen when my mother dies. Because who will be left to love me unconditionally? I've already lost one parent. If a friend or lover were accused of sexual misconduct or being horribly prejudiced, I would cut them out of my life. Because I need to take care of myself and I need to prioritize relationships with people who aren't run by hatred, you know? But don't abusers and bigots deserve to be loved? If they are hated and abandoned, won't that exacerbate the problem? I'm still not sure who should be the one to love them. (Doesn't this job usually fall to the women, the ones who are expected to put their own well-being aside, to love their abusers, to make excuses, to keep trying?) I wonder if my approach to sex makes this easier. Because once you realize that your days of being loved like you once were are over, the best you can hope for is some sort of pity. And being pitied is a huge turn-on for me.

Part of me, when I read these stories, sides with the bad people. It's easy for me to go along with a crowd rather than say what I feel and disrupt the peace. I never even really know if what I'm doing is the right thing, and so I just try to surround myself with people who seem to know what they're doing and hope they've figured it out. I sat through enough women's studies seminars to know there are people who think my sex life vetoes me from being a feminist. I do try to be good. I try so hard. I listen and learn, and I don't want to be motivated by hatred, ever. But I've made mistakes. And what if the only thing keeping me from being a hated public person is circumstance? What if it's just a matter of time before I'm one of the bad people, the unlovables?

I remember once, before our date, we spoke on the phone. We started role-playing (though is it still playing a role when you really believe in it?); you told me that even when I needed to be punished, it wasn't a judgement of my character. You said some people need discipline, but that doesn't mean you're going to like me any less. And then you disappeared. You literally left the continent and then ended things in a text message. Whatever we had was casual, a fling, whatever you want to call it, but it was also one of the most intimate relationships I've had with another person. You saw the parts of myself I was afraid of the most. And then you disappeared.

Lucy

21

Nora is back from her trip, and I squeal when I see her. It's only been a little over a week since we last worked together, but I squeeze her tight, breathing in her sandalwood perfume and her natural scent of safety and home.

"I've aged a million years since you left," I say, still refusing to let go.

"And I've reverse aged," she says. "I Benjamin-Buttoned myself. I'm now negative a million."

"You really are glowing." I take a step back to look at her. "Wait, you're not pregnant, are you?"

She scoffs. "That's really mean, you know. I know you mean it as a compliment, but that's downright cruel. I do have some news, though." As she says this, she brushes a piece of hair behind her ear with her left hand, revealing a silver ring, inlaid with a simple clear-cut amethyst, on her fourth finger.

"Wait, do you mean . . ." I grab her hand and stare at the ring.

She nods. "Yep! You're looking at the future Mrs. Nora Goldstein. I'm keeping my own name, of course."

"But you are marrying Christopher?"

"I'm marrying Christopher!" She bursts out giggling in an incredibly un-Nora-like manner. I hug her again, even tighter than before if that's possible.

"I just . . ." Sometimes I take it for granted that Nora is a person who is still a human. She seems so comfortable

184

in her ways, like life was something she lived in her youth, and now that she's figured it out, there's no need to change anything. That marriage was simply an experience relegated to her past, like playing in a punk band or reading Bret Easton Ellis novels. "I mean, I can't . . . It's so . . . Congratulations!"

"I know what you're thinking. After my last two divorces I always said I wasn't going to do this again."

"I wasn't thinking that," I say, even though I was totally definitely thinking that.

"Christopher and I first started talking about doing it for tax purposes, you know? Plus he gets all these benefits from work that will cover me if I'm his wife. But then when we went away this weekend, we had fun. And not just new-romance stuff; did you know we've been going out for four years now? Ugh. 'Going out.' I sound like a teenager." I nod in agreement, although I never went out with anyone as a teenager. "Anyway, I really started to imagine what a life with him would be like. Then he shows me this ring—we never talked about getting a ring—and it's gorgeous, and like no other engagement ring I've seen."

"It's very you," I agree.

"And now, all of a sudden I'm excited about getting married! Specifically, I'm excited about getting married to Christopher. I'm going to marry Christopher Moretti. I'm going to be Mrs. Nora Goldstein, married to Christopher Moretti!"

I move to hug her again, but a waspy woman appears at the counter, her honey-coloured hair pulled back into a tight bun. "Excuse me. Do you have that new Harper Lee book that just came out?"

"Oh," I say. "Yeah. We do. It should be in the fiction section, against this wall here. Under .L." Normally I would get the book for her, but I don't want to leave this conversation with Nora.

"Christopher told Marcella about his plans to propose," she says.

"Marcella, our boss, Marcella?"

"Yes! Turns out she's a huge romantic and supported this fully. Who knew?"

"Have you started planning the wedding?"

"According to Christopher's accountant—he has an accountant, can you believe it?—if we get married before the end of the year, we can file this year's tax returns together."

"How romantic."

"We want to do something small at city hall next month, right under the wire. Maybe have an after-party on New Year's Eve. His brother owns a bar we can rent out. Just close friends and family. My kids, Christopher's brother and mom, a few of his friends from work, you and Danny, and Marcella obviously."

"Oh, are we friends? This is so awkward. I always saw us as casual acquaintances."

"So here's the thing," she continues, ignoring me. "I made Justine my maid of honour at my last wedding, the one to Jeff that lasted less than a year." She rolls her eyes. "That was a mistake. The wedding, not the including-my-daughter bit. Anyway, she put on a brave face, but I think she hated the experience. *She* says I was a nightmare about it, but also she was like, fucking twelve at the time, what does she know. When I told her about this wedding, she said, 'I love you, Mom, and I'm stoked about this, but please, as a Hanukkah present to me, don't make me go through that again.' I know it's dumb to even want a maid of honour at a city-hall wedding, but since she's out, and you're my next closest female friend, I thought maybe—"

"Wait. You want *me* to be your maid of honour?" I never thought I was a person who cried over weddings, but my eyes immediately start to prickle with tears and my lower lip trembles.

"Again, it is really no big deal. I'm literally giving you this job after my own daughter rejected it because apparently I'm a terror. There's not going to be a bridal shower or bachelorette party or anything. It just always feels weird standing in front of a crowd, even a small one, declaring your love for another person, and it would be really neat to have someone in my corner standing next to me. Besides my future husband."

If I was speechless before, now it's like I've never known language. Tears are streaming down my face, and I can feel the telltale sign of mucus running out of my nose that only comes during a really ugly cry.

"Uh, hello?" the customer from before interrupts. "I couldn't find the Harper Lee book on the shelf where you told me to look."

"Oh, it's a terrible book anyway," says Nora, waving her hand at the customer before handing me a tissue.

"This is incredibly unprofessional," says the woman. "Do you have a manager I can speak to?"

"I got this," I say, finally finding the words, and amble over to the fiction section, still a blubbering mess. I grab the prominently displayed Harper Lee and hand it to the woman— "Here"—still aware of the tears and snot on my face.

Nora rings her through at the cash, and the woman leaves, giving us a glare over her shoulder.

"God, who knew you cared about weddings so much?" asks Nora. "Have you checked your period-tracker app recently?"

"I think I just care about you so much. And of course I'll be your maid of honour. I would love to. I'm so honoured to be your second choice."

"Thank you, Lucy. You can bring a date too, if you'd like. Do you have any updates about that fellow you're sleeping with?"

There is so much I've been waiting to talk about with Nora: the intoxicating times with Malcolm and the weird moments with him that I'm not sure how to handle; the not-fight with Sasha that I still haven't taken any steps to resolve; the death of my *Smash* magazine collection and the lack of progress I've made on writing anything. But everything in my life suddenly seems so petty and juvenile compared to her news. Nora asks if I want to see a picture of the dress she found at a vintage store in Vermont, which of course I do, and I push the thoughts out of my head.

22

I used to be very good at being by myself. Now, I can't seem to focus on anything alone in my apartment. I can make it through about half a page sitting and reading before I realize I'm not absorbing any of the words. I count the passage of time in between texts from Malcolm. I am still outpacing him in texting frequency. I scroll back through our message history, and there are large chunks of blue sent bubbles, with significantly smaller white return bubbles. Sometimes it will take him six, seven hours to reply. I know he keeps his phone on him at all times, the way I do, the way everyone does. I try to match his slow response times, to hold off from replying for several hours so he doesn't think I'm needy, attempting to distract myself by reading books I don't absorb.

Come over tonight, I text him as my shift ends. Nora's news has filled me with a different kind of nervous energy, a sudden overwhelming sense of the world, of life and its major milestones and the ways people find to delineate their relationships with ceremonies and institutional backing. Not that I ever want to get married myself. It's a patriarchal institution. I am just emotional for my friend.

Hey sweetheart! Tonight's a no-go . . . busy week ahead . . lots of work.

I tell myself not to respond and to pretend not to care. But then isn't the whole point that I'm needy? He has the power, but that's what makes it so hot. I'm supposed to text him more. It's part of the game. The one he agreed to play too.

The thought settles me, like ginger ale on an upset stomach. I can give myself permission to follow my basest instincts, the ones that are supposedly turnoffs in other relationships. Normal relationships.

I'm horny and I want to see you, I type back.

It takes several hours to get a reply, excruciating hours that I spend washing exactly three dishes and refreshing my Facebook profile about fifty times. When my phone buzzes with his response, I jump to my feet like it was choreographed.

impatient little girl. im going to have to punish you next time I see you.

Yeah, like you even have the time for that, I reply. *You might as well figure out a way for me to punish myself when you're not around.* I hesitate for a second, then send a follow-up: *Daddy.*

This gives Malcolm what he believes is an original idea. He tells me that I have to find something he can spank me with, something other than his hand, for when he comes over tomorrow night. He says I have to leave the item on my desk, so I can see it all day, a reminder of the punishment I have coming.

I tell Malcolm that's a great idea he came up with on his own. It's now 11 p.m.; he spent the whole evening texting me back, and I spent the whole evening waiting for it. I get dressed and go to the 7-Eleven around the corner, figuring I'll know what I'm looking for when I see it. There's a sale on fly swatters: a pack of two in pink and yellow plastic for $2.99. Perfect. I pick them up but then decide it looks suspicious, a woman alone at 11:15 on a Tuesday night in November, buying a fly swatter. I look up at the clerk, a guy with weak facial hair in his early twenties looking like he'd rather be anywhere else. I wonder if he's onto me.

I decide to stick around a little longer, looking at the pest-control section. I pick up bug spray and roach traps, look at them conspicuously to compare prices. I ask the guy if these are all the pest-control products they have. He says, "Yeah."

"It's so weird to get a bug infestation like this in November," I say. "Not roaches. Just flies." He looks at me blankly. I shrug. I tell him I'm on a budget and maybe I'll just stick to the fly swatter for now, maybe I'll come back later for the other stuff. He doesn't react. I pay and I go home and I hang the fly swatters on my wall on a loose nail. I take a picture and send it to Malcolm. He won't reply *Good girl* until noon tomorrow, but it's worth it.

Wednesday is my day off. Malcolm and I agreed to meet at 7 p.m., which means I have the whole day to spend by myself. I wake up, masturbate, buy coffee, read three pages of an Anna Akhmatova collection hoping that maybe poetry will stir me the way novels haven't been lately, put the book down in favour of porn, masturbate again. I clean my apartment. I am a grown woman. I know exactly what I'm doing.

Four hours to kill before Malcolm is supposed to come over. That's more than enough time to finish the Akhmatova. I look at the book. I look at my computer. I open my laptop, going to my favourite porn website.

The page doesn't load. No Wi-Fi signal. I go to the side of my room with the bed, rap loudly on the wall.

"Mr. Fillipelli!" I call. "You there? I need you to unplug the modem and plug it back in again!" Silence.

With nothing else to do, I begin clearing old files off my laptop, periodically refreshing the porn window in the hopes that the Wi-Fi has come back. The task is steady enough that I can lose myself in it, until I open the interview I did with Jennifer Flounder and realize I never finished transcribing it. I try to recall the last time I finished writing anything, even something small. I sell books and send horny text messages. I look at the fly swatter hanging on the wall and think, *You're supposed to be a good girl right now. You're supposed to be working hard so you have something to show for your day. It's part of the game.* I start transcribing.

It's a long, slow process that forces me to listen to my voice, my awkwardness, my transparent attempts to impress. *You're a fucking fraud, and she can tell.* But I keep typing through it. I get to the part where Jennifer mentions frequently working with a photographer, Buck Swinton. That sounds like the name of the hero of a 1980s serialized drama. Are there parents out there in the world who actually name their kids Buck, or did he just happen to luck into an actually cool nickname in grade school? It's not a name you hear every day.

I pause. It's *not* a name you hear every day. Definitely not one that appeared on the masthead of the magazine. I click over the browser window again and refresh the page. The internet is back, and the porn homepage loads. A video I haven't seen before, "BARELY LEGAL WHORE GETS SPANKING SHE DESERVES," is at the top of the screen, but I don't have time for that now.

Buck Swinton has a website. He exists, and he has an online photography portfolio. The website is a little janky; Buck Swinton isn't the most computer-savvy person in the world, which makes sense when you consider his heyday was forty years ago, but it's definitely him. There's a folder on his website labelled "music photography," and in there is an image of Virginia and the Woolfpack, the same one I saw in the magazine. There is also a photo of him. I look the name up on Facebook and find a profile that matches the image from his website. I start scrolling through his Facebook friends, and there it is: Chester W., Los Angeles. Could it really be that easy?

My heart is racing now. I send Chester a direct message.

Apologies for this informal means of communication, but I couldn't find another way to get in touch with you. I'm a writer researching a piece on Smash magazine. Would you be the right person to talk to about this?

I hit send and then exhale sharply. The act has reinvigorated my interest in this project. I go back on eBay to search for more copies of *Smash*. Nothing—the original seller I bought the last batch from is out, including the doubles that I didn't get last time. I go back to my transcription, trying not to cringe at myself, still unsure what the end goal is but feeling something starting to coalesce. By the time I finish, I realize I only have two hours left to make myself beautiful for Malcolm.

By six thirty, I've finished blow-drying my hair and applying my false eyelashes, which I hope aren't too much—Malcolm said before he doesn't like it when a girl looks like she tries so hard, because he's not into patriarchal beauty standards—but I figure if I get *so* dressed up it sort of wraps back around on itself and becomes almost ironic, like with burlesque. As I'm applying more cheek tint, my phone dings with an incoming text. Malcolm. He won't be able to make it. A work thing. I tell him it's fine. I'm fine. I'm always fine. The next rational thing to do would be to take off the false eyelashes and maybe try to get some work done, but it seems like a waste to look this good and have no witness. I put on the tallest shoes I own and walk down to the 7-Eleven to buy a bag of chips. Why not.

Later, I'm eating Cool Ranch Doritos in bed while idly scrolling through IMDB forums arguing that the recent *Fifty Shades of Grey* movie is just a cheap *Secretary* knockoff. People are discussing how the former is a toxic representation of BDSM that doesn't compare with the emotional stakes of the latter. Nobody brings up my main critique of *Fifty Shades*, which is that the sex scenes aren't even that hot. I lean my head against the wall. Mr. Fillipelli is home; I can hear the faint melody of *The Golden Girls* theme song tinkle from his room. The longest male relationship I've had in my life, I think.

My phone buzzes with an incoming call, and I wipe the Dorito dust onto my stockings, answering without even checking the display. *Probably Malcolm, deciding he can make it after all. Maybe at least I'll get some phone sex.*

I put on my sultriest voice.

"Hello," I start to whisper, in what I imagine is a sexy husk, but instead choke a bit on a Dorito.

"Jeez, Luce, don't die on me before we make up," says the familiar voice.

"Oh. Hi, Sasha," I say, disappointed that it's not Malcolm. Then it hits me who is calling. "Oh! Hi, Sasha!"

"Is this a bad time? You sound surprised. Didn't you look at the caller ID? What if I was a serial killer?"

"Then I would be scared but also thrilled at the prospect of adventure." I hear her exhale through her nose, a kind of silent laugh, and the only obvious reason for the call lingers in the air. "Are we in a fight?"

"No," she says quickly, and I exhale in relief. Then she adds, "Well. Not really. I hate not talking to you."

"I hate not talking to you too." Another silence. "I overreacted. At Nigel. You know I love her."

"Nigel loves seeing you. She gets excited though. And that's no excuse. She destroyed something important to you. And . . . she's sorry."

I feel it's my turn to apologize, but I'm not sure for which part. For losing my patience a couple weeks ago, or for the years of friendship beforehand in which I left Sasha emotionally drained. *Do you know how exhausting it is to be your friend, Lucy?* I settle on, "Well, tell Nigel I appreciate that. And I'm sorry too. For being so harsh. They weren't even that important. I'll be able to find more, somewhere."

"Well, that's one of the reasons I'm calling," she continues. "When I went home the other week, I really did feel bad for—Nigel. Making a mess of things. So I looked online and found this guy on Craigslist in, like, Florida who had a bunch of issues. I bought what he had. They came today."

"Wait." I sit up. "You did that? For me?"

"Well, obviously. You sound so shocked!"

"I'm not, it's just . . ." The right words aren't coming. *Do you know how exhausting it is to be your friend, Lucy?* I can't not think it. "Do you like being my friend? Do I really exhaust you?"

I hear her exhale now. Another pause, and I fight every instinct to be the one to break it. *She hates you, Lucy. Just like Malcolm, who couldn't come tonight. Just like Henry and everyone you went to middle school with and probably Nora, somehow. She doesn't want to answer that question because she hates you, and she's trying to find the words to say it.*

"I said some things I didn't mean when I was tired and hungover—" she starts, but I cut her off.

"Please just . . ." I start. I squeeze my eyes shut, unsure if I believe the next words out of my mouth are what I really want to be saying. "Please just tell me the truth. I need to know what I'm like. To other people. Please."

"I think you are a human being with needs. Like every single other person on the planet. And sometimes I feel like you have no idea what those needs are, and sometimes I think you know what you want better than anyone else, and maybe both are true at the same time, and it creates this kind of chaos in you. Like putting Mentos in a Diet Coke."

"Am I the Mentos in this analogy?"

"And that chaos, it's . . . what makes you you. It makes you curious about things, and sensitive to all the bullshit in the world, and really fun when you give yourself permission to be. And maybe, yes, I wish you could give yourself that permission more often. But I never for one second have disliked being your friend."

The double negatives in that last sentence trip me up. "Wait, sorry, did you say you have *not* disliked, or—"

"It means I fucking love you, you moron."

I laugh. Relief. "I fucking love you too," and then, for good measure, add a "Dipshit." She laughs at the other end, and it sounds so beautiful. "And I want to be there for you. The way you've always been for me. I'm serious, if you and Nigel ever need a break from Ryan—"

"Ryan and I broke up," she cuts me off.

Silence again as I take in this news.

"Wait, really?"

"Well, I broke up with him. I told him I loved him, which was true, and that I would probably always love him, which was a lie, and that our lives were just in different places, and I needed to be on my own for a while."

"And how did he take that?"

"Terrible. He cried a lot. It was a mess. But at least he accepted it this time."

"What does *that* mean?"

"It means I tried to break up with him twice before. Once about six months ago, again last month. Both times he told me that I was being reckless, that we could work through it, and I believed him. This time I said it was for real, but I can't be responsible for his feelings."

This is the first I'm hearing of this. And I realize, if Sasha didn't tell me, she likely didn't tell anyone; she was dealing with this part alone.

"Do you want to come over?"

"No. I'm actually at home right now. He's staying with a friend till he can find a new place to live. I told him that I can't be the one who leaves every time, that it stresses out the dog. *That*'s what finally convinced him."

"Wow. How do you feel?"

"I don't know. Awful. Incredible. Relieved, mostly. And ready. Lucy, I want to take a trip somewhere. I want to have an adventure. I was looking it up: you know, there are discount airfares to the States right now? And that's not even counting the air miles I have saved up."

"You want to take a trip?"

"I want us to take a trip. Somewhere dumb and amazing. Let's go to Vegas! Or Austin. Somewhere warm. I can't deal with the weather, and I need to mix it up. I don't even care where we end up. My sister will watch Nigel for a few days. Here, I'm emailing you a link to the airfare sale."

"Hold on, I'm opening my computer, stay there." I hit the speaker button on my phone and put it down next to my laptop, which was already open on my bed. I'm about to click over to my email inbox when I see the Facebook page I left up is dinging with a new notification. There's a message there from Chester.

Dear Lucy,

You found me! Smash was a lifetime ago, but such an exciting one. I would be happy to talk to you about what it was like. Maybe you can turn it into a book? Are you in LA? Let's meet up.

Chester Wright

"Sasha?" I say, my eyes still glued on the screen.

"What's up?"

"How do you feel about going to California?"

23

It's Nora who helps me come up with an excuse when I need to ask Marcella for time off. At 6 a.m. the morning after we buy the tickets, I call Sasha's cell phone in a panic.

"Is everything okay?" she answers.

"How am I supposed to take time off work?"

"Jesus, Lucy, what time is it? You woke up the dog."

"This is serious. We're taking a trip two weeks before Christmas. I work a retail job. How are we going to make this happen?"

"Well, the tickets are nonrefundable," she says. "Can't you get one of your coworkers to help you?"

I turn to Nora, as I always do.

"We would definitely be back in time for the wedding," I tell Nora at the store later. "It's just a few days. I feel like I'm fucking you guys over like this."

"Honey, are you kidding?" she says. "Can I tell you what a relief it has been to see you this excited over something that is not a guy? And," she quickly adds as I open my mouth, "I am not slut-shaming you. I just think it will do you a bit of good to get a change of scenery."

"But what about Marcella? No way in hell she'll let me take time off work this close to Christmas."

"This is a problem with an easy fix. Here's what you need to do."

Nora then instructs me to go to Marcella with a sob story; my grandmother has died, and we are holding off having a memorial until the extended family can visit. I'll only need a few days, and Nora will cover the shifts.

"What kind of terrible person lies about a dead grandmother?"

She shrugs and starts rifling through a stack of invoices behind the cash. "I did it all the time when I was waitressing. I've lost about a dozen grandmas so far, and three grandpas, though grandmas garner more sympathy."

"But that's different. *You* can do that."

"What are you saying? That it's okay for me to be a terrible person?"

"No, that's not what I mean." I throw up my hands. "Look. When you do things, it's because you have a reason. Usually a good one. But I know you, and I know you're a good person, and a kind and helpful person, so if you tell one lie or kill a fictional grandmother here or there, it's not a big deal. But it's different for me. I know what my reasons are. I know they're not pure. I know deep down what I am and what I'm not, and I'm not a good person. I have my own motivations for this trip."

"Are you kidding?" she says. "I used the dead-grandma excuse when I wanted to see a B-52s concert."

"That doesn't make sense. I thought you said you were a punk with the occasional foray into goth. Why were you listening to the B-52s?"

"This is exactly why I had to keep my love for 'Rock Lobster' a secret. Look." She turns to face me. "You have this habit of forgiving other people for things you'd never dream about doing yourself. This here?" She waves her hand around, gesturing to the store. "It's a job. They come and go. You can go see the world and come back and when you're fifty still be working here, or whatever the equivalent of a bookstore is by then. A vape store or something. But, and I say this with love, you need to get a life." She resumes her task with the invoices.

"Did you imply that I'm a loser?"

"No, I implied that you will be a loser if you don't go."

It still seems so reckless. But I remember Sasha's words. *I wish you'd give yourself permission to be fun.*

"Okay," I say, hoping I sound more decisive than I feel. "Okay. I'm going to LA. But I'm not going to say that my grandmother died. I'm going to use my great-aunt. That doesn't feel quite so bad. And nobody's dead, she's just in the hospital, and this is my last chance to see her."

"Atta girl," Nora says and claps me on the upper arm. "Although if you ask me, visiting a relative on their deathbed is way more dramatic than a memorial. Either way, you better text Marcella sooner rather than later so you can have a chat with her."

"Chat with me about what?" a voice comes from the door, and both Nora and I snap to attention to see that Marcella has just entered. She doesn't come by that often but tends to materialize whenever somebody is talking about her. I used to imagine that the owner of an independent bookstore would be warm and matronly, like one of Nora's twelve dead grandmothers. Marcella comes from a different world. Old money. She's a few years older than Nora, and though she isn't very tall, the way she carries herself makes her seem larger than she is, like she's done a lot of yoga. She and Nora get along pretty well, but Marcella scares the crap out of me.

"I was, uh, hoping I could talk to you for a minute. About the schedule for the next few weeks."

"Yes?" she takes off her coat, her face a reddish chill from the cold outside in a way that looks intentional. "Well I was wondering if . . ." I start. Nora is looking at me pointedly, waiting for me to speak. Having an audience makes me feel even more self-conscious. "See, I have this aunt. Well, this great-aunt, really. And she's—"

"Dead." Nora interjects. "Poor Lucy here is dealing with a bit of a family crisis. She needs a few days off in December, the fourth to the seventh. I've already agreed to work the extra shifts."

Marcella says nothing but stares straight at us both, and I try to look forlorn, like I am devastated over the loss of my great-aunt, but not, like, too devastated, because I still want to make it believable. Finally she nods.

"Well, if you've already figured out how to cover your shifts, I don't see why it's a problem." She picks up her coat. "I'll be in the backroom. I have a meeting with a rep from HarperCollins. Can you fix the new fiction display? It's looking dishevelled."

"Oh, um, right, of course." I breathe out a sigh of relief. "Thank you." I move to the display and immediately get to work reorganizing the books.

"Oh, and Lucy?" she says, and I pause. "I'm terribly sorry." Shit. She's already changed her mind. "Why's that now?"

"About the loss of your aunt. Your great-aunt. My condolences to you and your family." She turns back and finishes her trip to the backroom, closing the door behind her.

"I thought you and Sasha weren't even speaking to each other," Malcolm says from his position behind me as the

202

big spoon after I finish telling him about the upcoming trip. We're in his bed in his Parkdale apartment. We finished having sex twenty minutes ago, but I've been too comfortable in his arms to bring myself to get up and shower to wash his dried cum off my chest.

"We made up," I say simply. "We've been best friends for years. It's not like this fight was going to last forever." I reach up and scratch my nose. My wrists are still bound together with a shiny crimson bondage tape. Malcolm hasn't moved to untie me, and I haven't asked.

"So she apologized." He brushes his lips against the back of my messed-up hair.

"Yes. Well, we apologized to each other." He doesn't say anything, but I hear the soft change in his breath, a deeper exhale nearing a sigh that signals his disapproval. "We had both lost our tempers with each other," I say, defensively. "I was just as much in the wrong as she was." He still doesn't say anything, and his silence fills the room, creeping around the edges of his bookshelf filled with James Salter and Maggie Nelson titles and the opened pack of Dunhills on his bedside table. "She's always been super supportive of me when I was going through tough stuff and upset about things, and I could have been more supportive, and I felt really guilty about how we left things and really good about how we made up, and I don't know, I just, I don't know, I don't know." I am talking a mile a minute now, my shoulders tense, my stomach churning, the way it did when I was a kid and I got into trouble, like I did something wrong and I needed to keep talking until I could find the correct combination of words to make things right so that people would stop being mad at me. I need for Malcolm to not be mad at me.

"Hey," he breaks his silence and squeezes me tight.
"Hey. Sweetheart. There's no reason to get worked up."

"I'm sorry," I say, embarrassed by my obvious display
of feelings. "I just . . . I get so anxious about things sometimes. I can't help it."

"It's all right." He rubs his hands up and down my
shoulders, my arms, my body. "If you really believe that
things between you and Sasha are better, well, I trust you.
LA sounds like it could be a really fun trip. Just make sure
she's nice to you, you know?"

"We don't always have to talk about me and my problems, you know," which I don't believe in the slightest but
also seems like the quickest way to take the focus off Sasha.
"I mean, you're a good listener. But we never talk about you.
I don't want to be, like, selfish." He doesn't say anything for
a few seconds, so I quickly add, "Daddy," in a small, girlish
voice, and he gives my shoulder a tender squeeze in response.

"Never, sweetheart." He kisses the back of my hair.
"I like hearing about your problems. I like being able to
take care of you."

"You don't care that it's so one-sided? Our—this?"
I almost said "our relationship," which is dumb, because
whatever Malcolm is, he's not my boyfriend. Not that
we've had that conversation. He probably would be my
boyfriend if I asked him to be. Probably.

He's kissing my neck now. "That's what makes it so
hot," he breathes into my ear, before tracing his lips down
my neck and biting my shoulder.

"You like that I'm such a mess." I match his tone. He
flips me on my back and positions his legs on either side of
my hips, leaning over and kissing me on the mouth. "You

like that I'm so fucking helpless." I smirk as soon as he comes up for air.

He slaps me across the face. Hard. "Don't swear. It doesn't become you."

I wiggle my jaw, trying to get some of the sting out my cheek. I've never been hit that hard before. "Sorry," I gasp, and as soon as I get the words out, he slaps me again.

"What was that?"

"Sorry, Daddy," I correct myself.

"That's better." He raises his hand as if to hit me again, and I flinch. He laughs softly at my reaction and brings his hand down gently, resting it on my cheek and sliding his thumb into my mouth. "You're adorable," he whispers, and then in one swift movement he takes his hand off my face and uses it to grab both my wrists, still bound together, and pin them above my head. I gasp, and the look upon his face as he stares down at me is pure animal. Instinctively, I open my legs, manoeuvring them out from under him so they're spread on either side of his hips. Still pinning me and not breaking eye contact, he reaches out with his other hand and grabs a condom from his nightstand. He tears the package open with his teeth and slides it over his already-erect cock. "Wait, can we—" I'm about to suggest that maybe we use lube this time, but before I get any words out, he enters me with just the mildest of fumbling. It's a little uncomfortable—I wasn't as ready as he was— but he starts thrusting, and soon my body catches up, and I forget about my hesitation and allow myself to be his.

Dear Sir,

Did we have a healthy relationship? Would that be an accurate assessment? I know, even the word relationship *is loaded, but I don't mean it in the boyfriend/girlfriend way. I'm looking at the most literal interpretation—two people who have some kind of connection with one another. I have a relationship with my mother. And she and I communicate. Or, she communicates with me.*

You and I communicated with each other. Isn't that the basis of a healthy relationship? My friend Nora would say it's not enough; it concerned her how entrenched I was with you, a relative stranger. But at least you knew what your boundaries were.

I resented the methodical way you negotiated all our intimate moments, the textbook pursuit of affirmative consent was a total lady-boner killer. And yet, I know what the opposite is like. To be with someone who doesn't need to talk. I get there are stakes at play for you, being a socially conscious man and a dominant: you don't want to be an accidental rapist. Fair enough. I don't want to be raped. As a feminist, I know the threat of rape is supposed to be everywhere. I get it. I've marched in two SlutWalks and three Take Back the Nights. But I hardly ever obsess about being raped the way I think I'm supposed to. Not the way I obsessively think about consensual relationships, the ones that aren't supposed to be traumatic but overwhelm my brain.

The person I'm with now, I wonder if it's my fault that I can't vocalize my own boundaries. I don't think he thinks he's hurting me; or rather, I think he thinks I'm into it, the way he is. And the problem is, in many ways, I am into it. He will hit me harder than I would like, and I wonder if I should say something, but then I go home and I touch myself to the memory. I mean, that's not normal, right? Or if it is, it's not healthy. And I guess a healthy relationship is supposed to be what I want. I don't know. I don't know!

My ideal sexual fantasy—and you've heard a lot of them—my ideal sexual fantasy would be being with someone who knows what I want without my having to vocalize it. We could skip the formalities of discussing what "red/yellow/green" means, but he would instinctively know what my limits are and when it was okay to push them. I know that's a paradox: intimacy comes from knowing someone, and knowing someone comes from communication, and if I want to get to that level, I have to put the work in, like I assume you did with your girlfriend who has the perfect tits. I'm searching for something I know not only doesn't exist but can't exist. And so, I'm making a choice. The sex is hot with Malcolm, mostly. I feel comfortable and close to him because we are role-playing as people who are comfortable and close with each other, even though we still barely know each other. He hasn't expressed a problem with this—in fact, he seems to get off on how warped all this is—so I guess I don't have one either.

And even if he did, what does it matter? I'm leaving for LA in two days. I'll figure all this out then.

Lucy

24

"Okay, I made a Google map with every single taco place in LA the internet says we should check out," says Sasha, pulling up said map on her phone. We're sitting near the gate in the airport waiting to board our flight, and it's way too early to make sense of all the little icons that show up on her screen. "I cross-referenced the ones that the food blogs recommend the most against their Yelp reviews, just to make sure we aren't being suckered into anything. There are at least a dozen within a fifteen-minute drive of our Airbnb. God I already love LA."

"Amazing." I pull out my own phone. There's a text from my mom—*make sure you pee before you get on the plane in case there is turbulence or hijackers and you can't get to the bathroom*—which I ignore. Chester has agreed to an interview at a bar in Laurel Canyon tomorrow night, but when I emailed him back last week to confirm the time, he never responded. I've been refreshing my email every fifteen minutes since. Sasha notices my fidgeting.

"Hey." She gives my shoulder a squeeze. "He'll show up, okay? And regardless, it's going to be a good trip."

Sitting and waiting makes me restless, but I am genuinely excited. I arrived at the airport before Sasha this morning and stood by the doors inside the departure area to ambush her as soon as she showed up.

"LA!" I had exclaimed, while she made her way through the rotating door, serious men in business suits giving me a look as they pushed their way back.

"LA!" she shouted in return.

"Did you take the subway in that?" I said, eyeing her jeans, sneakers, and hoodie. "Jesus, Sasha, it's freezing out there!"

"We're going to California! I'm not bringing my parka."

"And where is your suitcase?" Sasha had a backpack and an oversized tote bag and that's it.

"I didn't want to be weighed down with a suitcase. It's LA! California! America! Land of the free!"

I couldn't argue with that logic. "LA!"

"LA!"

When the TSA agent asked me the nature of my travel to the United States, I puffed my chest up with pride and said, "Business. I'm a writer going to research a story." Then she asked if I had a travel visa, and I said, "Oh, do I need that?" She said legally she couldn't allow me to enter the country to work, and then I explained that actually I'm a bookseller, and I was just researching something for fun. "So you're not a real writer. As in, nobody is hiring you to write this piece. This isn't for work; this is just for you?"

"Yes," I said, my voice small and meek. "This is just for me."

"All right then." She stamped my passport. "You can go through. Have a nice vacation."

Now, we are only minutes away from boarding our plane and hours away from landing in LAX, where a rental car will be waiting for us. Sasha has arranged and planned everything, and I am just along for the ride. I check my email again while we're in line to board, but Sasha plucks the phone out of my hand and confidently turns it off.

"There." She drops it in her backpack. "Now you have no choice but to live in the moment."

"My boarding pass was on there!"

"Shit." She plops her backpack on the floor so she can rifle through it. "Hold on, I think it fell behind some other stuff." The gate agents eye us impatiently as I wait for Sasha to hurry up so we can live in the moment.

It's only midday by the time we begin our descent, but as I look out the window, the sky has an entirely different hue than it does back home, like a painting God did on acid. The whole city—or at least the small portion we can see that surrounds the airport—is filled with artificial lights, adding a hypnotic purple haze below the clear blue sky, with palm trees silhouetted against the technicolor backdrop.

The plane lands, and all the passengers do that thing where they stand up as soon as the seat belt sign goes off, even though the doors haven't opened and the line isn't moving and they all have to do that awkward crouch-stand. I'm sitting with my head against the window considering how dumb everybody is except for me when I realize I'm one of only two passengers left on the plane. The other person is Sasha, a few rows ahead of me, waving to get my attention.

"LA!" she exclaims.

"LA!" I reply.

We pick up our rental car—Sasha does all the driving; I never got my licence—with several hours to kill before it's time to check into our Airbnb in Highland Park. Sasha curses softly under her breath as we merge directly into traffic, while I fiddle with the car's Bluetooth and my iPhone before blasting a Santigold song about being young and free to sum up the mood, even though, I realize, the song is technically about New York. I think it counts as long as you're in the United States.

"I thought of a few things we can do to kill time until check-in," she says.

"You don't *kill* time. Haven't you read the most important book ever, *The Phantom Tollbooth*? Time is meant to be savoured and experienced."

"Okay, okay." Sasha shifts gears while keeping her eyes on the road. "There are a few things we can do to live our youths to the fullest and suck the sweet, sweet nectar out of life until it's time to check in. Do you want me to go through all our options, or do you want me to surprise you?"

"Ooh, surprise sounds fun. Pick the thing that will look coolest on our Instagrams."

"Naturally." She punches an address into her phone's map, tilts the screen away from me so I can't see ("It's a surprise!"), and the traffic starts to move as Siri's reassuring robotic voice tells us where to go.

"I want this to be a trip where things *happen*, you know?" she says.

"Totally," I nod. "Today is the first day of the rest of our lives." We stare at the road ahead. "How exactly do we make things happen?"

Sasha is quiet.

"Sasha? Do you have a plan for how to make things happen?"

"No. I do not have a plan for how to make things happen."

"We'll figure it out."

Sasha focuses on the road while the GPS issues more commands.

Sasha's super-secret mystery location turns out to be the Natural History Museum—maybe not the craziest place in the world to start a new life of adventure and intrigue, but we take some pretty solid selfies in front of a taxidermied bear and learn some cool facts about dinosaurs. After, we find a hole-in-the-wall Mexican restaurant for lunch, and I order potato tacos, which I didn't even realize were a thing.

"That's a good sign," she says. "I'm getting good vibes from this city, I'm telling you."

"LA!" I say, my mouth stuffed with potatoes. Sasha pulls out her phone to take a picture of me, and I hold up my taco.

"I paid too much for this international data plan. We have to upload a lot of pictures to Instagram to get my money's worth."

"Challenge accepted." I affect a pout.

"That's hot. Just wipe all the salsa off the side of your mouth and do that again."

"You know, when I'm trying to make things happen, I go on hookup apps. You can't go wrong on them." I hope she doesn't challenge me on all the ways hookup apps have gone wrong for me.

"I wouldn't even know how to start with those," she says.

I've already taken Sasha's phone out of her hand and am downloading the app. My finger hovers over the sign-up button. "I'm not gonna make you an account until I get your explicit consent, 'cause it's 2015," I say. "But this is LA. You could meet some hot movie star, or at least their weird cousin."

She sighs and shrugs. "Fine, let's do it." I clap in response and start building her profile.

Sitting in the car in the parking lot, Sasha is scrolling through one of the colour-coded travel plans on her phone. "Want to see something cool?" she asks.

"No, I hate cool things."

"I'm abandoning you on the side of the road." She sets the phone down and reverses out of the parking spot.

We drive for about twenty minutes. Then she pulls up to what looks like a playground. A series of jungle gyms rise up into long, pointed towers, a skeletal stack of rings made up of colourful tiles. We get out of the car and walk around. There are more than dozen structures, some connected; the tallest must be almost a hundred feet tall. I get as close as I can—the area is fenced in—and look up. The tall tower sticks out against the cornflower-blue Los Angeles sky, not a cloud in sight. Up close, the structures look spindly and delicate yet stand so tall and imposing.

"What is it?" I touch my hand to the fence in front of me, itself made up of a mosaic of tiles in turquoise and blues and oranges.

"It's called Watts Towers," says Sasha, as I move around the border. "I read about it on Atlas Obscura. They were made by an Italian immigrant. He wasn't a professional artist or anything. I think he worked in construction."

"Construction worker and tile mason. Built seventeen towers over a period of thirty-three years. An example of outsider art."

"How the hell do you know all that?" she asks.

"There's an info plaque." I gesture to the spot in front of me.

Actually, there's a whole info timeline. It tells about how Sabato Rodia made the structures out of a special concrete and wire mesh, as well as 7UP bottles, ceramic tiles, seashells, mirrors, and other objects. He called the end result "Nuestro Pueblo," which translates from the Spanish as "Our Town."

I walk up and down the length of the fence, letting my fingers trail over the mosaic, sliding over the bumps in the tiles.

"It's beautiful," Sasha says.

"Somebody just made this," I say. "Somebody saw this spot and decided they could build a whole new beautiful world here, and they just did it." I wonder if he had help, how much of the task he undertook on his own, if he needed to get permission first, if he received any pushback. If he hesitated, at any second, to take up space in order to make something grand and sweeping that forced anyone passing by to look, to have such faith that what he was doing deserved to be looked at, and to create something so worthy of that magnitude.

"'I had in my mind I'm gonna do something, something big,'" Sasha says.

"What's that?"

"It's a quote," she says. I walk over to where she's standing and look at the nondescript placard where the words appear, beautiful in their simplicity. *I had in my mind I'm gonna do something, something big.*

Our Airbnb is part of a house, a single bedroom and a kitchenette and a small living room with a couch that looks into a yard filled with cacti.

"I call the bed." I flop down face first and spread my limbs like a starfish

"Where do I sleep?" says Sasha.

"Also the bed," I say into the pillow. "But right now I'm not sharing. I'll move over in . . . five minutes. Also, do you have an extra toothbrush? I just realized I forgot to pack mine."

"Of course you did." She sits down on top of me, her bum resting squarely in the middle of my back. "And of course I packed an extra one. You literally always forget."

"I know you think this tactic will get me to move. But joke's on you. Your ass is so skinny I barely feel it."

Sasha stretches and lies down next to me, filling the tight space between my body and the wall. I shift over to give her some room but don't move from my facedown position.

My head hurts from the travel and sunshine. "Did you happen to pack any ibuprofen with that toothbrush?"

"I'll have to check," she says. "But I don't wanna get up right now. It'd be in my cosmetics bag."

I force myself up to go find Sasha's backpack, thrown carelessly on the living-room couch. Inside is a zippered pouch, which I rifle through. Benetint, Great Lash, two new toothbrushes, and a few pill bottles, including one of Tylenol 3 with codeine.

215

"Why do you have the super-hardcore Tylenol?" I call out to her. "Should I be worried about you?"

"What?" she calls back. She appears in the doorway, her frizzy hair sticking up from her ponytail, accentuating the confusion on her face. She sees the bottle. "Oh, right. Don't take those. They're leftover from a medical thing I had a few months ago."

"What medical thing?"

"Remember, when I was dealing with that birth-control stuff?"

"What kind of birth control requires opioids?"

She takes the bottle and her cosmetics bag out of my hands gently, avoiding eye contact. "It was more like a morning-after-pill situation."

"Like Plan B?"

"Like Mifegymiso."

The name is familiar, though it takes me a second to place it. It was in the news this last summer, covered on some of the feminist blogs I read, newly legal in Canada. "Jesus, Sasha, that's not the morning after pill, that's—"

"It's not a big deal, okay? It's done."

I try to think of what I was doing the night Sasha reached out to me about coming over to watch *Buffy* when she wasn't feeling well. This would have been when Henry was controlling my life over text and I was unsure how to fit her into that. She had an abortion, and she didn't tell me.

"Was Ryan supportive?"

"Ryan doesn't know," she says. She pulls a bottle of normal Advil out of her bag and fidgets with the child-proof cap. "I told him I had food poisoning and really bad period cramps. He was gone for most of it but brought me home a ginger ale after work." I imagine Sasha, weak, sick, and bleeding in bed, and all I want is to be able to go back in time and take care of her. She sees the look on my face. "I wasn't alone though. My sister came over. It's really not that big a deal. Yes, it hurt like a motherfucker, and I ruined, like, a dozen pairs of underwear in the weeks after with spotting, but it's done."

"How do you feel now?"

"Relieved, mostly. Glad I didn't have Ryan's baby. But mostly I don't really think about it. It was just a thing that happened. I've moved on."

"Sasha, I'm sorry," I say. "I should have been there for you."

She tips a couple of Advil into her palm and passes them to me. "You're here now."

25

The next morning, Sasha and I find another hole-in-the-wall Mexican restaurant and go for huevos rancheros. I try to bring up last night's conversation, but she says, "Please, Lucy, if you want to be a supportive friend right now, you can help me get laid." We are able to glom onto the Starbucks Wi-Fi next door and sit across from each other in a booth, focused on our phones, swiping through a parade of potential Tinder matches.

"This is so bizarre," she says. "I have to make a split-second decision based on someone's appearance. I feel like such an asshole."

"It's feminist for us to objectify men. We're modern heroes. Did you come across Chip, age thirty-two, with the golden retriever yet? I think he'd be maybe your type." She doesn't answer. I look up, and she's intently reading some guy's description, chewing her lip. "Sasha! Skip the bios. We're only here for a few days. Don't think, just swipe. I've gotten a dozen matches already."

"What happens if we match with the same guy?"

"You get dibs. I have to prepare for my interview with Chester tonight. I don't have time to go out with anyone."

"Why are you even on Tinder?"

I shrug. "Why is anyone on Tinder? Distraction. Force of habit. It's just something I do."

We resume swiping on our phones in silence, and a minute later Sasha jumps like she's just been shot with an electric volt.

"I got one!" she says. "I got a match! The first person I swiped right on, too."

"Obviously. You're a catch. Let me see."

Emil is twenty-eight and the exact opposite of Ryan. He's wearing a white tank top and too much hair gel, and his bio says he likes CrossFit and EDM. He is not my type at all but, I decide, perfect for Sasha right here and right now.

"What do I do?" she says.

"Send him a message. Something flirty and nice that lets him know you're only in town for a little bit and are down to eff."

"Hm." She chews her lip. Then she suddenly has a burst of inspiration and types out a quick message. She turns the phone towards me so I can see what she's typed out.

hey ;)

"Perfect," I say, and she hits send.

"Okay, now what?"

"Now, you keep swiping."

My interview with Chester is this evening. I have read every issue of *Smash* that I can several times and have a notebook filled with questions, but still I feel unprepared. Sasha and I go to the Museum of Jurassic Technology and then to In-N-Out next door for lunch where she introduces me to the secret menu, but I'm suddenly so nervous I can barely eat. I flip through my notebook while she eats her animal fries. She ordered a grilled cheese sandwich for herself as well. I haven't seen her touch dairy in years, but I don't question it. If Sasha needs a quiet break from veganism,

I decide I can quietly support it, even if she was the one who made me read *Eating Animals* in undergrad.

"Just breathe," she tells me, and I snort in response. "All you have to do is keep the conversation going and make sure your recorder is turned on."

"Since when do you know so much about journalism?" She slides her fries towards me. "Eat."

"All I've had in the last day to eat is tacos and fast food. I'm gonna get stress diarrhea before this interview."

"That's fine. Just make sure you go here before we go back to the Airbnb. That's one small bathroom we're sharing."

Sasha takes a nap in the afternoon, while I change my outfit three times, trying on every combination of the clothes I packed. I finally decide the only appropriate outfit is what I wore yesterday, a black dress that stops mid-thigh and seems both professional and cool. It smells ripe, though; it lasted me through a plane ride and a day around downtown Los Angeles. I search in the bathroom cupboards and find a patchouli-scented perfume. I'm supposed to meet Chester at a bar in Laurel Canyon, so maybe patchouli and B.O. are appropriate. I overcompensate for my hippie stink with too much eye makeup, deciding I can look a little sluttier than I would for a regular interview, given the subject matter.

I'm putting on my third coat of mascara as Sasha stirs from her nap.

"Damn, girl," she says. "You get invited to a party in Hollywood and forget to tell me?"

"My Uber's on the way." Obviously I'm against Uber for labour reasons, but I don't know how to get around without Sasha driving me.

"Right. Well. Knock 'em dead."

"Do you know what you're doing tonight?" I check one last time that both my digital recorder and my phone are in my purse.

"Yeah, I dunno." She looks away. "I'm thinking about maybe trying this bar I heard good things about? It might be lame, whatever."

She looks like she has more to say, but my Uber is arriving.

"Text me the address if you're out late. Maybe I'll join you after." I zip up my boots. "Either way, text me if you're still out by midnight so I know you're not murdered."

"Ugh, that would be so cool if I was. So *Helter Skelter*."

"You're weird." I head for the door, then stop, turn back, run and kiss her on the forehead, and then leave.

The most interesting thing about the bar where I meet Chester is its plainness. It's large, more of a restaurant really, and the booths are filled with patrons my moms' age eating spinach dip and drinking beer. I was expecting . . . I don't know, something glamorous? I feel overdressed. I pull on the hem of my dress.

I approach the hostess. "I'm meeting someone. My name is Lucy. His is Chester. Chester Wright. I think I'm a little early."

"You can wait at the bar. I'll let your date know where you are when he arrives."

"Oh, ha, it's not a date," I fluster. "No, I'm a writer? Doing a story? I'm interviewing him. As research. I'm here on business."

"Take a seat at the bar, and I'll let him know you're here."

I sit at the bar and order a vodka tonic. Minutes pass as I shift awkwardly in my seat. I check my phone; no calls or texts. I consider messaging Sasha, but I plan on using an app on my phone as the backup recorder, and I don't want to drain the battery. I try to pace myself with my drink, but Chester is now twenty minutes late. What if I have the wrong time, or worse, the wrong bar? I open my messages on Facebook, where our correspondence was; I never even got his phone number, which seems like journalism 101. *Stupid Lucy. So stupid. You came all this way to work on a story, and you fucked it up.*

And then Chester shows up. The hostess brings him to me, as promised. I had asked him for a photo when we messaged on Facebook so I would know what to expect, but the photo he sent must have been taken thirty years and thirty pounds ago. He's tall, clearing well over six feet, broad and paunchy, covered in the shadows of former muscles gone soft with age. His hair is a mess of frizzy white, pulled back in a short ponytail. He's wearing jeans, a stained, faded T-shirt, and a threadbare suit jacket. He is smiling broadly and warmly, and my first thought is *homeless Santa Claus*. I stand up from my barstool and extend a hand to shake his, but he surprises me by pulling me in for a tight hug. I can smell that he's already been drinking.

"So you're the girl who's writing a book," he says, sitting down next to me.

"Oh, it's just an article right now. I'm still just researching—"

"You know," he taps me urgently on my bare knee, which I quickly move back under the bar and away from his reach, "I think we could cowrite something great. I know people in publishing." He says this last phrase in a whisper, like he's sharing a secret that is supposed to impress me.

"I think we're getting ahead of ourselves," I start, but he cuts me off.

"Of course, those jackasses never know anything good. Do you know about Amazon dot com? They let you publish your own books. E-books. They're the future. That's where I published my novels. I assume you found them in your research?"

"I didn't see anything when I googled—"

"Of course, I didn't publish them under my own name," he continues, apparently not hearing me. "I didn't want people to confuse Chester the media mogul with Chester the novelist. They're very erotic, you know. I can send you the links. I think a girl like you would enjoy them."

"Why don't we just focus on *Smash* magazine for now." I hold up my recorder. "I'm going to turn this on so I don't miss anything, okay?"

"Just a second, honey," and he turns to the bartender to ask about their bourbons. The bartender takes his order, then asks if I want a refill, and I say, "Please!" maybe a little too loudly. I open my notebook with my list of questions, but before I have the chance to ask him, he spins off into a monologue.

"You probably want to know about all the celebrities," he says. "Let me tell you. I started my career at a talent agency, fresh outta college. Gave me a lot of contacts. The stories I could tell you about the famous people I met, Lisa, you wouldn't believe it. Anyone in the biz I needed to get, if I didn't know them personally, I knew someone. You like Marc Bolan?"

"There was a lot of post-punk in your magazine. A lot of smaller bands too. Stuff that didn't seem to be covered elsewhere. How did you get published by a place like Sanderson?"

"Oh that." He takes a swig of the drink the bartender puts in front of him. "Sanderson had a lot of trade magazines: cars, motorcycles, stuff you probably wouldn't be interested in. But they hired a new associate publisher there, someone who used to work at *Seventeen* magazine, Joe something. I knew him because the talent agency I was with, we booked big stars. Donny Osmond. You like Donny Osmond? Let me tell you, all the girls liked Donny Osmond back in the day; he was huge. And I had worked with Joe to get him Donny and other boys when he was working at *Seventeen*. Joe knew that things for teen girls could sell. They were the car magazine guides of the entertainment world."

"Sure," I nod, not because I agree but to keep him talking. He drains his drink, motions to the bartender for another, and keeps going.

"He wanted to make another magazine, something Sanderson wasn't doing, and he called me into a meeting about getting the biggest stars for a teen-girl magazine. And I tell him, I say, 'Look, *Seventeen* already has that market cornered.' I said, 'Joe, there's so much more that teen girls are interested in.' My girlfriend at the time was seventeen, and she thought *Seventeen* magazine was cornball. She didn't care about Donny Osmond. She was listening to the Sex Pistols! On the Sunset Strip or at Hollywood High, you see these teenage girls tarted up, waiting to see Led Zeppelin or Bowie—that's David Bowie, I met him twice—and no one was catering to these girls!"

"So you started a teen magazine," I say plainly. It seems my energy levels are inversely proportionate to his. *Smash* didn't care about empowering teen girls. They cared about marketing to them.

"Did *Smash* look like a teen magazine to you?" I'm not sure what kind of answer he's expecting; it did and it didn't, which was its appeal. He doesn't give me time to answer. "I knew those girls wouldn't buy anything that was too obvious for them. What they wanted was to feel cool, to be older, to be where the boys were. Glam rock was doing that, but it was on its way out. Punk was big, but how long was that going to last? I didn't know exactly what was going to come next, but I knew the people who did. I told him to give me a budget and I'd do the rest."

"So you hired young women? Because there were only two female names on the masthead."

"I hired whoever was right for the job. I hired youth. I hired cool. The girls we had around served a purpose. One of them was really smart." He stops, takes another big drink. "And angry!" He laughs at this part. "A lot of girls were angry at that time. It was a big thing in the seventies."

"Jennifer Flounder," I nod. "I talked to her."

"The other girls around were more fun. Here's a story you can put in your book. This is a full chapter." He reaches out to tap my knee again but seems to forget I have already moved it out of the way, and instead he taps air. His eyes are glassy, and his voice is loud, and I wonder just how much he had to drink before meeting me. I'm nodding along politely, but he is riveted by the words coming out of his own mouth. "I had an assistant. Meg. Absolutely adored me. Cute as a button, except for her nose. She wanted to go out with me, and I said, 'Meg, baby, you gotta update your look.' I had no problem going home with her, but going out was something different. She had a huge beak, you know?"

"Sure," I say, but he doesn't even seem interested in my reaction.

"So here's what I did. I took her out to lunch on the Strip one day. I said, 'Look, Meg, I hope I'm not out of line, but I know how I can get you a nose job, free.' And she said, 'Oh, really?' And I said, 'Yeah, we'd assign you to write this story, and we'd get a nose job for you, and you do a diary of it.' So she did it, and that's how we got the story. She wrote it under a pseudonym and left out all the parts about working for the magazine. And do you want to know the funniest part?"

"Okay," I say, unsure if I actually do.

"As soon as she got her nose job, which turned out great, she was good too for me." He laughs loudly enough that a customer on the other side of the bar turns their head to look. "Had a whole new lifestyle after that. Wouldn't see me anymore!"

"So Meg and Jennifer were the only two women on the masthead." I shift in my seat. He orders another drink. "But you said there were other girls around."

"Oh sure. PR gals. Or student workers—what you'd call interns now. We weren't a fashion magazine, but we did take original photos. Sometimes pictures of bands, but for the others we needed models. And girls loved us. Loved me in particular. Let me tell you, they'll let you get away with a lot if you tell them you're going to put them in a magazine." He laughs again at this, slapping his own knee this time, completely oblivious to the grossness of what he's saying. I'm several drinks behind him, but I start to feel queasy.

"Were these models from agencies?" I almost whisper.

"Oh, sometimes," he says casually, like he's describing his favourite places to shop for produce. "We would find girls on the Strip that wanted to be stars or send scouts to the high school. The good schools, with the lookers. It was an incredible period to be working. And a great time for women too. They didn't have to worry about being judged, the way they are now. In some ways I think we've gone backwards. Not you, of course. It's good to see you're not afraid to show a little leg. You wouldn't need to write a nose-job story for us. Maybe you could get a different job done, write about that." He's eyeing my flat chest as he says this.

I pull at the hem of my skirt. *A real reporter would have dressed appropriately.* I try to think of what a real reporter would even look like, and my mind turns to Malcolm. I picture him sitting in my seat, dressed in a suit, completely unfazed by Chester's words, knowing exactly what questions to ask next, sitting tall. Malcolm understands how power works. But then, I realize, so do I. I shake my head briefly, square my shoulders, and look Chester in the eye. "Were you physical with these girls?"

I worry the question will offend him, but he keeps talking like I asked him if he wants to get another round. "Did I do my job, you mean?" He laughs heartily. "We gave each other what we wanted. I always made sure they had fun."

"What does 'fun' mean?"

"They probably got a better deal out of it than I did! Not only with photo shoots in the magazine they could show off to their friends. We let them raid the record closets after, and they could take as much free music as they wanted. And they came to our parties. We threw great launch parties. Those girls probably ingested half of our budget in champagne and ludes alone. And those girls could not keep their hands off me. Even when they were dead sober! What man could resist?"

"Do you remember any of these girls specifically? Do you know what they're up to now?"

"Girlie, they came and went so quick that you couldn't keep track," he says. "Though every once in a while someone came along who burned in your memory. There was this one girl, Lois. She had just started high school, and she wanted to be an actress. We had these photos we took, other magazines would call them stock photos, but we took our own to illustrate our articles. They could be really artsy and abstract; our audience ate that shit up. So Lois comes to my offices one day, and let me tell you, she was a fox. Wore short, short skirts with no panties, which she made very clear the first time she sat on my couch."

I blink, unsure if what he's telling me is actually what he's telling me. I'm tempted to get up and leave, but I've made it this far. *You're a reporter. Be a reporter. Report the truth.*

"Every man in the office wanted Lois," he says. "I was no different. But I never got the chance."

I exhale, relieved. "So you had a crush on her, but nothing happened." I do the math. Chester would have been in his forties at the time. Lois would have been fourteen or fifteen. Him having a crush on her is unsettling, but not illegal. But Chester keeps going.

"I didn't get the chance!" he repeats. "We had a lot of movie stars coming to our launch parties or just hanging around our offices. We had a reputation for being a place where you could have a good time. Sometimes we put them in the magazine. Did you ever read our interview with Jack Franklin?"

"The actor from *The Greasers*?" Of course I remember the Jack Franklin interview. The boring handsome guy my mom had a crush on. The one she said reminded her of Dad.

"He was absolutely crazy about Lois! Started finding more excuses to come by just to see her. His movie career was taking off—*The Greasers* had just finished filming—and here he was, infatuated with this teenager! Can you believe it? It's every schoolgirl's dream."

Franklin was at least thirty when *The Greasers* came out, double Lois's age. I read some of the eulogies and remembrances in the weeks after his death, mostly Instagram posts from younger celebrities who played his kids in nineties movies and described him as "one of the good ones."

"So he had a crush on her too?" I ask Chester, wondering if he can sense the trepidation in my voice.

"You could call it that!" Chester says. "It drove me crazy at first. I wanted Lois for myself, but of course I couldn't compete when this hunk was around! But I was a good sport about it. I let them use my office."

"Use your office," I repeat.

"Well, they certainly couldn't go to her place, not with her parents around! And he was trying to promote this image, you know. He needed people to think he was single. Helped sell movie tickets and magazines. It couldn't last of course. He broke her heart eventually, and it crushed me to see, but how else are these things supposed to end?"

"Did the other people in the office notice that this was going on?" Did Jennifer know? I want him to stop. I want him to walk it back. I want him to keep going. He keeps going.

"I don't think anyone was keeping track," he says. "My office was used for all sorts of things once the door was closed. Some more interesting than others. Happy hours. A place to shoot the shit. Plenty of business meetings." He laughs, loudly. "Let me tell you though, Lisa, Jack Franklin was not using it for business meetings. Once I went to sit at my desk after they had done their, you know, their business. Lois was always so polite to me after she left. 'Thank you, Mr. Wright,' she'd say. Called me 'Chester' on other occasions, but those moments when I showed up to my office after they had used it, she'd suddenly be all bashful. So one day I went to sit at my desk, and what do I find bunched up underneath but a pair of red lace panties, size extra small." He chuckles, shakes his head incredulously, picks up his drink. "I guess it was one of the few days she had decided to wear them. She was good at this innocent act, but we all knew she was this wild animal."

All I can do is hope the recorder on the bar in front of me is working properly so I can make sense of what he's saying later. I touch it gently, sliding it a fraction of an inch in Chester's direction. His eyes follow my hand, and he does a double take when he sees the recorder.

"What the hell is that?" he asks.

"Oh, I um," I falter. I try to think about what a real reporter would do in this situation, if she would have drawn attention to her recorder at all. "I just wanted to make sure I'm getting everything. It's a little loud in here, and you're telling me such interesting stories—"

"Are you recording this?" he asks.

"Yes?" I say, more a question because he seems so incredulous. "I told you, at the beginning."

"I don't think you did." The cheerfulness is stripped from his voice, replaced by a steeliness that is genuinely intimidating coming from his large, drunk frame. "What's the idea here?"

"I told you, I'm a writer. I'm here to interview you."

"For the book, yeah," he says. I start to correct him, but he keeps going. "I thought we were just trading stories today, Lisa. I didn't think you were going to swindle me like this."

"I'm not—" I start, but I don't know how to finish that sentence. I'm in the right. I *know* I'm in the right. But he is so large and loud and aggressive and sure he's been double-crossed, and my instinct is to diffuse the situation. More people are turning to look. "I think there's been a bit of a misunderstanding."

The bartender comes up and asks if everything's okay, and everything feels very much *not* okay, but I am determined not to lose whatever professional credibility I have, so I say quietly, "I've got this." Chester becomes aware he's causing a scene and sits back down. For a second I naively think this is all behind us, but he puts his face in his hands and inhales deeply.

"I'm going to need to see everything," he says.

"Excuse me?"

"I'll need to see everything you write before you publish. Or else I'll have to call my lawyers."

"Whoa. That's not—I'm sorry, but that's not how I work."

"Then delete the tape recording," he says. "Delete it, right now, where I can see it, or I will call the cops."

I don't know if he has anything the cops will be interested in, at least not on me, but his eyes have gone ferociously dark, and I think, *He could kill me. He could follow me outside this bar and kill me.* Could he actually? I don't know. I just want to get out of there. I push some buttons on the recorder and show him the screen. "All gone," I say. "See?" The bartender comes back. "The bill please."

"Will you be paying together?"

"Sure. Whatever. Fine," and throw down my credit card while Chester keeps his eyes on me, a wildcat stalking his prey.

"You're a tricky kid, you know that, Lisa?" He slams down the rest of his drink.

"It's Lucy," I mumble.

"What did you say?"

"My name," I repeat, louder and clearer. "It's Lucy. Not Lisa."

The bartender brings me a receipt to sign as I say this, and Chester uses the moment I'm distracted to huffily stand up, extending himself to his full height. He sways for a minute, like he's about to pass out or hurl, but steadies himself a second later. "What a fucking waste of my time." He turns around, swiftly exiting the bar.

It's still relatively early in the evening by the time my cab takes me back to the Airbnb. *Jennifer Flounder warned you,* I think. *You should have been prepared for this.* And I was, or at least I thought I was. I thought Chester would be like Nora in that he might rant about kids today and not understand what words like *microaggression* mean but would still be, at the very least, *cool.* All the space he gave in *Smash* to covering women that I thought were liberated when really he was looking to get his dick wet. I shudder thinking about how gleefully he described finding a teenager's dirty underwear in his office.

I consider texting Sasha to see what bar she's at, but I don't want to be in a crowd. I don't want to be inside; the thought feels claustrophobic. I sit on the curb, pull out my phone, and before I can consider the cost of roaming fees, dial Ohio.

"Hello?" Jennifer picks up after a couple of rings. I realize it must be considerably later where she is, but I speak before my bravery leaves me.

"It was Jack Franklin," I say. "The actor, at the party, back in the seventies?"

"Lucy?" she says and then, after a second of processing, adds, "Who told you?"

"I'm in LA," I say. "I met Chester."

"What? Are you serious? When? How is he?"

"I don't know. Tonight, and drunk." I exhale, kick a rock on the ground in front of me. "Why didn't you want to name names? With Jack?"

"This isn't being recorded, is it?" I assure her it isn't. "Well, he's dead, first of all. And I'm not interested in getting my name in any tabloids. And, like I told you, nothing happened. He was a pushy drunk guy at a party. That was it."

"Yeah, nothing happened to you, maybe," and I immediately regret how harsh that sounds.

"What does that mean?"

I tell the story that Chester told me, about Lois and his office. I hear Jennifer sigh wearily at least twice. And then, trying to keep the accusation out of my voice, I say, "Didn't Lois ever try to talk to you about this?"

"I don't even know who Lois is," she says. I wonder if she's lying to me—covering her own complicity in the situation, because surely she would have known that what Chester was doing at the time was wrong, even if he didn't—but I let her continue. "I meant it when I told you girls were always coming and going from the office. And actors, musicians, and drugs. It wasn't a typical job. A lot of stuff went on, and yes, Chester sometimes kept his door closed when people visited. There was a lot of chaos, and I just kept my head down and focused on the work."

"So it was normal for teen girls and grown men to party together? Did you ever try to stop anything?"

"If I saw any girl—or any woman—who was visibly uncomfortable at a party, I would step in, sure. Or someone else would. Men too. There were a lot of good guys who really cared that everyone was having a nice time. But did I follow these girls around and babysit them every time they walked into another room? I was barely older than most of them and dealing with the same creeps they were."

I'm not sure what to say to this. I can't decide what the more depressing reality is—that Jennifer didn't care, or that she did and was powerless to do anything. I sit silently on the curb, taking all this in.

"Are you going to put all this in your article? Chester and Jack?"

"I don't know." It feels unprofessional to admit this in a phone call with a source, but then, I remind myself, I'm not a professional. I never have been. "I don't even—I don't know. You really didn't know this was going on? The Lois stuff?"

"I really didn't."

"She was a child. I mean, you must work with children all the time doing speech therapy stuff." My conception of speech therapy is limited to helping kids with lisps and stutters. "Are many of them that age? Fourteen or so?"

"I work exclusively with adults, actually. I specialize with patients who have acquired dysarthria after illness or injury."

"Oh. I didn't know that was even a thing."

"I got into this work after moving to Ohio. My mother-in-law had Parkinson's. I saw how hard it was for her to lose her ability to express herself." I try to take this in—*Parkinson's, like the Michael J. Fox disease?*—while Jennifer adds, "This is all on the About page of my website. The same spot where you would have found my phone number."

I have had, until this point, very little interest in Jennifer's life in Ohio or her career after *Smash*. I assumed she had traded in an interesting life for a stable one.

"I must have missed that," I say. "I'm learning a lot of new things today. I'm not sure what to do with it all."

"I can't tell you what to do, Lucy. You know, I hadn't thought about *Smash* for years before you called me last month." I can't tell if this is meant to be reproachful.

"I'm sorry," I say.

"Don't be. I wouldn't have talked to you if I didn't want to. I don't idealize that time at all. But I think I managed to put out some good work, in spite of everything."

I thank her, and we say our goodbyes. I stand up and head inside. Right now all I want to do is lie facedown on the bed, maybe see if I can get some tacos delivered. I'm so caught up in my thoughts I don't notice the lights are on and Sasha's bag and shoes are by the door.

I open the door to the bedroom and see that Sasha is still home. Correction: I see all of Sasha. She's on the bed naked, her skinny tan body covered in sweat, straddling a man, caught up in the moment. I should close the door and make a quiet exit before anyone notices me, but I'm caught off guard, and the vodka has muddled my head.

"The *fuck?*" is what comes out of my mouth.

Two shocked faces turn to me, and I see that the man on the bed is none other than Tinder Emil. Sasha shrieks, grabs a pillow, and uses it to cover herself, still impaled by her date. "Lucy!" she stammers. "I—we—I didn't think you'd be back so early."

"Sorry, sorry." I hold my hand out to shield my vision. "I didn't mean to—I'll leave you to it." I back out of the room, quickly closing the door behind me.

"Lucy?" Sasha's voice calls from the other side of the door. "Lucy, I'm sorry! We'll be done in a minute!" I hear a quiet male voice say, "We will?" and a sound of Sasha hitting him with the pillow.

"Please," I shout, putting my shoes back on and grabbing my keys, "take your time! I'm going out."

I end up flipping through magazines at the 7-Eleven down the street, almost identical to the one back home, eating soggy taquitos from the grill roller by the cash, also identical to the ones back home. My phone buzzes fifteen minutes later with a text from Sasha. *Omg Luce im soooooooo sorry,* it reads. *We couldn't go back to emils because he's living with his parents right now, and I swear I thought u would be out till later. I shoulda texted u or something. He's gone now!!! How was the interview?* *Don't apologize dude,* I reply. *I'm glad you got yours. But I'm sleeping on the couch tonight.*

26

Sasha stays in the bedroom the rest of the night, so I don't
see her until the next morning. We mumble good mornings
to each other en route to the bathroom. She showers while
I sit at the kitchen table, drinking coffee, listening to the
interview with Chester that I recorded on my phone. By
the time she joins me, Chester's voice emanates from the
speaker, working a mile a minute, sounding totally manic
with my shy little interruptions every couple of minutes.

"Fun night?" I ask, squinting at my computer screen.

"It hit the spot, so to speak," she says, pouring herself a
coffee. "What's going on there?"

"It's such a mess, Sasha. The interview."

"What happened?"

I tell her the full story with my voice rising in pitch as
I go.

"So what are you going to do?" she says once I finish.

"I don't know," I say, and the answer feels so incon-
sequential coming out of my mouth that I say it again.
"I don't know! I thought this would be a fun project, and
now what? Do I expose the seediness orchestrated by this
random guy at a magazine nobody has heard about from
forty years ago? Do I want to call out a B-list actor for statu-
tory rape a year after he died?"

"Well, what do you want to do?"

"I don't know that either. I feel like—I feel like stories
like Chester's and Jack's are a dime a dozen. Chester

238

doesn't see anything wrong with how he acted. I mean, he does, but only when he saw I was recording. I wanted to write about this moment in time I thought was unique, and now it's another story about another man on another power trip." I drum my hands on the table. "A real journalist would know what to do with this."

"I can't believe he just told you about the teenagers they slept with. No shame whatsoever. Like he was proud of it."

"I know. I think I know the one he's talking about. I brought a bunch of issues with me, and I was flipping through them last night. I found a model named Lois in some of the shoots. It's gotta be her, right?"

"Show me."

I go to the couch where my stuff is spread out and grab the magazines. "See, here's the thing," I say. "I remembered the shoot he was talking about, and the model is credited, Lois LaMarr." I flip to the page and slide the magazine over to Sasha, who studies it. "But *then*, in an earlier issue, I found this. Clearly the same girl, but here she is Lois Schwebb."

"LaMarr definitely sounds more glam than Schwebb. I can see why she'd change it. I'm not saying she *should*," she adds quickly. "I'm just saying, working for someone like Chester . . ."

"I wouldn't be surprised if he was the reason for the change."

"Have you tried tracking her down?"

I nod. "There are a couple of Lois Schwebbs and a bunch of Lois LaMarrs on Facebook, but none is the right age. No Loises in Buck or Chester's friend lists. But I was searching through the *LA Times* online this morning, and I found this." I turn my laptop screen towards Sasha so she can see the wedding announcement I found from the 1980s, in which Lois Schwebb weds real-estate agent Gerald Hartley. There is no job title listed next to Lois's name, but the grainy photo accompanying the announcement shows her unmistakable face. She looks young, even there. I shiver, thinking about what must have happened between her and Jack Franklin.

"Wow, Nancy Drew," Sasha says. "I'm impressed."

"Nancy Drew didn't have Google or Facebook. She probably would have solved crimes way quicker if she did."

There are a lot of Lois Hartleys when we do a search, but Gerald Hartley Real Estate is still in business, and his web presence is easy to find. Comically easy. "Gerald Hartley Real Estate: 40 Years in Business!" his website says. It links to his official Facebook page, and scrolling through the people who liked it we see one Lois Angela. No last name, but when we visit her profile, it's clearly her.

"Wow," says Sasha. "Literally everyone in the world just gives their information to Facebook. We're so fucked if Zuckerburg wants to take over the world." There's no option to message Lois on Facebook, but we can see where she works.

"She's a manager at the Gap. Look. Right here in LA. Do you think she knows that information is public?"

Sasha has pulled out her phone and is looking something up, her brow furrowed in concentration. "What are you doing?" I ask, but before she answers, she has put the phone to her ear.

"Sasha what—" I start, but she holds up a finger to silence me.

"Hi," she says in a chirpy voice. "I was in your store a while ago, and there was one sales associate who was so helpful. She said her name was something like Louise? I think she was actually a manager. Oh. Oh right. Lois, that's right. Anyway, I wondered if she was working today? I'm planning to come in later, and she just, you know, she really gets my style. Really? Excellent. Thank you." She hangs up the phone, and I stare at her, impressed. "Lois's shift starts at 1 p.m." She sees my agape mouth and shrugs. "I told you, LA Sasha is making things happen. Do you want to get tacos for breakfast?"

The Gap where Lois works is in a mall that exists as its own ecosystem. We grab lunch at the food court and find a bench that gives us a good view. We both pull out our phones and hold them in front of our faces, pretending to text while not letting our eyes stray from the store.

"What are you going to say when you talk to her?" Sasha asks.

"I don't know."

"Are you even going to talk to her?"

"I don't know."

"It's pretty fucked up, when you think about it," she continues. "Showing up at someone's work to ask them about an abusive relationship they had with a celebrity years ago for—"

"Sasha, please. I don't know. I just want to see her, I think."

We wait until 1:02. What *am* I doing here? But then Sasha throws our empty food containers in the trash. "Let's go."

She grabs my hand with the confidence of the Sasha I met in undergrad, and the next thing I know, we're in the store, surrounded by sensible slacks and cotton T-shirts in every colour of the rainbow, and I see her, I see Lois. Her face is lined and her cheeks gently sag and her hair is more grey than brunette at this point, but it's her. It's the girl from the magazine. She's at the back of the store, neatly refolding a table of long-sleeved crewneck tees. *Go,* I think. *Go talk to her.*

"Can I help you?" a sales associate asks, and I jump. The air conditioning in the mall is heavy, but I'm sweating profusely. I wonder if I look as suspicious as I feel.

"We're just browsing, thanks," Sasha smiles.

"Well, let me know if you need anything!" the associate says and leaves us alone. Were the lights in the Gap always this bright? Do they turn them up in America?

"Listen," Sasha says, and she grabs my elbow. "Whatever you decide to do, I support you and I love you, okay?" I nod and slowly walk, float really, to the back of the store.

"Excuse me?" I say once I reach Lois's table, and she looks up at me with the same eyes of the teenager that posed for Chester years ago.

"Yes? Can I help you find something?"

She's at work. This fact hits me like a revelation. *She's at work, at her non-glamorous retail job, trying to get through a shift so she can go home to her real-estate-agent husband and the life she built for herself, and you are here, you are here to harass this working woman for your weird vanity project with no real purpose. You are bad. You are a bad person.*

She's still staring at me. I need to say something, but all I want to do is be far away from her, far away from LA, far away from anything to do with *Smash.*

242

"Do you have a bathroom?" I whisper.

"Not in the store." She looks back down at the table and resumes folding. "The closest one would be in the food court." The conversation is done. We have nothing more to say to each other. I have nothing more to say to her.

I choke out a quick "Thank you" and turn around, walking quickly out of the store. "Are you okay?" Sasha says as I pass her, but I don't stop. I leave the store and find the bench where we sat earlier, mercifully unoccupied, and sit down, put my head between my knees, and breathe deeply.

"What happened?" says Sasha, catching up to me. "Oh. Oh shit. Are you hyperventilating?"

"It'll pass in a sec," I say between breaths. Sasha sits down beside me and tenderly puts her hand on my back, gently rubbing until I calm down.

"Nothing happened," I say quietly to the ground. "I saw her and immediately began to panic." I look up at Sasha and see her concern. Her hand is still on my back. "What am I doing here?" As soon as I say it, I realize I have no idea what I'm doing. In this mall, in LA, with this story. Another day in my life of waiting for someone to tell me the right steps to take.

"You're a twenty-five-year-old on vacation with her best friend. Maybe today doesn't need to be any more than that."

I shake my head. If I don't pursue talking to Lois, then this was for nothing. I've wasted everyone's time. I am a fraud. If I do try to talk to Lois, I risk confronting a woman for a project I'm not even sure the scope of, and she'll know I'm a fraud. I have once again tangled myself up in expectations I've invented for myself, a test I've failed with nobody keeping score. Sasha doesn't say anything else, doesn't ask me any more questions. We sit beside each other in an approximation of silence, the hum of shoppers around us creating an ambient wall of sound. A couple of twenty-five-year-olds on vacation. It's time to make a decision. I ask Sasha if she wants to leave the mall, and we do.

27

The sun never really sets in Hollywood. Like everything else here, it seems to follow its own laws. The night sky in Southern California glows amethyst from haze and light pollution.

Tonight, the final night of our trip, Sasha and I head off towards Griffith Observatory and park at the bottom of a hill.

"Looks like no public roads from here on out," she reads off her phone. "But there's supposed to be a shuttle that takes you up."

We wander around a little, and eventually find a long line of tourists boarding what looks to be a municipal bus.

"This bus might be the only way up," I say.

"It looks like people are walking over there." Sasha points to a wide dirt path that snakes up around what I assume is Mount Hollywood.

"Are you sure that goes up to the right place?"

"No. But we're going to a planetarium to learn about the mysteries of time and space. Do you really want to take a *bus* there?"

The walk up is steep and long and beautiful. The dirt path winds through the flora, and though there was still daylight when we started, dusk begins to fall. On the way up we pass a few people coming down, but for the most part, we're there alone.

"Look at this." I walk to the edge of the path, right where it twists around avoiding a deep drop of rocks and dirt. The city below us is vast and sparkly. To the right are the hills, with the Hollywood sign standing proudly and clearer than I've ever seen it before. The sky is a tie-dye of mauves and fuchsias, expanding into a rich velvety purple through which I can see what is maybe a star, likely a satellite. Sasha steps up beside me, and we look out.

"You know, it's actually my anniversary with Ryan tomorrow," she says. "The first time in years I'll have been alone on this date."

"Yeah, but you're not alone. Look at that city. Look at how big it is. How can anybody be alone here?"

Sasha grabs my hand and gives it a squeeze. I squeeze back. We walk the rest of the path up in silence.

We watch a planetarium show about the history of the universe, which is as beautiful as it is artificial, and then wander back outside, where there is a long snaking line of tourists, seemingly with no beginning or end.

"Excuse me," I approach a family, "what are you lining up for?"

"Telescope," the father answers in a thick German accent. "They let you see the sky. For free."

"Do you want to line up?" I ask Sasha after thanking the tourist.

"I do if you do. I want to see the sky for free."

"I want to see something real," I agree, and we find the end of the line. Within minutes, more people line up behind us, and soon we are just a couple more tourists ourselves, lost in a constellation of people.

"I might accidentally trip out if I think about the size of the universe for too long. You know. Infinity."

"Shit, I forgot!" Sasha opens her purse. She pulls out a small bag of gummy bears.

"What's that?"

"Weed gummies." She hands me one. "Emil from Tinder gave them to me last night. I wish I remembered them before the show."

"No, this way works out perfectly." I tear a little red guy in two. "We were on Earth while watching the show on Earth, and we'll be up high when looking at the heavens."

"Don't say shit like that before we get stoned." She pops her half in her mouth.

It takes half an hour for us to end up at the front of the line, and by then the gummies have kicked in, a mellow high. We enter the dome that houses the telescope, a large structure that both overwhelms with its size and feels claustrophobic with all the equipment inside, a reminder that the world is both too big and never enough. I'm in front of Sasha. The guide explains to me what I can expect to see, but I don't catch what he says, and I'm too shy and embarrassed to ask him to repeat himself. Instead, I just peer into the telescope and into outer space. The view is an algae green, reminding me of slides under the microscope from high school. But in the middle of the green is the unmistakable brightness of a heavenly body.

"What star did you say that was?" I ask the guide.

"That's Saturn," he answers.

"That's *Saturn*?" I turn to look at him incredulously, then back into the telescope. "*That's* Saturn. Saturn with the rings, Saturn the planet, Saturn the god, everything Saturn is, Saturn's just *right there*?"

"Please keep the line moving. A lot of people want to see Saturn."

The idea of hogging Saturn in that moment seems indescribably selfish—Saturn belongs to all of us—so I step aside and wait for Sasha to look through. She catches up to me when she's done.

"That was Saturn!" she says.

"I *know!*" I grab her hand tightly, and we find our way outside of the dome and into the universe.

After the observatory, we walk through Los Feliz and Silver Lake, waiting for our highs to fade. It feels like a good night to wander.

There's a bookstore that's still open, Skylight Books, and we go inside. We silently separate. I head over to the fiction section and browse the glossy spines of candy-coloured paperbacks. They have so many different titles than the ones at Prologues.

Then I spot a familiar title. *Bad Behavior* by Mary Gaitskill. My spine stiffens, like I've been caught, like Mary has witnessed me breaking a secret rule I had agreed to follow. I pick up the book and flip to the contents listing the titles of stories I guiltily remember I never read. "Secretary" jumps out, and I flip through to where it begins on page 132.

"The typing and secretarial class was held in a little basement room in the Business Building of the local community college," it starts. I sit down on the floor and continue reading, resisting the urge to skim for the sexy parts. I read every line. It's a lot bleaker than I remember, not romantic, barely even erotic. The boss, played by James Spader in the movie, is described as "a short man with dark, shiny eyes and dense, immobile shoulders." By the time Sasha approaches me, I still have a few pages left, but I am very aware the story is not going to end with a mutually satisfying relationship.

"Watcha reading?" Sasha asks.

"Short stories," I mumble, not looking up.

"Any good?"

"I don't know. I mean, yes, they're good. But I don't know if I like them."

"You ready to go?"

"Yes. But hold on. I wanna buy the book."

It's midnight by the time we get back. "I can't believe we go back to our lives tomorrow" says Sasha, flipping on the lights in the apartment. "Is there even anywhere you can see Saturn in Toronto?"

"'The world is wide, wide, wide and I am young, young, young, and we're all going to live forever,'" I say, flopping on the couch.

"Did you just make that up?" she asks.

"That's Elaine Dundy, *The Dud Avocado*. Everything I do is a quote."

We're too buzzed to sleep, so we flip through a tall stack of DVDs in the small living room for something to watch. I ask if we can watch something old and Holly-wood, and Sasha finds a copy of *It Happened One Night*. Neither of us has seen it. Sasha pulls out the bag of gummy bears. Clark Gable plays this rakish dom and Claudette Colbert is a bratty wildcard and they hate each other and love each other and at one point he actually throws her over his shoulder and spanks her in a way that is problematic because, you know, they never established a safe word, but also turns me on. I guiltily think about the copy of *Bad Behavior* in my tote bag. *You can't build a life based on what gets you off sexually,* I think, as Clark Gable declares his love onscreen for the woman he's known for three days, the way Lee declared her love for her boss in *Secretary,* the movie not the book. *What's going to happen tomorrow?* But it doesn't matter. The couple ends up together. They get married. The credits roll. They have no tomorrow.

Sasha turns off the movie and starts channel surfing until we land on a *Seinfeld* rerun. "We should probably go to bed soon," she says. "I just don't want to think about the trip being over."

I've stopped paying attention to the TV and am scrolling through my phone. There's a message waiting on Tinder from a new match. *I'm one of those rare guys who still opens the door for women so I think I get a few bonus points for that,* he sends, by way of opening.

"Do you feel like things happened?" I ask. I type out a reply to the Tinder message. *i dont want a guy to open doors for me i want a guy to pin me down choke me then cum on my face.* I turn my phone on silent and flip it over.

"I feel like I had a nice trip with my ol' pal Lucy," she yawns. "And I feel stoned. How do you feel?"

"I think I'm scared to go home. I think I have to resume my life where I left it." I'm staring at my socks while I talk. It felt like so much was beginning before I left, and maybe it still is. But the possibilities terrify me. Also socks are so fucking weird.

I look up. Sasha is curled up at the end of the couch, fast asleep. I reach out and kick her gently.

"Wassat?" Sasha says, groggily rousing. "Is the show done?"

"I think you're done, bud." She starts to drift off again, so I kick her harder. "Come on. Let's move to the bed. If you fall asleep here, you're going to hate yourself tomorrow."

She drags herself off the couch and shuffles to the bedroom. "You coming?" she mumbles, looking over her shoulder.

"I'm actually not feeling that well," I lie. "I'm fine, but the edibles made me nauseous. Toss me out a pillow, 'kay?"

Sasha is too tired to question this. I make myself a little nest on the couch with a spare blanket. I pull out my phone. Tinder is still open.

I scroll through my matches, each face a potential new person to lose myself in. Malcolm is back home, probably sleeping. I don't feel like talking to someone I already know. It's late here too, but I have a recent message from a man named Patrick. He sent me a quick *What's up?* ten minutes ago. I don't even look at his pictures. It doesn't matter who he is.

I'm restless and I can't sleep. I look at the time. It's 3:14 a.m. If he doesn't reply by 3:16, I will put my phone down and go to sleep.

His reply comes seconds later. *Too bad ;). Wanna meet up? Where you at?*

In bed, not leaving. But we can message.

Message about what?

What would you do to me if I were there? And then a few seconds later, *if you could make me do whatever you wanted.*

My hands slide down the front of my panties; I'm already more turned on by my boldness than by whatever Patrick might reply with. "LA!" I whisper to myself.

Patrick writes back with a detailed paragraph, surprisingly imaginative, about what he'd make me do with my mouth, my hands, the rest of me. I wonder if everyone is secretly kinky or if I just have instincts for finding people like me. Either way, it's exactly what I want right now.

Have you ever had a girl call you Daddy?

We continue to message until nearly 4 a.m., when I fall asleep, my phone still in my hand.

28

I reread "Secretary" on the plane ride home. Then I start the
collection from the beginning, but I can't get into the other
stories. I just go back and read "Secretary" again. I'm mad at
all the ambiguities in the story. I wish it could be didactic, like
the movie. I wish it could just tell me what to do, at least inso-
far as I pursue sex. Debby, the character who became Maggie
Gyllenhaal's Lee in the movie, ends up alone in the story.
Her boss is unambiguously abusive, and though she manages
to get off on it when she's alone later, she never romanti-
cizes him. There is nothing there to romanticize; the sado-
masochistic scenes are dull and uncomfortable and unsexy.
The first time I reread it, in Skylight, the story felt cold, at
least compared to the movie—Lee's untempered girlishness
and overwhelming desire to please. But on my seventh reread
I understand Debby isn't cold at all. She plays her yearnings
close to the chest, but they're still there. The humiliations
she suffers at the hands of the unnamed lawyer are enough
to temporarily distract her from a numbness before throwing
her into a depression. She touches herself often but is unable
to climax, and their relationship ends when she unceremo-
niously quits and he sends her a cheque in the mail, more
than what she's owed. In the movie, they fall in love and get
married. Lee doesn't end up alone. At least, not right away.
I suppose everyone ends up alone eventually.

Sasha and I have seats next to each other on this flight,
but she's watching some old action movie on the little

screen in front of her. I'm too restless to focus on a film, or anything else I can't control the pace of. I plug my earbuds into my recorder to listen to the interview with Chester.

Our conversation makes me wince even before any of the awkward parts start. Sometimes I imagine myself a reporter in an eighties movie, one of the ones where women had big hair and big shoulder pads and were confident at the office and still managed to end up with Harrison Ford. My voice sounds so meek on the recorder.

"You look as if someone farted," Sasha snaps me to attention. I didn't noticed her movie had ended, and she's taken out her earbuds to talk to me. "Was it—" She lowers her voice. "Was it the guy in front of us?"

"It's me," I say. "Not that. I didn't fart. It's this stupid interview."

"Everyone hates the sound of their own voice. I can't even watch my Snapchats once I record them."

"Do you think it's okay to expose men for having been pigs in the past if hardly anyone cares about them anymore?"

"Well, what about the women they hurt?" she asks. "Don't they care?"

"I don't know if they do. Jennifer had some things to say. But she mostly moved on with her life. I don't think Lois wants to be found."

I lean my head back against my seat. I wonder if the pursuit of pleasure and joy for its own sake is ever truly possible, without the other shoe eventually dropping. "I don't think I can talk about it right now. Can we please just watch a movie or something?"

"Yes, of course we can. They have *The Goonies*. Do you wanna sync up and watch together?"

"I thought we were already synced up," I say, as she leans over me and fiddles with my screen, pulling up the movie. Her hand brushes over the copy of *Bad Behavior* on my lap, and she picks it up.

"You decide if you like this book yet?"

I nod. "Yeah, I think I do."

It's late afternoon by the time I get back to my apartment, but I'm worn out from travelling. I could sleep for hours, and I start to doze off when my stomach grumbles loudly, waking me up. I'm reminded that all I've had to eat today is an Auntie Anne's pretzel and coffee at the airport.

I'm stiff from the flight, so I throw on pyjama bottoms and a sweatshirt before shoving my feet into my winter boots and worming into my parka. A quick look in the mirror reveals bloodshot eyes and a row of pimples on my makeup-less forehead. My long hair is a frizzy mess, and I attempt to pull it back in a bun before flattening it down with a toque.

There's enough change on my bedside table for a couple of doubles at the roti place around the corner, so I go. I place my order at the counter, then sit on one of the red plastic chairs, the table in front of me sticky with indeterminable sauces. I want nothing more than to put my head down on the table and close my eyes, but I feel like I'll never be able to raise my head again.

"Lucy?" a familiar voice says.

"Beard!" I reply, because that's what I see: a bushy beard hiding two crinkly eyes on a tall, broad frame. "Henry!"

"I thought it was you," Henry says, approaching. He opens his arms for a hug, but I'm caught off guard by seeing him, so I don't get up or make any kind of move to reciprocate. Instead, he just kind of pats my back awkwardly. "Do you mind if I—" he motions at the empty seat across from me, and I nod perhaps too vigorously.

"Please!" He slides in the chair and casually rests his forearms on the table. "What are you doing here? I mean, your work isn't anywhere near here?" For a second I wonder if he's moved up from his basement in Little Portugal, and I panic at the thought of us being neighbours.

"Oh, I had a doctor's appointment. Nothing serious. I come by here whenever I get the chance. Their goat roti is really good."

"Yeah, you have—" I motion to the side of my mouth. He touches his own face and rubs off some of the stray sauce just below his cheek. Some smears into that giant beard. I say nothing.

"Anyway," he licks the sauce off his thumb in a move I would have found irresistible a couple of months ago but now kind of makes me want to hurl, "I don't work there anymore. I decided to leave."

"You quit your data-management job?"

"I worked in digital branding. And yeah. The company was downsizing and laying off a lot of people, so I decided it was time to move on."

"It doesn't sound like you really chose…" I trail off. "How is Violet?"

"Oh, we split. She's a great girl. But I was in a transitional period of my life and didn't want to be tied down to anything. We decided it was for the best if we parted ways."

"How were you tied down if you weren't even monoga…" I stop myself again. "I'm sorry to hear that."

"Don't be. I'm a new man. I'm really focusing on me right now. Got a couple of projects on the go. Nothing I can talk about now, of course. It's all confidential. But it's a transitional time right now. Really exciting."

"I can see that. You got a beard and everything."

"Oh, you noticed, huh?" He grins, as if anyone could notice anything else. "I'm glad you like it." I offer a closed-mouth smile. "But what's going on with you?"

"Oh, you know."

"How's your writing going?"

"It's not really. I'm not really working on anything right now," I mumble. The *Smash* story feels too ambiguous to talk about. The last time I actually did write anything were those personal letters to him in my notebook, which he can never know about. "I am seeing someone new, though. It's really great. *He's* a writer. And I'm travelling lots. I literally just got back from LA this afternoon."

"It sounds like you're doing really well. I mean, you *look* . . ." He gestures to my pyjama-clad, pimpled, frizzy-haired self and trails off. "It's really nice to see you."

"Yeah. It's really nice to see your beard. You. It's nice to see you."

Neither of us says anything for a moment. Then, mercifully, the woman at the counter calls, "Two doubles to go!" and I pick up my order.

"Hey." Henry gently touches my arm. His voice is slightly lower than it was just minutes ago, the voice he used when he was dominating me. "I'm just heading out too. Let me walk you home."

"I was planning on staying and eating."

"I thought she said your order was to go?" he says. I shrug. "All right, Lucy. I understand. It was nice seeing you too." He turns and heads out the door, and I don't know what it is. Maybe it's hearing his voice again, the one that used to give me orders with an assuredness. Maybe it's the way he touched my arm. Maybe it's because, with his back turned to me, I can't see his stupid fucking beard.

"Henry," I say, and he stops but doesn't turn around, "will you please walk me home?"

He does that thing guys do when they follow you out a door, where he puts his hand on my lower back, and he makes sure to press firmly enough so that I can feel it through the puffiness of my coat. We're silent for the first minute of the journey, save for me gently directing the way back to my place. I forget that Henry doesn't know where I live; his presence in my life felt so pervasive, it almost didn't matter that he was barely ever physically in it. I finally break the silence.

"You were good," I say, softly.

"Well—thank you. I like to think so."

"No, not like that. I mean, you were good to me. At least, you were better to me. Compared to—well, you were just good." Henry doesn't say anything, so I keep talking. "I guess I took it for granted. All the safe words and stuff."

We've stopped walking now. We're already back at my place. Henry positions himself across from me and looks down, his brow furrowed.

"Lucy, that's not—" he starts. "Everyone should respect the people they sleep with. That's just how it works."

258

"I know. It's just, it doesn't seem natural for some people."

"Are you okay?" he asks. "Did something happen?"

"No, no. Nothing like that."

"Are you sure? I didn't want to say anything, but you seem a little frazzled."

"I just got off a cross-country flight!" I say defensively.

"You look very nice," he says, which is so clearly a lie but I can't help but smile a little. "But you know, Lucy, proper BDSM should always, always centre on affirmative consent with the submissive being the one who is truly in control—"

"I'm fine!" I say, mostly because I need him to stop talking. "Everything is fine. Things are going good for me. I'm just saying. For like, two seconds there, whatever was happening between us. It was nice." Until he dumped me over text, but that part feels so far away now.

"Well . . ." He crosses his arms across his broad chest. "Thank you. It was nice for me too."

Another moment while we both stand there in the frigid weather. I'm swinging the plastic bag where the doubles are nested in front of me.

"It really was good to see you," he says.

"Yeah. It was good to see you too." I almost consider saying something like "I'll see you around!" or "Let's keep in touch!" but I know neither of us wants that.

He opens his arms for a hug, and I reciprocate this time, allowing myself to be pressed against him, if only for a few seconds. He squeezes me tight, and as he starts to let me go, he gently tilts his head down and leaves one chaste kiss on my forehead. His beard tickles the top of my nose as he does so.

"Be good, Lucy," he says, his voice at his regular pitch, and he turns to leave. His beard remains truly unappealing. But I guess I can see how other women would be into it.

I'm so tired that I eat my greasy doubles in bed, a layer of paper towels on my lap, and then shove the mess of garbage on the floor, curling up and falling asleep with the lights on. Several hours later, I jolt awake, completely disoriented, realizing that I'm supposed to work soon. Kicking off my stale clothes, I roll out of bed, and my foot lands on the slick wrapper from last night's dinner. I pick up the trash and hop on one foot to the garbage can in the kitchen, trying to be careful not to track the mess through the apartment. Then it's a hop hop hop to the bathroom.

Congratulations on coming back from LA a changed woman, I think as I turn on the shower, as hot as the water will go.

Turning off a hot shower is ordinarily a hard task in a Canadian winter, but having just come back from sunny Southern California makes stepping out of my steamy cube into my chilly bathroom especially sadistic. *Be a good girl,* I mentally order myself. *Take the discomfort like a good girl, and suck it up, slut.* Counting backwards from ten, I turn off the water and step out of the shower in one quick motion, only to realize I don't have any clean towels out. *Dumb bitch. This is why you can't be trusted to think for yourself.* Soaking wet, I run into the main room of my apartment, rifle through the closet unsuccessfully, and finally dig out of the laundry hamper a dirty towel, which has been sitting there since before my trip. It takes me a few minutes to find my phone, forgetting that I left it at the bottom of my tote bag.

I hold my breath before looking at the screen, bracing myself for how late I'm running.

It's two in the morning.

Idiot, I hiss at myself.

There's text from Malcolm on my screen.

Are you back yet baby? I can't wait to see you.

It was sent a few hours ago. I type out a quick reply. *Ughhh sorry, I fell asleep. I'm working all day today but can I come over after?*

I shower, brush my teeth and wash my face, change into clean pyjamas, and go back to bed. It's no use. Wide awake, I look at the phone again. It's only 2:45. There's no use trying to force sleep. I clean my apartment. I scrub every surface, the nooks and crannies I don't usually get to, working quickly and quietly to not wake up Mr. Filli-pelli. I sort my bookshelves and clean out my closet. With-out the distraction of the waking world, I can lose myself in these tasks. As I unpack my tote, I pull out my notebook and flip to a fresh page.

Dear Sir,

I suppose it's strange writing to you, considering I just saw you, but you're not really you, are you? I mean, maybe you used to be, when I started this—one specific Sir, one specific intended future audience—but that stopped being true forever ago. So who am I writing this for? Not me, surely. Can you imagine? If I turned out to be the Daddy this whole time? Some freaky Sixth Sense *ending. Or maybe* The Wizard of Oz, *where I go on a quest to be spanked, and all I have to do is look inside myself and tap my heels three times and realize the power to be a freaky nasty dominant bitch was in my heart all along.*

But that's not true. Because here's what I do know: I do have another Sir in my life right now. I told you about that, right? He makes me happy, I think, or maybe he makes me horny. Is there a difference? And I still don't know anything. I still don't know what to do! And maybe I know more than I did a few months ago, just like a few months ago I knew more than I did five years ago, just like in a year I'll know more than I do today, just like I'll keep learning, or forgetting what I've already learned, every day until I die. And I'm awake, in the middle of the night, sorting through my underwear drawer (you like that, don't you, perv?), because I can't manage my own life enough to get to sleep at a real time. I'm going to be exhausted at work tomorrow. It's my own fault. Because knowing things doesn't necessarily preclude me from making the same mistakes, or having my shit together one day doesn't mean I will tomorrow.

Sometimes being an adult feels like spinning plates, where you have to keep everything going at once to ensure that you are both keeping yourself alive and keeping a balanced life—to eat, to sleep, to work, to learn, to fuck—and then, while you're working on all that, you also have to figure out how to be a good person. And every time you think you have it, a plate falls and crashes, or six more plates are added. And I keep thinking, if I just find the right person, they can help me spin all these plates and I won't have to do it alone, but then of course every new person comes along with their own plates, and their own method of spinning them, and sometimes they're really good at it, sometimes they can help you spin yours, and sometimes their plate-spinning methods are just incompatible with yours, but mostly everyone is trying to figure out how to spin the plates they've been given.

I should add, I have literally no idea how plate spinning works or what it's even for. Do they spin plates in the circus? Idk.

It was fun, when you spun my plates for a while, even though that sounds like a sex move I would definitely be into. I think I did that thing where I got so caught up with you I forgot that maybe you had your own shit you were dealing with. I think I do that a lot.

But again, "you" are not you, because you will never read this. But you know what I mean.

Goodbye for now.

L.

29

I manage to get a couple hours of sleep in before I have to show up at work. Both Nora and Danny are at the store today; we're in the heart of the holiday rush, all hands on deck. Even Marcella shows up for a couple of hours midday.

"Tell me all about LA," Nora says, during a quiet moment while she unpacks a delivery and I make my way through the gift-wrap orders.

"What's there to tell?" I say. "Sunshine? Good. Tacos? Good."

"And now you're back home where everything is depressing and grey."

"And now I'm back home where I can get excited about your wedding!"

"Honey, please," she says. "I'm just looking to get through these next few shifts. But it's nice to be working with you again."

"It's nice to be working with *you* again," I say, meaning it.

Nora has encouraged me to bring a date to her wedding. It seems like a counterintuitive gesture, considering how small she's keeping everything, but she said that was exactly the point. "Please, Lucy," she said, weeks ago. "I'm going to be busy making nice with Christopher's family. You're too old to hang out with my kids and too young to hang out with the other old folks, and I know you don't want to be making awkward small talk with Danny all night. Bring whoever you want. Bring Sasha!"

264

Naturally, I invited Malcolm. He agreed when I told him it was pretty casual and there would be an open bar. When I told Nora about this, her lips went a little thin, but she said, "Whatever you want."

I take the streetcar to Malcolm's after work. He opens the door, his hair messed up and his glasses slightly askew, looking soft and adorable. "I just woke up from a nap," he says, and I respond by leaning up to him in his doorway, kissing him right there, firmly and passionately. He wraps his arm around me, sliding one hand down till it navigates around my heavy winter coat and cups my ass, and soon we are in the middle of a full-on make-out sesh in the hallway of his building.

"Should we take this inside?" he asks, and I giggle in the way I only allow myself to when the prospect of sex is on the line.

"I brought you back a present," I say as we enter his apartment.

"Oh yeah?" he says, closing the door behind him.

"Mm-hmm," I nod coyly. I reach in my tote bag and pull out a keychain I bought at the airport gift shop, a tiny licence plate that says MATT in big letters. "They were out of Malcolms, so you'll have to change your name."

He takes it from my outstretched hands and turns it over, rubbing the embossed surface with his thumb.

"I love it. A true Hollywood relic."

"Absolutely," I say. "One of a kind. Local artisan made. Probably worth a fortune."

He pulls me in for another kiss, and we resume making out. The sex we have is familiar but comfortable, missionary with a minimal amount of foreplay. He spits on my face early on and grips my throat as he cums inside me, my legs wrapped around him in an attempt to pull him closer, but I'm mostly struck by how otherwise wholesome the whole affair is. He doesn't call me his slut or his whore. We barely talk. The rhythm is steady, almost gentle, and he stares into my eyes the whole time. I don't come close to climaxing myself.

I wonder if all sex, eventually, gets to be this boring.

"That was great," he says, rolling off from on top of me, and I give a noncommittal "Mmm" in agreement.

He silently strokes my hair before speaking again. "I've been working on a book proposal," he says. "One of my old coworkers at *The Hog* introduced me to his agent. I want to work on an oral history of the Montreal experimental-film scene of the early nineties."

"Seriously?" I crane my head to look up at him. "That's so cool!"

"Thank you. I think it could be really neat."

"I didn't even know Montreal had an experimental-film scene of the early nineties," I say.

"Nobody did. It's not like anything else now. Everything's gone so commercial. People just like to be spoon-fed their art. Nobody wants to be challenged. Carson's agent says there probably isn't a market for a full-length book, but I'm going to make it really good. I have a lot of connections in Montreal, you know."

"I think it's great you're doing something you're proud of." I lean over and kiss him gently on his mouth. The room is chilly, and as we lay motionless, the sweat from the sex is cooling on our bodies, and I let out a dramatic but involuntary shiver.

"Baby, you're so cold." He rubs my back with one hand and pulls the blankets up around us. I scooch my body down gently so I'm lying on top of him, resting my head on his chest, where I can hear his heartbeat and feel the gentle rising and falling with his breath. My fingertips run gently up and down his arm that's wrapped around me, grazing his bicep, touching the vein on his inner forearm that all men seem to have. My lids feel heavy, and I could easily fall asleep here.

"You're my inspiration for this, you know," he says, barely a whisper, the bass of his voice reverberating in my ear.

"What's that?" I murmur groggily, already drifting off.

"Seeing you work on this *Smash* magazine piece. How you went to LA to research it. It inspired me."

"Really?"

"Really, baby. Have you pitched it anywhere yet?"

I shake my head. "The piece doesn't really exist anymore. I'm stepping back from it."

He stops stroking my back. "What's that?"

"I did meet Chester in LA. He was a nightmare. Not what I was expecting at all when I started my research." I describe what happened during our interview, though I leave out how nauseated the whole thing made me.

Malcolm listens but is decisive when he says, "But this is what you wanted. All this time you were looking for an angle, and now you have one. There's a celebrity hook. Beloved Jack Franklin, secretly a predator, and the culture that enabled him."

"It's just not the story I wanted to write. Maybe a different writer could do something with it. I talked it out a little with Sasha—"

"Of course Sasha is behind this."

I roll off of him and sit up in bed, facing him, holding the sheet up against my naked chest. For some reason I suddenly feel very exposed, and not in the sexy way. "What is that supposed to mean?"

"Sweetheart," he says slowly, like he's spelling out something that should be so obvious. "Are you not concerned that her own lack of ambition is maybe rubbing off a little bit?" He reaches out to gently cup my elbow, and I let him, but I can't help tensing up at the same time. Of course I haven't explained the situation well enough. I tell Malcolm it's not like that, and he sits up too, swinging his body around so he's sitting next to me on the edge of the bed, his broad shoulders once again sloping over me. "Lucy," he says. "You just got over a big fight with her a few weeks ago. Now you've suddenly decided to give up on this project. You were so excited about it. Do you not see the pattern?"

"But I haven't given up." I try to sound strong and defiant, but my voice wavers. "Last night. When I couldn't sleep. I found this cool website. It's American, and it's geared towards older women. Not old women, just not, like, twenty-somethings or whatever. It's called *Grace*." I'm excited about this news, proud that I had managed to find something to do with my work so far, but Malcolm's eyebrows rise in a type of condescending disbelief, and I start talking quicker. "They have this series about women who make major career changes midway through life. They're not, like, little Q&As; they're really long and thoughtful conversations. And I was thinking about maybe redoing my interview with Jennifer Flounder there. Then

I can still help her tell her story without including Chester in it at all."

Malcolm is still staring at me, like he's waiting for me to finish. "Are you kidding me?" he says quietly. He is calm, but the hostility in his voice unnerves me so much that I instinctively inch away from him. He grabs his boxers on the ground and stands up, quickly slipping them on before adding his rumpled T-shirt in swift movements. Within seconds, he is fully dressed save for his socks, standing in front of me at his full height, while I continue to sit on his bed, wrapping the sheet tighter against my naked body, unsure of what I am supposed to do.

"Is it that big a deal?" I say, shyly. "Pieces change shape all the time. I hadn't even pitched it anywhere yet. It's not like I'm bailing."

"You had the chance to write something good, and you're backing out to submit to some website that nobody has ever heard of. Is this what you really want, Lucy? Mediocrity?"

"It's one piece. And I told you, it seems like a really cool website." Instead of going back to sleep last night, I ended up spending hours reading interviews with women in their thirties, forties, fifties, and older. They weren't celebrities. Some of them were boring. Most of them had jobs that didn't interest me. But they were given space to talk about their lives at length, and I was comforted by the promise that there seemed to be so many ways to live a fulfilling life past the age of twenty-five. I clicked around to other parts of the website which featured more interviews, essays, columns. Malcolm was right. It didn't seem to be a website that anybody I knew had heard of.

"Look." He takes a deep breath. "I'm not trying to pick a fight. But do you even want to be a journalist? A writer?" I don't know how to answer this, because I'm not sure if I do. Writing seemed like something to do with my degree, a natural next step, the thing I was supposed to want. Malcolm is a real journalist. He works every day, and isn't afraid of asking difficult questions in interviews. A career like his seemed like an admirable thing to try to work towards. But it also doesn't seem like the one I wanted, and I have never felt more clarity about this than I have in the last couple of days. Maybe it makes me a bad feminist, to not be more ambitious, to admit that Malcolm is in many ways a better writer than me, but for the first time, I feel okay with being a bad feminist. I made a decision, and I am sticking to it. He keeps going. "You're always asking me to tell you what to do. And here I am, telling you: Don't throw this piece away. Don't be dumb. Jennifer is not the story."

"Can we please just forget it? Let's not fight."

"You think this is a fight? I'm trying to help you."

Come to bed. Please. Just hold me. But for the first time with Malcolm, I can see the gulf between what I want in the moment and what I actually need. What I feel and what I know to be true. And I fight every part of me that just wants things to be safe and normal to say it.

"I don't want your help," I say. The words are coming out faster. I tell him, "I figured out what I wanted to do. And you're kind of being a prick." I regret it immediately. *Please just come back to bed. Please just shut me up, with your hands, with your dick, whatever, restore the natural order, make this easy for both of us.*

"You . . ." He's searching for the right word, something vicious, and what he stops at is almost laughable in its simplicity: "You're being a cunt." It's so cold the way he says it, so void of emotion.

My body reacts before my brain does. I climb out of bed. I stand in front of him. I don't know what I was expecting; I have no game plan. He squares his shoulders as he towers over me, like he's bracing himself for a fight—for me to yell at him, or hit him, I don't know. Instead, I drop to my knees. He looks confused as he stares down at me and opens his mouth as if to speak, but no words come out. I lower my gaze to the ground submissively. Out of my peripheral vision, I see his hand raise slowly, gently, and inch towards my face, stopping just before it reaches my cheek.

Just let him touch me, I think. *If he touches me, that means he didn't mean anything he said before. If he touches me, that means it was all foreplay. If he touches me, then it's all okay.* I can fathom Malcolm's cruelty when he's intimate with me, followed by him taking care of me, and I only ever have to concern myself with being his.

His hand pulls away, and I think, *That's it, we're done, he's going to leave,* but he reaches for his fly and unzips it. I don't think I've ever seen him so hard before.

I take him in my mouth, relieved that it wasn't a fight, that we didn't need to fight like other couples, as long as we can fold ourselves back into our roles. I hear his breath change as I suck him off, waiting for the submissive headspace to engulf me, waiting to feel okay again.

"Good girl," he whispers, in between his heavy breaths. His hand reaches down, holds my head in place, and he starts gently thrusting in and out of my mouth. "You're still a good girl."

I feel nothing.

"No," I say, but his penis is still in my mouth, so it comes out, "Nnnnn . . . I on anna o ish."

He stops, lets go of my head. I pull back, a thick line of spit connecting his penis to my lips. "I don't want to do this," I repeat.

"Do you need a second?" he says. "A break?"

"I don't want to do this anymore. With you." I'm still on my knees. I can't bring myself to look up at him, so I stare straight ahead, at his drool-covered dick, still erect, inches from my face. I close my eyes. "I'm sorry," I say. "But I think we should stop seeing each other."

There's a moment of silence that feels endless as he— we—take in what I just said. And then some movement, as I open my eyes to see him tuck himself back into his jeans, zip up his fly. "Well, fuck this," he says.

"I'm sorry," I repeat. For all that just happened, I still need to feel Malcolm likes me, still need reassurance that nobody is mad at me. "Maybe we can still be friends?" I offer weakly, not meaning it. He starts collecting my clothes strewn around his bed, my tote bag off the floor.

"Get up," he says, dropping my things in front of me. "You're pathetic." He turns and exits the bedroom, leaving me alone on my knees.

30

My mother will pick me up from the bus station on Christmas Eve. It's the first time in years that she isn't going to Nova Scotia for the holidays. I originally planned to stay in Toronto, taking shifts right up until the last minute and again on Boxing Day, spending Christmas Day with Sasha's family like I did last year. But two weeks ago, after Malcolm and I ended things, I had the strong urge to go home. My mother rearranged her plans as soon as I called her. Marcella gave me the days off without me having to kill off another relative; I suspect Nora talked to her. *Look at all those people who want to take care of you,* I think. It is comforting.

Work is so mercifully nuts in December that I rarely have any time to think. I work every day that I can, staying late to organize the massive influx of gift orders and reorganize the displays that have been trashed during the day by the hundreds of customers who have been through the store. Nora is busy planning her wedding, so most of these after-hours shifts are spent with Danny. It actually becomes nice, working with him. I tell him on our first late night together that I'm not in the mood to chat much, and to my surprise, he listens. I even let him have control of the store's CD player on the condition that he limit the amount of sad indie rock, and he starts bringing mixes from home of incredibly catchy sixties garage bands filled with fuzzy guitar riffs. I ask him about every band on the mix, and he promises he'll write them out for me. One day, he brings in a bag of candy from the international grocery store for us to snack on while we work. "I ate these guys almost every day Berlin," he tells me. I have never heard him mention Berlin before. He smiles as he says this, and I notice for the first time how nice his smile is.

The night before my bus ride home, Sasha and I go out for hot chocolate.

"Are you sure you're ready for this?" she says. "How many years has it been since you've been home anyway?"

"You make it sound like I'm shipping off to war," I respond.

"I've met your mom," she reminds me. "And I've met you after you've spoken to your mom. And now you're going to be on her turf."

It's true though. I think about how little I have to show my mother for my life in Toronto: a career in retail, a wardrobe of thrifted clothes, no relationship. So far from the life she wanted for me, the life she built for herself and that the Kenzies of the world are currently thriving in.

"Are you going to be okay this week?" I ask.

"With my brilliant parents and brilliant sisters and my brilliant cousins and no boyfriend or best friend there? It's going to be fucking terrible. And then it will be over, and then you'll be back. We'll get through it. Cheers." She holds up her hot chocolate to toast me, and I pretend to clink my paper cup against hers.

"You're the smartest person I know," I say, and she rolls her eyes in response but doesn't contradict me.

My mom spends the car ride home from the bus station filling me in on all the suburban gossip I missed, telling me about classmates from childhood whose names I can't place who are now married or divorced or gay. I hear about the one neighbour who is in rehab for opioid addiction and my old math teacher who left her husband for a man fifteen years her junior. I hear that Mr. Morris's agency is hiring junior copywriters, and I could be guaranteed a job if I ever decided I was ready to grow up and move back home.

We pull up to our house, and I'm struck by how big it is—a comfortable size for a small family but absolutely massive for a woman living alone. There are four bedrooms: mine, my mother's (which of course originally belonged to both my parents), and two more that have been turned into a guest bedroom and a home office. I asked my mom once if she ever thought of moving to a smaller place, and she dismissed me by saying she spent too long getting this home just right. We never discussed it again. It strikes me now, at twenty-five, that my parents bought this house with the intention of starting a larger family, and the realization makes me unbearably sad.

"Help me carry these in," my mom snaps me to attention. The back of the car is filled with enough grocery bags to feed a small army; she went to the store before picking me up. It takes multiple trips to bring it all in.

"Is this a Tofurkey?" I ask looking into one of the bags.

"For our dinner tomorrow," she explains.

"Mom, you hate fake meat."

"You're still on that vegetarian kick, aren't you? It's Christmas. Put the ice cream in the freezer before it melts."

It's fairly late in the evening, well past my mom's normal bedtime, and I expect her to go to sleep as soon as we unload the groceries, but instead she starts heating up vegetarian lasagna and saag paneer, both of which she made earlier today.

"You know I can use the microwave on my own," I tell her.

"I know you can, sweetheart," she says, before adding a few more spoonfuls of paneer cubes to my plate. "Make sure you leave your dirty laundry out before you go to bed. I'll put in a load in the morning."

My childhood bedroom hasn't changed since I moved out seven years ago. There's still the *Rushmore* poster on the wall, the Sylvia Plath poetry books on the nightstand, stacks and stacks of teen magazines that my mother subscribed me to in high school. My mother left a brand-new set of pyjamas folded on my pillow, patterned with little Santa Clauses, along with a new toothbrush. I realize I forgot to pack mine.

I get changed and then take out my laptop and sit on the paisley bedspread I begged my mom for when I was sixteen. With all the late nights I've been working lately, I haven't checked my email in over a week. There's a message from Keisha, the editor I've been in contact with from *Grace* magazine, with final edits on my interview. Jennifer Flounder and I spoke for over an hour last week, a conversation that I transcribed and submitted to the website. In the email, Keisha says that it "reads really well" and asks if I would be interested in more assignments. They're looking for someone in Toronto to cover a wellness and sexuality seminar.

I look at the time: 12:03 a.m., technically Christmas. I wonder if I should wait until the holiday is over to respond but then decide I don't care. I type back, "Dear

Keisha, I would absolutely love to talk more. Let's set up a phone meeting."

My mother and I exchange gifts the next morning. (I got her books, she got me peplum dresses from Banana Republic.) After, she asks if I want to come downtown with her, to church. This is new.

"Are you a Christian suddenly?" I ask.

"There's a group I work with," she says. "They give out hot meals to those who need it on holidays, when the service is done. Usually I go on Thanksgiving and Easter, but I told them I would be around today, and they told me to drop by."

My mother volunteers with the homeless. I was also not expecting this. We arrive to the church, where volunteers have already set up in the kitchen, putting together plates of sliced ham and mashed potatoes and carrying them out to the crowded makeshift dining hall. My mother is treated like a celebrity in the kitchen as word spreads quickly that "Anita is in town this Christmas." I'm put on carrot-peeling duty with an old woman named Beatrice, who tells me it's such an honour to "finally meet Anita's famous daughter."

"She talks about you all the time," Beatrice tells me. I look across the room at my mom, who is going over paperwork someone handed her. "Lovely Lucy and her exciting life in the big city."

"Has she been helping out here long?" I ask.

"Oh yes, must be six or seven years now," she says. "An organizational whiz. Immense help with coordinating all the donations we get from food distributors. We truly could not do this without her."

My mom's head suddenly raises as if she heard us talking about her, although we're way across the noisy room. She catches me staring at her and returns my eye contact, smiling. I suddenly feel embarrassed, unable to look at her, and focus back on the carrot, making sure I get every peel perfect.

That night, we sit on the couch, flipping through TV channels, every station playing *It's a Wonderful Life* or a holiday special of some classic sitcom.

"Lucy, you're going too fast. I can't see what's playing," says my mom, as I rapidly click through with the remote. "Wait! Wait! Go back! Channel 47."

I do as she says and see the thing that has caught her attention. *The Greasers* has just started; the opening credits are still onscreen. Jack Franklin's face appears, still objectively handsome, but now his features seem distorted by everything I've learned about him.

"Oh, I love this movie," Mom sighs. "I haven't seen it in years. Let's watch it."

I look to the screen, at this man I find disgusting, and then I look at my mother, so happy, so serene, in love with a version of Jack Franklin that existed in the public eye and nowhere else. I turn up the volume, set down the remote. We watch in silence for a few minutes.

"He reminds me so much of your father," she says. "Especially back when we were first dating."

I shake my head. "Dad was way cooler," I say. I rest my head on my mom's shoulder, and she puts her arm around me. We watch the rest of the movie together in silence.

The drive back to the bus station the next day is quiet. We listen to the radio, a classic-rock station turned down low so the jangly strains of Steely Dan come through faintly.

"Well," says my mom, as I pull my suitcase, filled with the new clothes I know I'll never wear, out of the trunk. "Wait, I almost forgot." She opens the back seat of the car and pulls out a small cooler. "Leftovers. Make sure you put these in the fridge as soon as you get home. Eat the lasagna first; the curries will last a little while longer in the freezer."

I take the cooler from her and look down at it, feeling as though I might cry. "Maybe I could come back for a longer visit soon," I say. "In January. When work slows down."

She tells me I'm always welcome to come home. She says my room is waiting for me. I nod and then put the cooler down on the suitcase so she can hug me goodbye. I squeeze her tightly, holding on for five, six seconds before letting go. She cups my chin in her hands and studies my face.

"You should pull your hair back," she says. "You look so much prettier without all that scraggly hair in the way."

31

I end up bringing Sasha as my date to the wedding on New Year's Eve. She asks me, "Aren't you going to be busy all day with maid-of-honour stuff?" but Nora has given me very little to do. Nora and Christopher have rented out a bar in the West End for the night, and true to her word, the whole event is low-key. I show up early to help her do her makeup in the basement of the bar.

"I'm not gonna lie, I was gearing up to deal with Bridezilla Nora," I say, steadily applying liquid liner above her lid.

"I should kick you in the shins for that remark, sugar."

"I figure if there were ever a time to go all in and indulge yourself—"

"What, my third wedding would be it? Listen. I have all my best friends and family members here. I'm marrying a guy who turns my underwear into a slip and slide—"

"Gross."

"His family is paying for us to keep the bar open all night, and I get to play dolly for your expert makeup skills. How'd you get to be so good at this anyway? I never see you wear any yourself."

"I was deeply insecure in high school and hid behind a mask of Maybelline. Now shut up for a second; I gotta do your lips."

"Mom?" a voice interrupts us. Justine has come downstairs. She looks like she's on her way to some kid of comic con in a hot-pink and black baby-doll dress filled out by a hot-pink tulle petticoat. Her eyes are coated in thick black makeup, and her red lipstick clashes with the dress. Her frizzy brown hair is pulled up in two tight mini buns. She looks like a mall-punk Minnie Mouse. Behind her is a skinny guy with stringy hair wearing a thrifted suit with a top hat. If I ever tried to wear a getup like either of them at any age, my mother would kill me, but Nora seems nonchalant. "You know how you said me and Randall could each have some champagne tonight? Well, the bartender says they can't serve us, 'cause we're minors. I told them you said it was okay, but then they said it was a legal thing?"

"Nobody is having any champagne for a while, baby," says Nora.

"Stop moving your mouth," I instruct, but everyone ignores me.

"*Moooom*," Justine whines.

"Have some pop now. We'll have champagne when we go home later."

"I'm literally almost done. I just need you to be still for, like, one second while I apply this coat."

"Wait," says Justine, walking up beside me as if she's seeing her mother for the first time. "You did *that*? Mom, you look awesome."

"The light down here is terrible," I say. "But it's all I got. We'll have to see it upstairs."

"No, I'm serious, this is, like, really nice," Justine says.

"You look real nifty, Mrs. G.," Randall says, his mouth awkwardly forming around the word *nifty* like he's testing it out for the first time.

Nora makes eye contact with me, and I nod at her, lifting my hands up and stepping back to signify I'm done.

She turns to Justine and hops off the stool. "Thank you, baby," she says, hugging her tightly. I open the door to the dimly lit, single-stall bathroom behind us so Nora can take a look at herself in the mirror. "Holy shit," she calls out from inside. "I'm a hottie!"

She does look stunning. She's wearing a sleeveless navy vintage dress from the 1960s embroidered with a silver pattern that hits her at mid-thigh, which she got for dirt cheap because there was a coffee stain on the hem. Her hair has been straightened and is pulled back in a loose, messy bun, with a few face-framing strands that have already rebelled and gone back to their natural curls. And her makeup, well. I'll have to see it in the light upstairs to judge it properly.

"Thank you, Lucy," she says, hugging me. "I'm so happy all of you are here today." She even touches Randall-the-narc's arm, seeming genuinely pleased that he's here. "I'm just . . . so happy."

"Don't cry!" I scold. "I didn't use waterproof mascara."

She laughs, dabbing her eyes. "If my memories of today include pictures of me with smeared eye makeup because I was so happy, well then, I'll roll with it."

Randall and Justine head back upstairs while I pack up all the cosmetics.

"So, um," I say, putting my stuff in a tote bag. "I know you made me swear not to get you any presents, but I couldn't help myself." I pull out a small rectangular gift from my bag, puffing up the wilted ribbon bow with my fingers.

"Lucy!" Nora comes out of the bathroom. "For me and Christopher?"

"I guess. But really for you. No offence to Christopher. I couldn't think of what to get him."

"He's already having the best day of his life," she grins, turning the package over in her hands.

"You don't have to open it now. But just don't open it in front of all the guests. It's nothing. It's dumb."

She pulls off the bow and slides her fingers under the paper, gingerly unwrapping it. Inside is a framed photograph. "Oh, Lucy," she looks at the image.

I scanned the photo of her as a teenage punk from the music book she showed me, the one of her snarling with the fork in her front pocket, and had it professionally printed. The quality of the final product isn't great, but it's both Nora as I know her best and a Nora who will always be a mystery to me. Young, weird, wildly independent.

"Do you like it?"

"I love it. I absolutely love it. It's my favourite thing."

She hugs me again, tighter than before.

"I'm so happy I know you," I say.

"I'm so happy I know you too, honey. And I'm so happy you're here today with me."

We embrace for a few more seconds, then gently break the hug.

"All right. Are you ready to go get married?"

"First let's double-check my makeup by the light upstairs."

Nora and Christopher are married by one of Christopher's childhood friends, who had himself ordained on the internet for the occasion. They wrote their own vows, sort of. Christopher says, "I promise to love, cherish, support, respect, admire, trust, and laugh with you." Nora says, "I promise so many things, things I can never possibly get through listing in this lifetime, so can we just skip through that part so I can hurry up and be married to you?" Christopher's friend says, "I now pronounce you husband and wife," and Nora and Christopher kiss a long, slow, passionate kiss, and I look over at Justine, and she is crying big, messy, beautiful tears that stream her thick makeup down her face, holding Randall's hand, and Danny is smiling, and Sasha is tearing up, and everybody looks touched to be included in this moment, the way that I am happy, for Nora, for Christopher, for their love, and for myself.

There is no exchange of rings, no first dance, no speeches or toasts. The DJ plays a mix of post-punk and disco, and everyone does their version of dancing, mostly awkward shuffles and shoulder shimmies. Nora, of course, is completely unselfconscious, turning the sticky floor of the bar into her dance floor, expertly spinning around jutting chairs and misplaced stools, looking like she will live forever. Christopher joins her for a few songs but mostly stands off to the side watching her, beer in hand, grinning ear to ear. Sasha manages to keep up with Nora for longer before taking a break to go to the bar. I see out of the corner of my eye one of Nora's aunts sneaking Justine a fruity-looking cocktail. I join the dance floor.

I'm a sweaty mess after dancing with Nora to "Disco Inferno" followed by Joy Division's "Disorder," spinning around, holding her hands, following her lead, and letting out spontaneous whoops of pure joy. By the time the next song—one by the Village People—starts up, I'm completely spent and have to go sit down. "JUST ONE MORE SONG!" Nora yells out over the music, but I tell her I need a breather and pass her off to Justine, whose lipstick has now been completely replaced by the berry-pink stain of her drink.

Danny is slipping outside to go smoke. I have never seen him smoke before, but he seems to have bought a pack of Gauloises for this occasion, and I grab my coat to go outside on the slushy sidewalk .

"Can I bum a cigarette?" I ask Danny. He nods, holding the pack out so I can grab one. I put the cigarette between my lips. He lights it with his own, huddling close to shield us against the wind. I've never seen Danny this close before. He smiles again.

"Are you having fun in there?" I ask, a question that seems lame as soon as it leaves my mouth.

"Definitely. It's really nice to see Nora this happy. She means a lot to me, you know?"

It feels strange, thinking that Danny and Nora have a relationship without me, even though it makes sense; they work so many shifts together. I also realize that we're an hour away from the new year, and I don't have anyone to kiss, and I'm pretty positive Danny doesn't either.

"Should we head back inside?" I ask as we finish our cigarettes.

"I'm actually heading home."

"Really?"

"I kinda find New Year's overrated. I already said goodbye to Nora and Christopher."

We exchange goodbyes, and I try not to hide the disappointment in my voice. As he turns and walks away, I realize that it's him; it's always been him. I've spent so much time chasing after messy masculinity when sweet, kind, adorable Danny was right there, madly in love with me and waiting, so patiently, for me to come to my senses.

"Hey, wait!" I call after him. He turns around, looks at me as if to say, *Yes?* "Do you—do you want to go out sometime? With me?"

"Excuse me?" he says, blinking rapidly. He needs a minute to absorb my words. I must be blowing his mind. "You and me. Let's go for a drink sometime. Only not actually a drink, because I think I'm going to cut back. New Year's resolution. But you know what I mean. Let's go out."

He is silent for a moment, still stunned, and I wonder if he needs me to be even more direct, suggesting a place and a time. The poor guy has probably been dreaming about this moment for years. But then he says, "Oh, god, Lucy. I'm flattered, really. But no."

"Excuse *me?*" I say, my turn to be caught off guard.

"I don't think it's a good idea. Thank you. But no. Happy holidays." He turns to leave.

"You don't understand," I say, and he stops walking away. "I'm asking you out. I *want* to go out with you. This isn't a pity thing. I'm finally asking you out."

"Are you . . . Are you serious right now, Lucy?" He doesn't seem amazed. He seems pissed off. "I don't want to go out with you. I'm telling you right now. I. Don't want. To go out. With you. Please respect that. I respected your decision when you said no."

"But . . . you're supposed to have a crush on me!"

"I *did*. When we first met. I thought you were pretty, and I wanted to go out. But in the two years we've worked together, you've *never* asked how I'm doing. I always have to force small talk with you. And, you know, I'm great to talk to. But you wouldn't know that. Besides," he says, while I'm still trying to take all this in, "I have a girlfriend."

"Oh," I say, which is the only response I can think of. "Oh. I . . . didn't realize you had a girlfriend."

"Yeah, well, you never asked. Happy New Year, Lucy." With that, he turns to go, for real this time, leaving me stunned in his wake. It's started to snow, big puffy white flakes. I shiver from the cold and head back inside.

Back in the bar, still stunned by the recent rejection, I grab a glass and one of the pitchers of water floating around and find a quiet-ish seat in the corner of the venue, surveying the room of drunk, happy people dancing and laughing. I open my contact list, scroll down to the *M*s, see Malcolm's name. Maybe it wouldn't hurt to text him one last time. Get some closure. But instead, I scroll down a few more names and click on the contact labelled "Mom." *Happy New Year,* I text her. *I love you.*

Nora approaches, sweaty but happy, and motions for my glass of water. I hand it to her, and she chugs it down. "I am working up a sweat out there!"

"You look like you're having the time of your life," I say.

She nods, sits down next to me, fanning her face with her hand. "I just need a sec."

She refills her water from the jug, drinks another glass.

"Did you know Danny has a girlfriend?" I ask.

She nods. "Candace. Sweet girl. It's too bad she had to work tonight. She's a nurse."

I nod, like this is all old information for me, and hope my desire to change the conversation isn't too transparent. "Any New Year's resolutions?"

"I don't know. Probably get into yoga. Seems to be the thing to do. Be nicer to my kid."

"You are *so* nice to your kid! You got into steampunk for her!"

She laughs. "I love her so much, you know?"

"I know."

"You don't. I'm sorry. Nobody does. This feeling's all mine."

"I can't imagine feeling anything so intensely," I say. "I can't imagine being able to take care of someone the way you take care of her. I can barely take care of myself."

Nora shakes her head. "You know, you're not as hopeless as you think. In fact, I'd wager you're going to be just fine."

"Thank you," I say, because she sounds like she means it. Suddenly, I remember where we are. "Nora, this is your *wedding!* We should be talking about you!"

"Nah. No more talking." She puts down the glass. "I'm gonna go dance some more. You coming?"

"Yeah. In a minute. I think I need to sit for a bit."

Nora leaves, handing me back the now-empty glass. I refill it with water from the jug. A couple minutes later, Sasha slides into the seat next to mine, two drinks in hand.

"I got us each a Sex on the Beach," she says. "I had a sudden craving. It's *so* nice being out at a place I don't have to bartend." She trades me one of her drinks for my glass of water and chugs the whole thing greedily. "God damn, I love water. Are we getting older?"

"Every second of the day."

"Well," she puts the empty water glass down and raises the cocktail. "To Nora and Christopher."

I raise my own glass. "To 2016. It's going to be our year, I can feel it."

We down our drinks just as the opening bars of a familiar song start to play. Sasha turns her head in confusion, looking over her shoulder around the room as if trying to see the music. "Is this the B-52s?"

I nod. "I think it is, yeah. We gotta dance to this song."

I jump up and grab her hand, pulling her with me. Nora is still on the floor, dancing with Justine, both of them looking happy and goofy.

"This is my favourite band!" Nora shouts over the music when she sees me.

"I know!" I respond. I spin her around drunkenly, and she ungracefully flails her arms to the music. "You look like such a narc," I say.

"I'm so glad you're here!" she shouts.

"Me too!" I reply, and neither of us says anything else as we shut up and dance for the rest of the song.

Acknowledgements

First, I owe a huge thank-you to those who made the material conditions possible to write this book. Thank you to the Ontario Arts Council for their generous grant, and to my roommate, Lara Desjardins, who did way more than her fair share of dishes while I was busy writing (and also when I wasn't).

I started writing *Good Girl* in the fall of 2016, never imagining anyone else would read it. Thank you to Heather Karpas at ICM, who saw a blob of words and recognized the potential for a story, and to editor Emily Keeler, a truly kindred spirit who helped me shape so much of this narrative. Martha Sharpe at Flying Books, you poured your heart and soul into making this book happen and refused to let me give up even when I really, really wanted to. Thanks to Stephanie Sinclair at CookeMcDermid, designers Leanne Shapton and Lisa Naftolin, eagle-eyed copy editor Liz Johnston, proofreader Khalida Hassan, typesetter Mark Byk, publicist Jessica Rattray, and everyone who read early portions and provided invaluable feedback, including Haley Mlotek, David Iserson, Lola Pellegrino, Darcie Wilder, Emma Rice, Esme Blegvad, Amy Jones, and Kathleen Hale. Thanks also to Stoya, Emma Straub, Tamara Faith Berger, and Zoe Whitthall for the hype.

To my loving and chaotic family, where would I be without your endless support? Promise me you'll never read this book.

Oh jeez, how do I even begin to approach this next section? Let me start by shouting out the group chats: the Space Potatoes, the Coven, the Sex Martini, #DReis AndButthead, my Instagram close friends list, the "Come Here to Feel Great and Validated and Share Memes about Boats" group. Extra gratitude to: Leigh Beadon; Mara McCormick; Allison & Cam; Ali & Laura; Sarah Hagi; Serah-Marie & Ted; Naomi Skwarna; Estelle Tang; Graham Wright; Ave Smith; Monica Heisey; Emma Healey; Gabe Appel; Lydia Ogwang; Palmer Fritschy; Katie Merchant; Jared Bland; Alexandra Molotkow; Sarah Niedoba; Laëtitia Lancellotta; Steve Sladkowski; my colleagues at *The Believer*; the Toronto Public Library; the discography of Joanna Newsom; the staff at Le Swan. There are so many people I'm missing, can I just say thank you to all my communities past and present in Toronto, New York, LA, and beyond? Here is a blank space to fill in with your own name: _____.

Thank you to all the publications that have ever published my work, but especially *Worn Fashion Journal*, *The Hairpin*, *Rookie*, *Hazlitt*, and their editors. They turned me into a writer, so if you hated this book, please take it up with them.

Last but never least, to Caitlin Ellis, you're a pal and a confidant. Thank you for being a friend, but thank you even more for letting me put Nigel in this story. I couldn't have done it without her, or you.

Anna Fitzpatrick is a Toronto-based writer. She is the author of the children's book *Margot and the Moon Landing* (very different from *Good Girl*) and has written for *Rolling Stone*, *The New Yorker*, *The Globe and Mail*, *Elle*, *Rookie*, *The Hairpin*, *Hazlitt*, and more. *Good Girl* is her debut novel.